*Please Don't Stop the Music*

# Please Don't Stop the Music

Jane Lovering

Published 2011 by Choc Lit Limited
Penrose House, Crawley Drive, Camberley, Surrey GU15 2AB
www.choclitpublishing.co.uk

A CIP catalogue record for this book is available
from the British Library

ISBN-978-1-906931-27-8

**Mixed Sources**
Product group from well-managed
forests and other controlled sources
www.fsc.org  Cert no.TT-COC-002063
© 1996 Forest Stewardship Council

Printed in the UK by CPI Cox & Wyman, Reading, RG1 8EX

In memory of Peggy Thomson, 1922–2010

# Acknowledgements

To everyone who has so patiently encouraged me, laid
trails of chocolate to encourage me to my laptop and
listened to me whinge about how *haaaard* writing
is; everyone at LLS, especially Fran and Heather for
spending hours plotholing. For Lyn and Linsey for being
so long-term, the rest of my kids, Vienna, Fern, William
and Riyadh for … umm … give me a minute, I'll think
of something … My husband, Kit, for putting up with
me, as always. Not that he always puts up with me,
sometimes he just leaves the room with a tense smile.

To Sarah Williams, wonderfully talented owner
and creator of www.butterflybuckles.com, for
all the information on jewellery making and for
letting me rummage around among her crystals
for inspiration. For all guitar-related stuff, for the
Metal Hammer tip-off, and also for an *incredible*
amount of posing, my eldest son, Tom.

And, because I've been told that people mentioned
feel obliged to buy the book, I dedicate this
novel to everyone whose name appears in
the York District Telephone Directory.

# Chapter One

You know you're in for a bad day when the Devil eats your last HobNob.

All right, it was Saskia, not Old Nick, and any hoofed tendencies were well-disguised in sling-back Manolos, but from there on the resemblance was remarkable, down to the slightly reddish-tinged eyes and the air of immoral superiority.

'Bad news I'm afraid, Jemima. Well, bad for *you*, obviously, not for me!' She tinkled a laugh that I wanted to hit with a brick. 'I've decided to start sourcing elsewhere.'

Her tight little lips mouthed another few crumbs, nibbling slowly around the biscuit's edge until I wanted to scream, 'Just *eat it*!' but I didn't dare. 'Sorry, what?'

'Your jewellery is very – well, it's quite lovely of course, very *intricate*, but it is rather expensive you know.' It takes weeks to build each piece. That's why Saskia started stocking them in her shop – because they were exclusive. 'I've been talking to one or two people in the States who make very similar pieces, and they can supply me at roughly half what you charge.'

*Half?* What are they using, I wanted to ask, plastic and polyfilla? I'd already got my overheads down as low as I could by renting a room in Rosie's little house and sharing workshop space in Jason's barn. 'I could, maybe, give you discount … use less expensive materials …' I tried, but Saskia was already standing up.

'Anyway, I've decided to give the shop a more cosmopolitan look, buy things in from all over the world. That's what this darling little rural corner could do with, right? A touch of World Culture? All right, better trot now, busy, busy!' She dropped the remains of the biscuit casually onto the edge of the table, paused for a moment as if waiting for the butler to sweep it off, and then with a quick shrug, was gone through the door in a waft of Arpège tinged with brimstone.

'Coast clear?' Rosie snuck half a shoulder round the bottom of the narrow stairway. 'Thought I'd stay out of the way until she'd gone, she doesn't need any more ammunition in the great Unpleasantness War. Sssh, lovey, Cruella's gone now.'

This was addressed to her baby son, Harry, who lay in her arms like a damp rucksack, grouching slightly.

'She … she's just dropped me.'

'Dropped you?' I tried not to look as Rosie pulled down the front of her pyjama top and fastened Harry to a boob as though buttoning him on. 'From how high? Ow! Yes, go on, Jem, I'm listening, breast-feeding doesn't leach away your brain you know.'

'Yes, I know, it's just … distracting, you sitting there with your chest hanging out and Harry grabbing you, farting and squelching.'

'Sounds like a really good party,' Rosie said wistfully. 'Remind me again, Jem, what parties are?'

'Excuse me, I'm just about to become penniless thanks to the Diamante Demon and you're smiling indulgently at me whilst having a head full of fluffy mummy-moments! You might want to throw me out into the snow when I can't pay my bills. And – and this is the clincher – she ate the last HobNob.'

Rosie sighed. 'She really is evil, isn't she?'

Rosie supplied the shop with her handmade greetings cards so she was well up on the Awfulness of Saskia. She, however, had long since branched out and now also supplied most of the card shops in this part of North Yorkshire. We'd first met at Saskia's one afternoon when I was delivering a series of belt buckles, each a bejewelled representation of the Seven Deadly Sins, and discovered that we both loathed Saskia with a passion bordering on unhealthy fixation. Which came in handy six months ago when Rosie's pregnancy meant that she'd had to ease up on the work front and the short-term lease on my flat in York had begun to seem restrictive. It was a near-perfect situation, except that the result of the pregnancy now had to sleep in a carry-cot jammed in beside Rosie's wardrobe; when he needed to move into a proper bed we were probably going to have to fence-in the bath.

'You'll find another outlet.' Rosie tucked herself away and hoiked Harry up to her shoulder where he belched like a lager-lout. 'You're twenty-eight. Blonde and gorgeous. You make the most exquisite jewellery I've ever seen, and you're thin, you bitch. Honestly, people will be eating their own knees to have a chance to buy your stuff. Anyway, Saskia never marketed you properly, you should have worldwide recognition for your designs, not a cramped corner of a jumped-up knick-knack shop!' She pondered for a moment, flicking her chicane of black curls out of her eyes. 'And I can't throw you out into the snow. It's not winter.'

'I was being figurative. Honestly, Rosie, what am I going to do for money? What am I saying, it can't get much worse, I already share workspace with a guy who reads *Shunters' Weekly*, and not in an ironic way.' Jason is an artiste (his 'e') who lives in a beautiful flat in the roof-space of the barn, like a materially successful pigeon, and he builds things out of scrap locomotives. Thicker than a bed sandwich, his chief saving grace is looking like a mixture of Johnny Depp and Jack Davenport. 'And we both know she only stocked my things in Le Petit Lapin because I'd got friendly with Jason and he put in a word for me. Saskia fancies him so much she'd buy Liverpool FC if he asked her to. I mean, yeah, everyone loved my stuff but they didn't like the prices.'

'Le Petit Lapin.' Rosie sniggered, ignoring my tirade. 'Honest to God, Jem, I can't hear that name without thinking that it sounds like a strip club. I'm surprised the York Board of Trade didn't make her change it.'

'With a husband as rich as Alex is she could call it "Rub Me With Your Willy" if she wanted to.' I stared at the walls. 'I really thought I was making a go of it,' I said quietly.

Rosie touched my arm. 'You *are* making a go of it,' she said gently. 'People love your pieces, you only need to read your e-mails to know that. Don't let Saskia get you down, other shops will take you on, don't worry. Anyway, what's she so uptight about money for?'

Saskia's husband Alex 'did something' in property. They lived in the same village as us in a much, much larger house. Saskia regarded living twelve miles outside York as the class equivalent to just-off-Knightsbridge, while Rosie and I privately agreed that she put the 'colic' into bucolic and couldn't wait until she was driven back to town by the pitchfork-wielding locals. Sadly improbable, with the money that she and Alex threw at village institutions, but we still found ourselves backing away slowly whenever she complained about the 5 a.m. cockerel chorus, or the smell of cows.

'Maybe her marriage is on the rocks?'

Rosie snorted. 'Yeah, right! She'd take Alex to the cleaners! Anyway, what did she pay you for the last lot? Two grand? Two thousand pounds is the kind of loose change she'd give to a beggar in the street, if she ever gave anything to beggars apart from a sneer and a kick in the ankle.'

'She doesn't actually *kick* them does she?'

'Well, no,' Rosie looked down at Harry's sleeping head and dropped a soft kiss on it. 'But she looks as though she would if no-one was watching. Anyway, my point is … oh sod it, Jem, what *is* my point? I thought my memory would improve after Harry was born. D'you know I'm beginning to think it wasn't the placenta that came out after him, it was my brain?'

'Well thanks for *that* image. Your point, I think, was that Saskia isn't exactly short of a few quid.'

'Yes. Yes, that was it. And she ate our last HobNob? Hang on a minute, nursing mother here, aren't I entitled to *any* privileges? Look, I'm going to put Harry in his cot for a sleep and get on and do some cards. I've got a few orders to fill before next week so I'd better make a start now while it's quiet.'

'Are you sure you wouldn't rather go to bed for a bit?' Harry, bless his little babygros, wasn't exactly the calm, relaxed baby Rosie had somehow been led to believe she'd have, despite all the whale-song CDs and the hours of pregnancy-yoga, during which she'd looked more and more like an egg on a stick. Since his arrival she'd acquired shadows under her eyes and a pale, stretched look as though she was co-existing in several universes at once.

'Nah, I'd better get on. I'll catch a snooze later.'

'Have you thought any more about … maybe …' It sounded incoherent but Rosie knew what I meant.

'I can bring Harry up on my *own* perfectly well, just as long as Saskia doesn't decide she wants to turn him into a baby-skin coat or sausages or something.'

Harry's father was something Rosie never talked about. She'd not had a boyfriend for at least a year, or, obviously she *had*, for the duration of copulation if nothing else, but she refused to say anything about him. *My* money was on Jason, but then my money was on Jason for everything from funding terrorism to dropping litter. Despite this, I harboured a kind of hope that he was the father. He was well-off, good-looking and wouldn't necessarily mean Harry was doomed to being several nails short of a shelf unit; Rosie was quite bright enough to make up that particular deficiency.

'Well, if you're sure … I'd better get back to the marketing drawing board. Again. "Cosmopolitan" huh! I dread to think what she's going to turn that lovely little shop into! Should have seen it coming, I guess, she's

6

always wanted to be El Supremo of York City Centre.'

'Wouldn't she have to be black?'

I stared at Rosie for a moment then my synapses managed to switch to new-mother mode of thinking. 'That's the Supremes, dear. Look, I'm going into York, trolling round the jewellery shops for another outlet. Do you need anything?'

'New body? One where all the bits that are meant to go in, go in and don't flap around in the breeze?'

'I'll buy you some big pants.'

Rosie looked down at herself. 'Can you get them neck-to-ankle?'

'You're not that bad. Anyway, you had a ten-pound baby less than two months ago, it'll take time for it all to go back to where it was.'

'Yeah.' Rosie sounded tired and I suddenly had a brilliant idea.

'How about if I take Harry with me?'

She came over all protective, wrapping her body over Harry's slumbering form. 'Why?'

'Distraction. I mean, last time I went round with my stuff, everyone was so dismissive. If I've got a pram and a baby, people might at least feel sorry for me.'

'So you want my baby just so you can have a crack at the pity vote? Jemima, that is very immoral.'

'You could get on with your cards. *And* probably fit in a snooze.'

I watched her eyelids droop as though even the promise of sleep was enough. 'All right. There's a couple of bottles of expressed milk in the fridge, in case he wakes up.'

'But you just stuffed him.'

Rosie gave me a Look, which expressed the gulf between mothers and non-mothers. 'Just in Case. That's my motto.'

'I thought your motto was Biscuits, Bustiers and Orlando Bloom?'

'Yeah.' She sighed. 'Then I had a baby.'

# Chapter Two

York has numerous streets and alleyways which fold in upon themselves to fill a small area with an almost limitless number of retail opportunities, like a kind of fractal purchasing reality. However, I soon discovered (a) that most of the shops, despite looking exclusive and designer from the outside, actually stocked depressing shades of the same eco-friendly woodwork and mass-produced earrings and (b) that you can't push a pram over cobbles. Cobblestones might be picturesque but they take a toll on childhood constitutions, and Harry looked a bit wan as his head rolled around on the mattress for the third or fourth time. He was beginning to grouse tetchily. I peered down at his matinée-jacketed form. He was wearing a pale crocheted effort over a green babygro that Rosie liked because she thought it made him look cute; I actually thought it made him look like a string bag of sprouts but, hey, he's not my baby.

'One more, Harry. Promise. Then we can go home.'

I lied, of course, because he was eight weeks old and couldn't hold it against me. Much good it did me. I might just as well have quit after the 'one more', no-one was keen and most of the shops were so narrow that I had to push in and back out, risking taking most of the stock with me. Leaning over the pram, spreading my portfolio over Harry's head, didn't really give the opportunities for selling either. The answer was always, 'Sorry, they're beautiful, but a bit expensive,' until eventually I had tried every jewellery stockist in the central York area.

Harry had begun to complain seriously now. I shushed him by pushing the pram energetically to and fro, making his rabbit mobile oscillate dangerously, while I perched on the edge of the fountains outside the art gallery and wondered what to do. I mean this was *York*! City of horse-drawn carriage rides and medieval stone work. If I couldn't sell hand-crafted belt buckles here then I might as well go back to France. Where I hadn't exactly taken the Continent by storm either, but at least my failures had had an edge of Gallic glamour. Or Italy; I could go to Italy again, where I'd discovered the population possessed a whole range of elegantly dismissive shrugs when faced with a belt buckle in the shape of the Venetian Bridge of Sighs. If the jewellery didn't start selling I could write a book, 'How to tell you're being given the brush-off in ten European languages' – hang on a minute. Wasn't that another little alleyway there, between those two sandwich shops?

Sure enough, the sun was shining down a passage I hadn't noticed previously where the walls of the two shops didn't quite touch. Dragging the grumpy Harry, although there was barely room for the pram to pass without scoring a line in the brickwork, I emerged into a small cobbled yard behind the shopping street. It contained two kiosk-sized constructions, one of which was closed and boarded but the other had a window display of technicolour music posters and T shirts with various tour dates emblazoned across. It also contained, coiled in one corner like a sleeping snake, a big leather belt. Belts need buckles, don't they?

I jostled the door open with my shoulder and backed the pram in, realising as I did so that there wasn't room for both Harry and me to fit inside the shop at the same time. In a spirit of compromise (and also because if I'd left him outside Rosie would have found out somehow and killed me), I left the front half of the pram hanging over the step. It lacked a certain dignity for a sales call but I reckoned I'd shot my bolt on the dignity thing, what with the fluffy bunny hanging toy and the Thomas the Tank Engine changing bag.

As the door opened a broken bell let out a buzzing sound which I could feel in my teeth. Beyond the immediate doorway the shop widened, giving room for the racks of music, the guitars hanging on the walls and the stand displaying posters of the latest bands. Between the Fenders the walls were coated with neon flyers for gigs by a DJ called Zafe. At the back of the shop there was a counter with a cash register, but no-one standing behind it. It was dark and there was a smell of polish and old paper, the kind of librarianish smell that asks you to be quiet and not eat anything which might stain.

'Hello?'

My voice made Harry step up the whingeing a notch. I hoped he wasn't hungry or wet. I had to admit to a slight squeamishness about both ends of Harry and their products.

'Anyone in?'

Harry upped the ante on the grouching stakes and he'd gone a bit pink, too. Maybe he was too hot? Did babies get too hot? I knew they had to be protected against getting chilled, but Rosie hadn't mentioned the heat. Cautiously

I reached over and tweaked the blanket further down his little green body. 'Are you all right?' As I drew the blanket lower a tell-tale yeasty smell floated out of the pram and I could see the stains spreading all the way up the back and sides of his sleepsuit. 'Oh, Harry ...'

Harry, very male all of a sudden, looked rather proud of himself. Great. Food I could do, nappies I could do. A complete change of clothes and pram sheet – nope, bit lacking in the total clean laundry department.

'Can I help you?'

The voice came from the dark recess at the back of the shop. Male. Great.

'I ... no, sorry, it's just, he's got a bit ...'

'Hold on.' There were footsteps, a slammed door and a pause, during which Harry kicked his legs like a trainee can-can dancer and gave me a full view of just how bad things were. Not to be too graphic, it was even in his *hair*. Then there was someone in front of me in the doorway, prevented from coming in by Harry and his malodorous transport. 'Hi. That's better, now I can see you. Did you come for the guitar?'

'Guitar?'

'That'll be a no then. Look, why don't you shove the pram outside, bring the baby in with you and we'll find out what I can do for you, yes?' The pram was being tugged from the outside and I had no choice but to follow it into the yard and confront the man who was pulling it.

To call his appearance weird was to leave myself short of adjectives to describe his clothes, but a few moments with a thesaurus opened to 'urgh' would rectify that. He was tall and skinny and wearing a shirt made for a much larger man, or at least one with shoulders. His dark hair straggled at various unkempt lengths outlining how thin his face was, and he had on multicoloured trousers which clung so tightly to his legs that I hoped they were lycra. Otherwise he was doomed to a day standing up. Around his desperately bony hips was wound an enormous belt which probably doubled his bodyweight and ended in a silver buckle with a death's head motif. Overall he looked like a man who'd been dressed from the rag-bag and then run over by a lawn mower.

I couldn't take my eyes off the belt buckle. Eventually the man coughed to attract my attention. 'I don't usually like to stop women staring at my groin, but ... you're a bit intense, I'm starting to worry.'

'Oh, I'm sorry.'

'Don't be. I'd have shoved a pair of socks down if I'd known, to give you something to look at. Now, shall we go inside? This young chap looks as though he could do with some attention.' The man leaned forward as though to lift Harry out of the pram, but I leaped across to forestall him.

'No!'

The man jumped back, hands held up. He had a curiously concentrated expression as though my face was the most important thing he'd seen all day. 'Hey, it's all right, I'm not going to molest him or anything.'

'No, it's just that he's absolutely filthy.'

'Filthy? Why, what's he been doing, working on a building site?' He shook flopping locks from big brown eyes and stared down at Harry. 'You're a very forward little guy, aren't you?'

'I meant, like, pooey,' I said, but he didn't seem to be listening, staring at the baby again with that concentrated look. The lines on his face and the slight tightness of his mouth which was just visible amid some fairly serious stubble, indicated that this was his customary expression. Then his nose began to twitch.

'Ah. So that's what's causing the complaining. Well, I've got a kitchenette out the back there, if a bowl of warm water and a towel is any use to you.'

I did my best. Honest. I could *feel* Rosie's presence in that little room as though I was psychic. However, I think I ended up doing pretty well for someone who's never really been at the sharp end of parenting, and eventually carried Harry back into the shop, wrapped in every clean tea towel I'd been able to find. My unlikely saviour was lounging against the till.

'Good God! He looks like a junior Roman Emperor!'

'I'll get them washed and back to you.'

The scruffy, tight-trousered man eyed up the little shrouded figure and gave a small shudder. 'Don't worry about it. I'm not sure I could ever wipe a mug rim again without thinking about, well, you know. Keep them.'

'He is wearing a clean nappy.' I'd replaced the pram sheet with an extra-large towel bearing the legend 'Glasgow, City of Culture' which, doubled over, completely covered the mattress.

'Even so. Now, what can I do for you?'

I gave him the full sales pitch, a guided tour of my portfolio and then brought out the *pièce de résistance*, beautifully apt. It was a belt buckle formed of interwoven musical instruments with the central pin in the shape of a microphone. He handled it carefully, running his fingers over the surface without taking his eyes off my face, as I told him about the history of the piece and how I'd made it. I described the heating and twisting of the wire, the careful placement of the crystals, the way each piece felt as though it had a soul and called itself into being, with me acting only as the instrument of creation. He did have nice hands, I had to admit, with very long and slender fingers. But his eyes – there was something hidden deep inside them.

'Ben,' he said suddenly, as I paused for breath.

'What?'

'My name. It's Benedict. Benedict Arthur Zacchary Davies. I thought you asked.'

'The middle fall out of the baby name book, did it?' This was a bit rude of me. All very well giving him the sales pitch but I hadn't even told him my name, so how could he order stuff? Duh. Come on Jemima, stop being such an amateur. 'Jemima Hutton.' Rather late in the day I held out a hand to shake, which involved a bit of Harry-juggling.

'Hutton? Like the place on the moors?'

'Er, yeah. I guess.' Change the subject Jemima. 'So, would you be interested?'

His eyes were tracing the contours of my face. 'Interested?'

'In my stuff.'

'Oh. Right. Your stuff.'

But now I was wondering about him. About the weird way he seemed to keep watching me. He was odd. Implacable. There was something about Ben Davies that felt like he was layers deep, that there was more to him than the superficially strange. 'My stuff. Yes.'

His hands played with the buckle, flipping it between his fingers like a magician doing a disappearing coin trick. His body language was confusing, at odds with his responses, as though he was saying one thing but thinking another and letting a little of that internal struggle seep out into the way he moved. At the moment his eyes were still firmly on my face but he seemed to be wishing me gone. 'I'm not sure.'

I *had* to get him to change his mind. If Saskia thought someone else was interested in me she might decide to keep me exclusive after all. Besides, I was bordering on the seriously broke. Even this weird guy with his tiny business tucked away down a back alley was better than nothing.

'How about if I come back? Say tomorrow? I could bring some of my smaller, less expensive stuff? Look, I'll leave you that buckle, on trust. To help you think it over?' Every marketing book said that you should be definite, give them no get-out, and I'd blown it, I could tell from his face.

'I haven't got the customers. People who come here already know me, they want the guitars, the gear, not jewellery.'

Frantically I stared around the shop. I had to find us some common point, some mutual interest, something, *anything*. My eye settled on a bright yellow star-shaped guitar hanging at the back of the shop, almost inside the kitchenette which had saved my (and Harry's) skin. 'Nice piece of equipment. My … cousin is into guitars. Do you play?'

He swallowed and put the buckle down on the counter. Rubbed his hands over his face. 'No,' he said indistinctly. 'Not any more.'

'You gave up? Why?' He didn't answer and when I looked at him he was staring at the floor. A muscle trembled in his cheek and his fingers were flexing, twitching, almost as though he was playing out a tune on the strings of a long-gone instrument. I felt suddenly ashamed; there was something naked on his face, something he couldn't conceal behind warped body-language and flippancy. A longing and a desperation.

On my shoulder, Harry stopped bumping his head against me and began to whinge. I fussed him into a new position and when I looked up, the man – Ben – was watching me again. 'Look, tell you what. I'll keep this,' and his hand closed over my sample buckle. 'If I sell it I'll order some pieces from you. If I can't, then no go.'

Hope flared through me. It wasn't exactly an unqualified yes, but then he hadn't dismissed me either. 'Thank you. Ben.'

A sudden smile lifted his face into the handsome category. 'Don't mention it. Jemima.' He flicked at the business card I'd given him. 'I'll e-mail you if there's any news.'

'Or phone. My mobile number's on the card.'

'You'd better get that young man home. He looks like he's working up to another eruption.' Ben nodded towards Harry, who did indeed have a very thoughtful expression. 'I've got no tea towels left to come to your rescue.'

As I tucked Harry back into the pram I glanced in

through the shop doorway and saw Ben take the blazing star guitar down off the wall. He struck a chord then played a riff, teasing his fingers up and down the frets like a man reacquainting himself with an old lover. He looked so poised, so natural, holding the guitar loosely with the body resting against his thighs, I couldn't believe that he'd given up playing. Yet, as I began hauling the pram backwards out of the yard, it almost looked as if Ben, with his head bent over the strings, was crying.

**21st April**

Weather fine. Sold — two guitar strings, one poster (Iggie Pop, reduced to £2.00). Breakfast — three Weetabix.

Is this the kind of thing you want me to write, doctor? Is this giving you the insight you thought it would?

Drank a bottle of wine. For lunch. Back in the day it would have been a couple of grammes of snow and carry on playing, with the world all feather light in my head and feeling like I owned the universe. Now I feel like I'm dragging each day by the neck. So, what do you want me to say? What am I supposed to write? You want the truth, you want to know how I am? I'm scared, that's how I am, scared and depressed. What's the point in any of this any more?

So, today was — a day. Wednesday? Maybe. Who cares? Who fucking cares? Nothing out of the ordinary, just hours passing here inside this box. Oh no, one thing, a girl came in with her baby, wanting me to buy some jewellery, stuff that she makes. Felt kinda sorry for her, she looked a bit out of her depth, bit unpractised, still she'll get the hang.

Come to terms with it, like we all have to do. Wade through the crap until you realise that there's only more crap on the other side. She was — cute, skinny. Bit scared-looking. Something about the eyes ... Told her my name but she didn't get it, so I guess ... hey, there have to be a few, you know? Yeah, I know what you're thinking, but no.

I don't need anyone.

# Chapter Three

When I went over to the workshop the following day, Jason was finishing off stretching a portrait of David Beckham across the front end of a Deltic diesel.

'Kettle's on.' He didn't even look at me, just hung from his ladder and welded another wire through the footballer's face. Poor Mr Beckham now looked as though he had a case of ferrous acne, and even the engine wasn't coming out of it well, but this was the sort of thing Jason did. And sold. Made you wonder about art, sometimes.

'Thanks.'

'Oh, and you got an e-mail. Two sugars.'

'I wish you wouldn't go through my mails, Jase. They might be private.'

Jason hooked a leg around a strut for stability and looked thoughtful. 'Right. So your secret lover is going to communicate by e-mail? Not very romantic.'

'Yes, Jason,' I said pointedly. 'And with you being such a romantic, and all, you feel able to comment.' I made the coffee, but to punish him didn't put any sugar in.

Jason gave me his best Johnny Depp look, lowering his head and peeping out from under his eyelashes.

'Aw, come on, babe.' He slid down the ladder and landed at my feet. 'It was only the once!'

'Taking a girl to see Hot Fuzz and then dumping her by text because she didn't laugh? Believe me, Jase, it only needed to be the once.'

Jason took a huge swig of his coffee then made a series

of faces which were an artwork in their own right. 'Jem, you trying to kill me, babe, or what?'

'By *text*, Jason,' I said sternly. 'It's never acceptable.'

'You sold something.'

'It's like being dumped by Post-It. I ... *what?*'

'Some guy mailed to say he'd sold your buckle? Now, presuming that's not kinda slang for having nailed you last night, which, babe, ain't happened since I've known ya and I'm thinking you've fossilised down there ...'

'You are *such* a pain, Jase.' I elbowed him out of the way and ran through to the office where we kept the computer. Jason liked his appliances like he liked his women so it was slim and sexy. And very, very slow. He didn't like to be intellectually challenged by his girlfriends, he said, but still managed to swim in an enormous dating pool. Mind you, he normally went out with supermodels, so, there you go. 'It must be from Ben. The guy I left the big buckle with yesterday? My only hope? I told you last night, remember.'

'Oh, right.' He hovered behind me as I logged on. 'The guy in the tiny shop, with no customers, who sold *guitars*. Yeah. Sounds a real possibility.'

I ignored him and opened my in-box. There amid the offers and deals was one from baz_davies@gmail.com.

Dear Jemima

I'm glad to say that I sold your belt buckle this morning. So, if you'd like to drop by with some more of your work I would be delighted to stock it.

Best regards

Benedict Davies

*Davies Guitars – Bessel Street – York. For all your musical needs*

' "Best Regards"! Bloody Nora, Jem! 'E talks like my dad!'

'It *is* meant to be a business e-mail, not like you'd know. The only e-mails you get hold the world record for the number of times you can mention sex in a subject line.'

'Jemima! Jason!' It was Rosie calling from the front. 'Are you in?'

'Hi, Rosie.' I popped out of the office. 'What's up?'

'Saskia just rang.' Rosie was slightly out of breath. She wasn't going to take up going to the gym again until her stomach stopped needing its own postcode. 'She's doubled my order.'

'Wow.'

'Yes. But she wants it by next weekend. So I wondered … would you mind Harry for me? Just for today, to let me make a start?'

And, sure enough, parked in the doorway was the pram. 'I assume he's in there.' Jason eyed up the changing bag and advanced on the pram with the gormless grin he always adopted when Harry was around. Whatever his faults may be, and there were earthquake zones with less faults than Jason, he doted on the baby. 'You didn't just bring the transport to, like, ease us in gently.'

'I don't know what else to do!' And Rosie suddenly had tears overflowing. 'I can't work with him there, I can't! He cries and I have to hold him, it's the only thing that stops him! And I can't do the cards with one hand!'

Jason was instantly all sympathy. Well, mostly sympathy, some of him was solder and rust. 'Course we'll have him, won't we, Jem? He's a lovely little lad,

22

no trouble at all.' And then, as soon as Rosie had gone, 'Can you take him, Jem? Only I gotta get Mr Beckham good to go.'

'But I need to get to York and drop some more pieces off!'

'You took Harry with you yesterday. Mr Stick-up-his-arse didn't complain did he?'

'No, but ...'

'I mean, he could stay here but, you know, the glue and everything. Don't want to turn out the world's youngest solvent addict.'

'All right. The guy is weird, at least if I take Harry I could use the pram as a weapon.'

Jason paused, half way back up the ladder. 'He's not, like, some kinda psycho, is he?'

'He ... what?'

'Or is he that kinda weird that you girls like, that mean and moody thing?'

'Wouldn't know. I'm not interested in *him*, I just want someone to sell my pieces.'

Jason looked at me out of one eye. 'So, guess you don't care if he's, like, some mass-murderer or something. You want me to come looking if you're not back by teatime, or are you gonna find that whole loony-tune thing attractive? Eh, Jem, is that what turns you on, that why you've not been with anyone? You waiting for some guy that nails bunnies to the wall to get your jollies with?'

I looked at Jason, who was wearing a Railway World T shirt under a set of grubby and frayed overalls, huge leather boots and enormous gauntlets. 'Any man that can out-weird you, Jase, is probably gibbering in a locked ward.' I seized the pram handle. 'And I don't want jollies, thanks very much. Just business.'

His snorting laugh followed me right the way across the rough patch of paddock that we liked to call lawn.

Harry and I, Harry's pram, changing bag, bottles, fluffy toy and spare nappies, got onto the bus to town. It took a while, with me holding everyone up while I tried to get the pram to fit into the space provided and find the brake pedal to prevent Harry suddenly vanishing down the aisle. Today Harry was resplendent in a crimson fleecy jacket like 'Little Red Riding Hood, The Early Years'. He sat in state, propped up by pillows, his chubby cheeks wobbling as the bus passed over the speed humps on its way into the town centre.

When we got off the bus next to the Art Gallery, Harry and I looked at one another.

'Right.' I tilted the pram so that I could fix him with a steely glare. 'Please keep your bodily fluids to yourself young man. I've got business to discuss.'

And I wanted a proper look at the skinny bloke. Yesterday's exploding baby incident, combined with the stress of needing to sell my stuff, had meant that I'd been left with the impression of a skeleton wearing hair and a pair of desperate eyes.

This time I wasn't quite as accurate getting Harry down the alleyway and sparks flew as we scraped our way along the brickwork into the yard. Once there the traffic sounds were muted by the buildings. A couple of hanging baskets trailed the smell of rose and honey through the dusty sunshine and a small ginger cat poked its head out from behind a dustbin. It was like a postcard of somewhere in Greece, with the white-painted buildings and the glossy flowers, the black railings with a bike tethered to it and the bench seat. Even the two small shops had a continental look, low roofed with eaves that sloped down to hide the doors in shadow. Having Harry sitting in the middle of it, slightly stained in his scratched pram, definitely lowered the tone.

Until Ben Davies walked out of his shop doorway, that is.

He was coming backwards at me down the step, shouting to someone inside. 'And *I'm* telling *you*, I will not sign!' today wearing a pale grey shirt and faded old jeans. He stuttered onto the cobbles of the yard and swivelled on his heel, which brought him face-to-face with me, at which point he closed his eyes. 'Oh, God,' he said with emphasis. 'Just when I thought I was getting the hang of today.'

'Well, sorry.' I wasn't at all and I think my lack of regret might have bled into my expression. 'I thought I'd better bring the rest of my stuff over. Since you sold the buckle.'

Ben opened his eyes slowly. 'Ah, yes, of course. I sold the buckle so you've immediately assumed that I'd be able to stock the rest of your collection, which you no doubt have somewhere about your person.' A quick look at Harry. 'Or his. What do you do, make him sit on everything like a drug smuggler? Nappy stuffed with crystal, is it?'

In the doorway to the shop a man appeared. He waved

a hand in Ben's direction.

'I think your friendly neighbourhood lawyer wants another word,' I said.

'What?' Ben blinked rapidly at me.

'The man in your shop. I presume he must be a lawyer, or legal in some capacity if he's got something he wants you to sign. Anyway, he's wearing a suit.'

'Impeccable logic there. Wearing a suit, must be a lawyer. What do you do for an encore, tell people their birth-sign?'

Harry made a gurgling noise as though someone had pulled his plug out. 'I suppose he could be a Man-In-Black.' I looked at the besuited and bespectacled figure. 'Seen any good UFOs lately?'

'I don't want to talk to him.' Ben said tightly. There were tiny lines of stress round his mouth. 'I've said everything I'm going to.'

'OK, well, looks like he's got other ideas. He's coming over,' I just had chance to say before Ben Davies leaned in, grabbed me by the shoulders and began kissing me.

I didn't see it coming and I panicked. His claustrophobic closeness, the touch of his mouth on mine; it called to mind memories I'd thought I'd buried, making them rise like dead things surfacing in a lake. I could taste him, a sweet muskiness against my tongue, smell the scent of coconut from his hair. My breath caught, my stomach leapt and I tried to move away but the pram handle was caught between our bodies. It dug into my middle, causing our joint movements to rock Harry dangerously from side-to-side so I had to stand still or risk tipping him out. Just as I was about to grab Ben's ears and lever him away from my face he moved back half a step, looked deep into my eyes and whispered:

'Has he gone?'

My breathing stammered in my throat. My heart was attempting to hijack my ribcage, driving my lungs into uselessness. 'Urrgh,' was all I could manage to say.

Ben half turned away until he could see the man still standing on the steps of the shop. '*Shit.*' His whisper licked against my skin, raised goosebumps and turned my stomach to water. 'He's just standing there, staring. Look I'm really sorry about this, but …' The mouth came down again, but this time it was more gentle and deferential, although his stubble grazed my skin and there was a gap between our bodies that would have given the lie to the situation had anyone come close enough to look.

This time I was stunned enough to stay still. And despite … well, despite everything, I felt the tiniest tingle inside.

'Now?'

I answered like a robot. 'Yes. He's gone.'

Ben let me go and stepped away. He blew out a long sigh and combed through his hair with his fingers. 'He'll be off to write a report. Great.' His voice was bitter enough to make his mouth twist. 'Still, I've bought myself some time. Thanks for that, by the way.'

I breathed out, hard, and wiped my hand across my mouth. Forced myself to relax. It was over. 'Don't mention it.'

'Is that all you have to say? "Don't mention it"?'

'Well, hold on just a second, I'll go and look it up in my little book of things to say when some tosser kisses you uninvited, shall I? Oh yes, here we are.' And I slapped him across the face. Not very hard, I still wanted him to stock my jewellery after all, but hard enough to let him know that I was angry. 'There. Or would you prefer my original answer?'

Ben stared at me for a second, putting his hand to his slapped cheek as though he couldn't believe what I'd done. Then, with a kind of snapping shut movement like a swatted insect he folded down to sit on the shop step, where he hunched himself forward over his knees and began to laugh.

I watched for a few seconds. 'You are weird, you are,' I said.

'I'm sorry.' Ben's voice was muffled. 'I'm just ... things are crazy right now.'

'You don't say.'

'You're the first girl who's ever slapped me like that. I'm not used to it.'

'Well, with you being God's gift and all, I'm not surprised.'

He looked up into my face and the laughs seemed to die in his throat. 'You really *are* upset, aren't you? I'm sorry, I didn't mean to compromise you or anything.'

'Compromise me? How? You haven't got photographers up on the roofs have you? Waiting to sell pictures of some back-street guitar dealer having a furtive snog? I don't think even *Hello* are that desperate.' Yes. We'd put my expression down to my being disturbed at being kissed by a man I hardly knew. That was easiest.

'Shows what you know.' Ben stood up again. 'Anyway, I meant with his father.' He nodded towards Harry. 'You can tell your – boyfriend, is it? – that it was only to get rid of Dr Michaels. I was just sick of talking to him today and I needed an excuse to get out of the conversation.'

'Firstly, I resent the implication that I'd have to go and blab to any significant other that I got conjugated by a freak up an alleyway and secondly, do I *really* look like someone who gave birth eight weeks ago?' I indicated myself. Today I was wearing an old pair of black jeans and a little satin and velvet top, which totally failed to disguise my lack of post-natality. 'Wouldn't I be all – you know, bouncy and stuff?'

Ben looked from me to Harry, then back again. 'What do you do then, rent him by the day?'

I gave a deep sigh. 'Look. I've brought my stuff over for you to put on display. If it isn't too much trouble. That's all.'

Ben leaned against the shop. The sun shining on his scruffiness didn't do him any favours, although it did make his hair shine. 'No, I'm intrigued now. This peculiar, bossy woman comes to my place and appears to be pushing around a stolen baby. You've got to admit it catches at the curiosity.'

I opened and closed my mouth a few times.

'Ah, right, now you're speechless.'

'I'm not speechless,' I protested. 'I'm just trying not to bite you. Do you have any idea of how unpleasant you are?'

He tilted his head to one side. 'Using what scale?'

'How the hell do you ever actually sell anything? Do you glare at people and mutter until they feel they have to buy something just to avoid the Evil Eye? Because you're not exactly Mr Winning Personality in the salesman stakes, you know.'

Ben gave a tiny shake of his head. 'Could I just have a recap – who was it that was weird, again? Because I'm beginning to feel that I'm being seriously outclassed.'

I bit my tongue, hard. Me being arrested for killing someone (provocation or not) was the sort of thing Saskia would trumpet about until the end of the world. 'Look,' I said, 'I just want to know whether you're interested in stocking the rest of my jewellery.'

'Yes.'

'What?'

'Oh, I'm sorry, did I slip into Latvian or something? Yes. Y.E.S. I'll stock your stuff.'

I opened my mouth a couple of times but the thought-gears wouldn't mesh. 'Oh.'

'Drop it in the shop, would you? I've got to go out for a bit, be back this afternoon, so if you could lock up and post the keys through the box.' Self-preservation cut in just in time for me to snatch the keys out of the air before they hit me on the head. 'Cheers.' And Ben turned and sauntered out of the alleyway, walking slowly enough for me to notice the quite spectacular tightness of his jeans, as he headed towards the main road.

'Baaawaaaah,' said Harry, succinctly.

**22nd April**
Weather – who cares? Opened the shop, no business, thought of calling an ad through to the paper but – really?

Who needs it.

Okay, yeah, you got me. I kissed her. But only to embarrass you out of doing another 'you have to come to terms with things' monologue. And she's cute, so shoot me, all this celibacy does things to a guy, you know? While I was kissing her – I just wanted a moment, a little fantasy that things were fine. That I was fine. And for that minute, that one sweet minute when she was still and quiet, I could feel her heart, taste her breath, it was like I was **real**, like I came into existence just for that.

Hell, she was scared though. I could see her pulse going in her neck like she'd got a rabbit kicking under her skin, and I wish I knew what made her freak like that. I mean – Jesus, I'm not exactly Mister Scary, am I? A six-foot-streak-of-piss. But she recovered well, give her that. Slapped my face and called me unpleasant. It was great.

And there's something about Jemima. Something that seems to look through me, makes me twitchy, to tell you the truth. Truth-telling, something I don't do too much of now, doc, you probably noticed that, yeah?

I'm guessing that's what this little exercise is all about. Making me keep a diary, the one place I can be really honest – good thinking. From your perspective. Me? I think honesty was one of those things that died, crawling on the back of comprehension and lucidity. Now I'm hanging in there and things like today make me realise how far I am from having a normal life. Funny, that one kiss from a reluctant stranger can make me see ...

# Chapter Four

I curled up on the sofa and stared into my glass of wine. 'D'you think I did the right thing?' I asked Rosie who was leaning over the table, glueing dried leaves onto card fascias. 'Leaving my stuff, I mean. He could flog the lot for stupid money and run off.'

'Mmmm. Do you trust him?' She looked up, her eyes bulgily magnified behind the glasses she wore for close work.

'Yes. No. He's a bastard.' I gulped some more cheap Chardonnay. I was really thinking about that forced kiss and my reaction to it, but I wasn't about to admit that to Rosie.

'Sexy?' Rosie stuck on a pink-tinted oak leaf, concentrating so hard that her glasses started to slip down her face.

'He's so skinny, I mean, it'd be like … I dunno, shagging a pogo stick or something. And his clothes! You should have seen them, today he'd got these jeans, right –'

'I should warn you, Jem, I'm taking this as a yes.'

'Huh.' I held up the bottle. 'You sure you don't want a glass?'

Rosie joggled her bosom at me. 'Breast feeding.'

'Yes, but you don't have to swear off everything you enjoy, do you?'

'Believe me, when you've got a tiny baby there's not much that you *do* enjoy. Or can even bear the thought of.' She jerked her head up towards the ceiling, as though her chin was on string. 'Oh, he's awake again.'

'I didn't hear him.' But two seconds later I did, as Harry's wails floated through the substantial structure of the cottage. 'Do you want me to go?'

'No.' Rosie sighed and took her glasses off. 'I'll try another feed, that might settle him.'

'Anything I can do on the card front while you're gone?'

She gave a long, slow blink as though her eyes were tired. 'It's all fine. I'll get Harry off again and come and finish these. Saskia wants them all by the day after tomorrow, so I'll have to make it a late one tonight.'

'Woah, I thought you said she wanted them by the weekend – even that would be going some.'

'She changed her mind.' Rubbing her back wearily, Rosie began climbing the stairs. I heard her go in to Harry with a rather curt, '*Now* what do you want?' and then the rocking sound of Harry being fetched from his cot. There was a loud creak as she sat on the edge of her bed, and then a silence which lasted until I'd finished my wine. I went up and peeped through her door. Rosie was stretched on the bed, fully dressed and fast asleep, with Harry alongside her, nipple still in mouth. His eyes were screwed tight shut and his tiny starfish hands had relaxed into sleep. I picked him up gently and laid him in the cot. Apart from a momentary jerk as the cool sheets touched the back of his head, he didn't move. I covered him and then his mother, although I drew the line at tucking her boob back into her dress. I pulled her duvet up and turned out the light. Then I went into my own room and flopped down on the divan.

Wine buzzed pleasantly around my head and gave rise to a pretty little fantasy, where my jewellery was discovered by a hugely wealthy woman – make that Madonna – who dragged me from obscurity to follow her around the circuit as her personal designer. Reality tried to intrude by asking what the hell Madonna would be doing hanging around Ben Davies' backstreet establishment, but I ignored it, and fell asleep to pleasant imaginings of a villa in Portugal, returning to Britain only to annoy Saskia with my new, famous friends.

At three o'clock in the morning I was woken by Harry. I pulled my pillow across my ears and reminded myself how lucky I was to have a roof over my head. Did a few nights of disturbed sleep really matter that much, in the scheme of things?

Harry let rip with another screaming bellow. How did Rosie stand it? In fact … I took the pillow away from my ears to check … why hadn't she gone to him? Rosie hated to hear Harry cry; she'd normally haul him up onto her shoulder at the merest hint of a grizzle.

'Rosie?' I got out of bed and whispered against the wall. 'Hello?'

Harry, hearing me, redoubled his efforts. I went across the landing and into the room in case Rosie had been stricken and confined to bed or something. She wasn't there.

'Rosie?' Picking Harry's warm, wet body out of his cot, I held him against me. He shuddered with the force of his crying, twisting his head away from me in rejection. 'Sssshh. It's all right.' I tried to soothe the baby, but all I could think was that something was very wrong. Rosie never let Harry cry himself into a state.

I tiptoed down the stairs, Harry's little fists clenched in my hair and his forehead banging against me like a heavy metal music fan listening to Motorhead. Rosie was downstairs, hunched over the table brushing powder paint over seed heads.

'Rosie? What's up, couldn't you hear him?' I touched her on the shoulder and went to pass Harry over, but she cringed away, holding up her camel-hair brush to ward me off.

'I … I just can't cope with him right now, Jem. That's all. I thought … I thought he'd go back off to sleep after a while. I really need to get these cards done.'

Her face was blotchy and streaked in the miserable light from the tablelamp. 'Are you OK?'

A frantic, desperate nod. 'I'll be fine. Honestly. I just need to do these cards otherwise Saskia won't let me keep supplying her. If I get all this done tonight I've only got the last bits to finish off before I deliver them.' She was avoiding looking at Harry. 'There's a bottle in the fridge, will you warm it up and feed him? He should go straight back down afterwards, and then I –'

'Rosie.' I spoke carefully but insistently until she met my eye. 'I'll gladly feed Harry and change him and settle him and anything else his little heart desires. But, and I want you to listen to me, but, I will only do it if you agree to go back to bed. Now.'

'Jem, I –'

'NOW, Rosie!'

I'm not usually this stern. Hell, I'm not usually stern at all. In fact I'm Miss Pussycat Pushover, but it had the desired effect. Rosie went all kind of limp and turned for the stairs as if she'd had a run in with a stage hypnotist. Harry stopped crying and gaped at me, with his mouth all round and just the right size and shape for the bottle teat I shoved between his lips a few moments later.

I stared down at his blissful little face as he sucked and wondered what the hell I was doing. Middle of the night and I'm feeding someone else's baby while they go and sleep. When did I get so altruistic? Although I had to admit it was nice, snuggled up while Harry fed, watching his body relax. Like being a mother without all the tedious nine months being sick and getting fat stuff. And no saggy belly or enormous tits either.

As though even the merest thought of enormous tits had beamed out through the ether, there came a tap at the window and Jason's shifty profile pressed itself against the glass. 'Anyone up in there?' he hissed.

'Only me.'

'Oh. I just finished pulling an all-nighter, saw the light was on. Got any coffee that doesn't taste like it's already passed seven sets of kidneys?'

I shuffled to open the door, Harry tucked under my arm. 'All right, but can you whisper? I've sent Rosie off to bed and I don't want her to find any excuse to come back down.'

''Kay.' Jason kicked his boots off and came in. 'I'll put the kettle on then, yeah?'

Harry's eyes began to close and his sucking eased off. He became a warm, damp weight in the crook of my arm and by the time Jason came back into the tiny living room bearing two steaming mugs and a spare packet of biscuits, Harry was fast asleep.

'Rosie been working then?'

I laid Harry down on the sofa so that I could take my mug. I'd only once attempted to hold a hot drink whilst cuddling him, and Rosie's resultant screech had been audible in Dorset.

'You know what Rosie's like for not wanting to let anyone down, if she's told Saskia that the cards will be ready tomorrow then she'll kill herself in the attempt.' I stared at Harry's downy little head. 'I'm a bit worried about Rosie, actually.'

'Mmm?' Jason looked at me over the rim of his mug. 'What about her?'

'She's just so tired. Is it natural?'

Jason lowered his eyes, giving me a glimpse of his fantastic long eyelashes. They were one of his major pulling attractions, apparently, although I *had* pointed out to him that camels have beautiful eyelashes despite smelling like a suitcase of offal. 'When Viv had her kids, she was knackered most of the time. I remember Lance – that's the brother-in-law – told me he hadn't had a decent shag in four years.'

'Jason, please!'

'You asked.' Jason blew steam. 'So, yeah. Reckon it's natural. But if she can get plenty of rest she'll be fine.'

I yawned a huge yawn that made my jaws creak. 'So you won't mind keeping an eye on Harry for what's left of the night then? Since you're awake anyway.'

He slumped down on the sofa next to Harry. 'OK. Seeing as you're so persuasive and all, I'll watch him 'til one of you gets up. Can I help myself to your cornflakes?'

I yawned again. 'Sure. They're Rosie's anyway.'

'By the way.' Jason began rummaging in the pocket of his overalls. 'You got another e-mail from your man. I printed it out so you wouldn't have to yomp over to the workshop.'

'Privacy, Jason? It's not just a word that means being alone long enough for a wank, you know. Anyway, I thought I changed my password.'

'You did. I watched. Honest, Jem, "Christian"? What kinda password is that? Never figured you for a God-botherer.'

'I didn't know one of your sisters had children.' I took the much-folded piece of paper from him, resisting the urge to start reading.

'Yeah. Jasper and Freddie. Names right out of the lost-puppy handbook, but they're okay. How about you, Jem, you're not an only child are you?'

'How do you know that?' I sounded frosty but Jason didn't seem to notice.

'Rosie and I, we got talking about you. Just after you come here it was. What with you bein' all mysterious and all. She said you couldn't be an only, 'cos you're too good at arguing.'

'I bet she didn't say it like that though.' I forced myself to relax, uncurling my fists.

'Nah. I'm just translating her words into the lingua franca. It means the language we have in common,' he added, seeing my face.

'Yes, *I* know what it means ...'

'... but you're surprised I do? Yeah, I know a thing or two, I went to Roedean.'

'Jason, Roedean is a girls' school.'

Jason gave me a wicked smile. 'Yeah it's amazing what you can pick up from those posh bints when you're giving 'em one up the Pavilion.'

I shuddered. 'That had better not be a euphemism, and if it is, please don't tell me.'

His wicked smile widened and his eyebrows waggled. He was reaching for the digestive biscuits as I took myself off up the stairs back to bed.

# Chapter Five

When I came down next morning – although actually it was the same morning, but later and it felt like another day altogether – Jason was sprawled asleep along the sofa with Harry sprawled asleep on him. They were snoring in contented unison, although I was glad to notice that the spreading stain of damp along Harry's bottom wasn't mirrored by anything Jason might have done.

I inched into the kitchen, put the kettle on and poured myself a bowl of muesli which I'd just started to eat when I was joined by Rosie. She looked pinker and better rested than she had at any time since Harry was born.

'How are you?' I asked carefully.

'Oh, Jem.' Her hands went to her black curls and she tugged at them distractedly. 'I am so sorry about last night. I was *exhausted*, but I had to keep doing the cards and then Harry wouldn't settle and –'

'It's fine. Honestly, Rosie. Harry went off like a lamb and he's been asleep ever since. It's probably the best night's sleep he's had since he arrived. Courtesy of our Jason there.'

We both peeped around the living room door. 'Bless him.' Rosie's face curved into a fond smile. 'Aren't they lovely when they're asleep?'

'I'm not sure "lovely" is a word I'd associate with Jason, but I guess he has a certain charm.'

'I meant Harry. But, yes, Jem, why don't you have a go at dating Jason? I think he'd be really good for you.'

'Rosie, do you actually like me *at all*?'

'He's not that bad.' Rosie dared another look through the doorway. 'He's quite cute, you have to admit. All leggy, and he does have a fantastic bum. And he'd take you out, you'd meet people, rather than being stuck between here and the workshop with your occasional forays into York, where you only seem to meet freaks and loonies.'

'And Saskia.'

'This is the sound of me resting my case.' Rosie poured herself a bowl of cornflakes, while I made us two cups of tea. 'Unless – forgive me for this, Jem, but you aren't into girls are you?'

The kettle carried on tipping while I stared at her and boiling water puddled on the floor. 'Just because I'd rather eat my own ears than date Jason doesn't make me gay, Rosie.'

'I know. It's just – well, I really don't know much about you, Jem and it's times like this that I realise it. After all, you never talk about yourself, do you? Before you came here I mean. All I know is that you're from somewhere down south. You don't flirt, you don't date, you're like some kind of woman of mystery type thing. Assuming you've not been recruited by MI5 to spy on the comings and goings of a deranged new mother and a bonkers artist – why the secrecy?'

'It isn't secrecy.'

'Really? When we first met we were just sort of drinking mates so I never really asked questions, and then when I found out Harry was on the way I guess I needed a friend, what with my family being so far away and all my other friends still thinking E's and vodka make a great night out. Particularly when I couldn't even *think* about vodka without throwing up. Asking about your background wasn't really on my list of things to do, not when I had a waistline the size of Montana and a memory like … what do they call those things that have holes in?'

'Honestly, Rosie, there's no secrets.' I bent down to retrieve a dropped spoon, taking care to hide my expression behind my hair. 'I've led a very boring life and I came to York to start selling my belt buckles and jewellery in a city where I thought there'd be more opportunities. That's all.'

Rosie gave me a long look. 'I've known you for, what, eighteen months now? And you've always been a good friend, always stood by me. And, after last night, I owe you one. But you can't blame me for being curious, Jem. I'm sorry if you think I'm prying.'

I gave her a quick hug. 'Nah. I'm just hiding my ordinariness and mundanity by being inscrutable, that's all.'

From the next room came the sound of an enormous fart and Jason saying, 'Whoah, sorry mate. Forgot you was there, like,' and Harry gurgling.

Rosie began spooning up her cereal. 'I take back everything. I wouldn't want you going out with that. Unless you had your own wind-turbine, then he'd save you a fortune.'

'It's got to be his looks they go for. Surely. It's not his urbane manner, that's for certain.'

Jason came into the kitchen with Harry tucked in front of him. Harry was beaming as though he'd seen the funniest thing ever. 'Two blokes in need of breakfast coming through.'

'Do you always fart like that first thing in the morning?' Rosie pushed the muesli packet towards Jason and began to unbutton her blouse.

He winked. 'Wouldn't you like to know darling.'

Rosie and I did a joint grimace. 'Er, no.'

'Anyway, ladies, I better run, catch meself some shut-eye before today kicks off. If you've not got any bacon?'

'No, sorry.' And Rosie raised herself on tiptoe and gave Jason a kiss on the cheek. 'Thanks for last night, Jason.'

Jason turned his head slowly and gave her a lip-smacking snog which went on until Harry, deprived of his promised feed, squawked. 'Don't mention it, babe.' And with a leer that was probably visible from Lancashire, he let himself out of the cottage.

Rosie was even pinker. 'Bloody hell,' she said. 'Sorry, Harry but, *bloody hell*!' She breathed out until her fringe rose several inches. 'I think I just found out how he gets all those girls.' She sat down on one of the little stools and clasped Harry to her chest.

'Good was it?'

She blew again. 'Phew. Put it this way, if I didn't feel like I could launch jumbo-jets out of my lower regions, I'd give him a go.' She looked down at Harry's busily sucking face. 'If he'd promise not to speak.'

'Or fart.'

She patted Harry's bottom. 'So. Are you down at the workshop today or what?'

'Thought I'd go back into town. Have another crack at Saskia maybe.'

'Or ...' Rosie peeped at me from under her hair. 'Have

another crack at the bloke you left your stuff with.'

'He sent me another e-mail last night asking me to pick up the money I made from the belt buckle. So if I *do* see him, it'll be strictly business.'

Rosie made a face. 'You should invite him over. We could all have dinner – I'd cook and everything. Go on, Jem, it'd be nice for me to meet someone new.'

'We don't really have that kind of relationship. He's a bit, I dunno, sharp. Edgy. Not dinner-party material certainly.'

'Doesn't matter. Ask him anyway. I could do my Mexican bean thing and Jase could come over and we'd be like two couples eating dinner like real people, not like big fat blobbery things that never go anywhere and have to have the TV on for company.'

I was about to laugh when I saw the shiny glimmer of tears in her eyes. 'I'll ask him. But don't hold your breath.' I stood up. 'Better get on. You know what Saskia always says about the early bird –'

'Yeah, it gets eaten by the even earlier cat.'

'Quite.'

It felt strange to be heading into town without Harry but it was a damn sight faster. I found myself standing outside Le Petit Lapin just as Saskia's assistant Mairi was putting the blinds up and unlocking the front door.

'Is Saskia in yet?' I asked.

Mairi paused to consider the question. She was a stunningly lovely girl, slim as a young tree and with hair so unreasonably shiny that I was convinced it was nylon. What she wasn't, however, was particularly bright.

'Well, she was going over to the Harrogate shop first thing,' was her final and very considered answer. 'But I heard someone moving about in the back.'

'Could be ghosts.' I squinted through the trendily dark windows to see whether Saskia still had any of my pieces on display.

'You think so? You hear so many stories, don't you, about these old buildings? Across the road there, they swear they've got plague victims buried in the garden.' Mairi followed me up the step and into the shop. 'I don't know what I'd do if I saw a ghost. What would you do, Jemima?'

'I'd probably try to sell it something,' I muttered, looking around the new improved interior of Le Petit Lapin. Saskia had swept away the hanging displays and the little cluttered corners which had been ideal for browsing. Instead a few choice examples of what I supposed must be native art stood in the centre of the floor reflected in long mirrors. I stared and wondered which long-term institution the manufacturers were natives of.

'Gorgeous, isn't it?' Saskia swept into view. The mirrors reflected her too; it was like being surrounded by Lucrezia Borgia. 'It's called "Femininity".'

I looked closer at the largest item. 'It's a twig.'

Saskia flipped her hair. 'That remark just shows how little you understand about Art, Jemima. That is a central representation of the essential core of womanhood. It's American.'

'Right.' I stared a bit longer. 'Americans must be very

different, if that's their essential core. Looks like a bit of old firewood. Are they flammable generally, Americans?'

Saskia turned her back and began fussing with a small glass case containing what looked like a phial of urine. 'Did you want something Jemima? Mairi darling, put the machine on would you, I'm absolutely dying for an espresso.'

I made the sign of the cross behind her back but she didn't crumble to dust as I was hoping. 'I was just wondering if you'd thought any more about carrying on selling my jewellery.' Even I could hear the note of desperation. 'You must be able to find somewhere to put it. Now you've got all this space. Or, you could stock it over in Harrogate, I wouldn't mind travelling over there with stuff, if you wanted.'

'Jemima.' Saskia looked up at the ceiling. 'Take a teeny tiny peek around you. What do you see?'

'Space. Loads of it.'

'And?'

'And a twig.'

Saskia spun around. 'Shall I tell you what you can see, Jemima? Shall I? Class, that is what it is. Class, exclusivity, rare items available only to the discerning purchaser. Now while I admit that your pieces are lovely, they are a little – oh how to put this to cause the least offence? – they are a little *obvious*. Darling.' she added as though the endearment would make me less likely to want to kill her. 'Mairi, do we still have any of those invitations to our official re-opening?'

Mairi tippytoed forwards on her immaculate little feet. 'There's still a pile here,' she pointed out helpfully. 'And over here.'

'Right.' Saskia pulled a leaflet forward. 'Look, Jemima. *This* is my stock. *This* is the clientele I am aiming at.' The brochure contained photographs of Saskia herself, often holding various odd items. In many she was standing next to people who had the sharp edges and branded hairstyle of the upper class. Everyone wore plastic cocaine smiles and showed too many teeth. 'But do come to the opening, darling.'

I stared at the shiny oblong. 'When is it?' I asked dully.

A perfect nail tapped. 'Next week. You never know you might make some contacts there. I am inviting all sorts of people, even the kind that might buy your things. Chavs with money, you know.'

Even though I knew this had been a futile errand I still felt slightly sick. 'Who's the celebrity you've got to do the honours then?' I asked, reading the gothic typescript.

Saskia looked uncharacteristically shifty. 'I've a few names up my sleeve,' she said, turning to reposition her centrepiece in a way to make it look less like something swept in on a breeze. 'Contacts, darling. That's what it's all about. Take some invitations. Bring all your friends.' She smirked. I was hardly known for my huge social circle. 'There will be nibbles but if I were you I'd eat first.'

Mairi and I exchanged a look. She had my pity, at least I could walk away. 'Thank you,' I said trying to be graceful in defeat. 'I shall look forward to it.'

'Hmmm. Now, Mairi, I wonder if you'd mind getting up onto the balcony with a duster ...'

I left them to it. Shoved the almost frictionless glossy invites into my back pocket and decided to go round to Ben's shop. He'd got some money for me and the way things were going he was my last, best hope. I had my website but that was never going to make me my fortune. I usually sold my smaller pieces that way; they were cheaper to post, easier to pack and a little bit more wearable than the big statement items I placed in shops … the shop.

Which surprised me by having two of my buckles in the window. One was attached to an enormous black leather belt draped over a dayglo-green guitar. It looked surprisingly sexy and also a little bit like an offensive weapon. The other buckle was attached to Ben, who was stacking amps to one side to make room for a cardboard cut-out figure I didn't recognise.

I waved at him. After a second he waved back. Apart from the buckle, today he was wearing a black T shirt and a grungy pair of black jeans with a ripped pocket and his hair was tied back into a ponytail. He was stubbled and his eyes looked fantastic in the middle of all that dark hair, although they had bags under them you could have lost a granny in.

'Thought I'd pop in. You know, see how things were.' I stood in the doorway slightly awkwardly, wishing he'd invite me inside. With the way he was carrying on working and avoiding my eye, I was beginning to feel a bit stalkerish.

'Things? Oh, they're great. Just great,' he repeated, wrestling the amps, settling one on top of the other and showing off a great set of biceps while he was at it. He had skinny arms but with guitar-player's musculature. I found myself staring for a moment, then wincing and hating myself, although not really sure why.

'Right. Only you asked me to come over.'

Ben stopped. 'Did I?' A grimy hand wiped his forehead, smearing it with grey. 'Are you sure?'

Now I did feel unwanted. Not that I wanted him to want me, of course, but ... well, he seemed to have forgotten that he'd asked me over and that annoyed me. 'You really know how to make a girl feel needed, don't you?' I waltzed into the shop in my best affronted fashion. 'You must be a real success in the dating world.'

'I don't date.' His words were flat, emotionless. 'All right?'

'You do surprise me.' I'd meant it to be sarcastic, but it came out a little softer, a little more rounded. Ben looked at me blankly.

'So why did I ask you over?'

'You e-mailed me last night. To pick up the money from the first buckle?'

'Okay, I did. But I didn't mean – I didn't think you'd come straight away.' He came out of the window display and squinted around behind me. 'Where's the baby?'

'He's my friend's son, not my conjoined twin. Does this mean you don't have the money for me?' I was relying on it to give Rosie something towards this month's bills.

'Are you always this confrontational?' Ben moved towards the back of the shop but watched me over his shoulder. 'I bet you're a real success in the dating world.'

Touché. 'Ha ha. All right, I'll engage in a little social chit-chat if you want, but since I'm here for the money I thought I'd save us both some time by coming to the point.'

Ben rubbed the back of his hand over his forehead again. His pony-tail was coming untied, wisps of hair curled onto his cheeks and made him look like a scruffy teenager. But one with very old eyes. 'Yes. Yes, you're right of course. I just thought maybe –' He stopped and went to the till. It was the old-fashioned kind with the push-keys and the little front drawer that pings out. 'We said a hundred and fifty, yes?' The till rang up a 'no sale' and opened. 'I'll give you two hundred. The other fifty is on account until I sell one of the other buckles.'

'You've got two hundred quid in there?' I craned my neck over the counter. 'Wow, you must have some turnover.'

'Guitars are expensive.' Ben pulled four fifties from a compartment which contained many more.

I slipped the money into a pocket and was turning for the door when I remembered my promise to Rosie. I turned back. 'Would you like to come to dinner one night?'

'*What?*'

'Dinner. At my place. Look, it's complicated, but my friend – that's the one with the baby – she doesn't get out much at the moment and I'm a bit worried about her, but she wants to have more visitors and meet more people and she suggested ...' I saw his expression and stopped talking. He looked scared. Not just creeped out as I would have been by an almost total stranger inviting me round to their place, but downright scared.

'I don't really do –'

'Believe me this isn't a date. I'm right with you on the not dating thing. This is ... look, forget it. I'll tell Rosie I asked, but you're – I dunno, spending the next ten years being criminally skinny or something.'

'Do you really think I'm skinny?'

I stared him up and down. 'Honestly? Yes. And those tight trousers don't do you any favours, you know. What's wrong with ordinary jeans?'

'Is this some kind of quiz?'

'Never mind. E-mail me if you sell anything else, and I'll go and make a few more bits to replace the ones you have sold so far.'

I had my hand on the door latch and was pushing the truculent door open when he spoke again quietly. 'I'll come.'

Puzzled, I turned to face him. 'Where?'

'To dinner. Your short-term memory is really shot, isn't it?'

Something deep inside me was relishing this banter. It was – now, what was the word again? Ah yes, *fun*. Something I had forgotten about, until now. 'It's all this having to restrain my intellect, use little *tiny* words that you'll understand. My address is on the card I gave you. Little Gillmoor. Near Kirkbymoorside.'

'Those are real places?' Ben came past me and pushed the door shut again. 'This dinner invitation. It is … I mean you obviously don't – you don't want to get to me for any reason?'

'No, Mr "I fancy myself more than a bit". I do not want to get to you, whatever you might mean by that. I'm only asking because Rosie wanted me to. Personally I don't care if you never eat again.'

'Wow. I bet you're fun to be friends with. Look.' He'd

clearly come to a decision, and one that had cost him. But he'd stopped rubbing muck all over his face. 'I need someone to help out in the shop. Only for a few hours a week that's all, but I have these ... appointments and at the moment I have to close so that I can go. If I had someone to just man the till – and with me selling your things, I thought you might be interested. Proper rate of pay obviously. And of course I am doing you a favour by coming to dinner.'

Say what you like about our man, he did have a lovely smile. For a walking anatomy lesson, of course.

'Well ...' I balanced the time that I'd have to spend away from making jewellery with the fact that I'd get paid regularly. 'All right. But you don't even know if I can work the till or deal with cash. I might sell everything while you're away and run off with the money.'

'You're trusting me with your buckles. I'll trust you with my shop. Deal?'

He held out a grubby hand. I hesitated, but shook it eventually. He had a warm grasp, and fingers which were so long that they met around my hand. 'Deal.'

'I've got an appointment tomorrow. Can you come in around ten? I'll hand over to you and then leave you to find things for yourself. It's not too difficult.' Ben looked around at the obvious lack of customers. 'We're hardly Marks and Spencer. Do you know anything about guitars?'

'Some. I had a friend who played.'

'I thought it was your cousin?'

Damn. I was usually better than this. Something about those deep eyes, his manner, made it hard to remember.

Or should that be *easier to forget*. 'Yes.'

'I'll run you through what you need to know in the morning then.' A pause. 'You were going,' he said, at last.

'I am.'

'And dinner will be … when?'

I shook my head. I was feeling a little bit shaky at my own inconsistency. Cousin. Yes I'd told him my *cousin* played … 'I'll ask Rosie. Let you know tomorrow.'

A nod. A dismissive turning away. I went out of the shop and stared for a few minutes at my buckle in the window.

**23rd April**

It's funny, y'know, how life is. There you go, strumming along, everything the same grey bassline, and then, wow, it's like the melody just kicks in and there you are, singing it all out again. Like you've done it forever. Today was one of those days.

I felt human again. Went out this afternoon and bought some clothes, just retro gear, nothing fancy, but … She thinks I'm skinny! Whoa with the pot-kettle interface there, babe! But there's something … she's hiding something. Her face when she talked about the guitars, like she's been told the apocalypse is coming on the back of a Gibson. And her eyes went all kinda deep and dark and I could hear this tune in the back of my head, up and down the scale like a warning. She's trouble. I can feel it, the music knows it, but it's like I can't move out of the way in time, it's gonna hit me and, you know what? Part of me wants that. Something

vast that hits and breaks and blows me open ... Sorry.
That's a lyric there. One of my better ones, from the days
when ... yeah. I know. Don't dwell, don't look back.

See, the trouble is, when you don't look back, you don't
see what's creeping up behind you.

# Chapter Six

I lay in my tiny bed in my tiny room listening to the regular breathing of Rosie next door. It was comforting hearing her snuffles and the musical plucking of bedsprings whenever she turned over. Being able to reach out and touch all four walls at the same time. Womblike. *Safe*.

Rosie couldn't understand how I could bear to sleep in such a small space. 'You'll only have to put on half a stone and we'll need special equipment to get you in and out.' I hadn't told her, compared to a cell, this cosy little room, with its bulgy plastered walls and the ceiling with the suspicious dip in one corner, was a palace. Everything in it, from the daisy-embroidered duvet to the collection of shells on the wonky window ledge, was *mine*. And I didn't have to fight to keep it. Didn't have to sleep with a wary eye open in case my random cellmate took a fancy to something and backed up her desires with some sharp edges collected earlier from the prison workshop.

A faint memory crept through. A room like this. A trail of perfume, a soft hand under my chin, a whispered conversation about – something. The anticipation-filled weight of a Christmas stocking pushing a pony-patterned eiderdown onto my feet, and a pink night-light showing me exciting shadows against a papered wall. A memory that hurt, despite its benevolence. There was so much more underneath than that one Christmas morning, but I was afraid to look too far back, and the pain made sure I never did.

The psychiatrists had a name for it, this deliberate blocking of all memory. It had gone on so long, and become so effective that I'd probably rate my own chapter in any given psychology text book. In fact, one of the prison doctors had written some kind of thesis based on me, a fact which made me quietly proud, in a horrible sort of way, an acknowledgement that at least I could do something, even if that something meant cutting dead any memory of anything that had once been good.

But, just sometimes, the urge to have some of it back forced me to let a little remembrance seep through, with a blinding snatch of pain as payment.

In the shapes made by the bizarre arrangement of cracks in the paintwork I could see faces. One reminded me of my brother Randall. The way the crack curved as it met the plaster looked just like the way his nose hooked round to the left, or had ever since he'd had that run-in with a guy who'd turned out to be a better fighter. I shook my head into a more comfortable position and forced my body to relax. Remembering my family always made me tense. Made me smaller, reduced the target.

And as for Chris – I wouldn't remember him. Not now.

# Chapter Seven

'What do you think?' I held up the finely twisted wire shape for Jason's approval.

'Yeah. What's it meant to be again?'

'It's a musical stave. With a treble clef.'

'Oh yeah, right, getcha now. Lovely.' Jason turned his attention back to David Beckham, who was proving a little troublesome. The material he was painted on kept tearing away from the bolts Jason had used, and shreds of canvas hung from the footballer like an epic disease.

'Right well. I'm off. If I get the nine o'clock bus I can be there in good time.' I pushed the beginnings of the new buckle to the back of my workspace and rubbed my eyes. I'd spent hours working on it yesterday evening and my eyes felt strained and boiled. I'd started early after a night of disturbed sleep and bad dreams, and didn't want to get caught by Rosie before I left. Didn't want to admit to her that I couldn't be a stand-in mum for Harry whenever she had work to finish, which made me dislike myself more than I usually did. Surely as a friend, blah blah blah, should be only too happy to help out with crying baby, blah blah? But something about Rosie just lately disturbed me. I had the feeling that if I was available she'd palm Harry off onto me whether she had work to do or not. A kind of blind hope had seized me that she'd find she could cope perfectly well if I wasn't always there to step in; hence the getting up early and sloping off to the workshop. At least Jason hadn't put in another night shift, trying to work whilst he alternately hummed and ran an arc-welder would have made Harry look like the peaceful option.

'Ah. You're here.' Ben was fussing around at the front of the shop when I arrived. 'Here's the keys to the till, those are the front door keys. If you have to pop out be sure to lock up. I'll see you later.' He was pulling on a ramshackle jacket as he spoke, something that looked as though it had been a horse-blanket when it was new.

'Is that it then?' I squeezed past him in the doorway, coming in as he was going out. 'Aren't you going to tell me how to deal with shoplifters or anything?' I tried to ignore the brief moment of contact when I'd felt the bones of his shoulder against mine.

'Are you serious?' Ben looked around the walls at the big heavy guitars. 'All right, if anyone comes in wearing a tent, search them before they leave.' And he was gone, trailing a surprisingly nice scent for someone who didn't date.

I spent a pleasant half-hour searching for any clues as to where he had gone with his newly shiny hair and his expensive aftershave. There was a calendar hanging behind the counter but today's date didn't bear anything more informative than a circle in yellow highlighter pen. I did establish that Ben kept a spare T shirt in a drawer in the little kitchenette and that he had 145 unread e-mails, but I couldn't log in to read them even if I'd wanted to.

After that I got a bit bored. No-one came in even to browse. I flicked through *Kerrang!* even though it was an old copy, straightened a few instruments which had become oddly angled under their own weight and finally started walking about reading the posters on the walls.

'Zafe Rafale!' they all screamed in various fluorescent colours. 'Brit DJ of 2008!' Zafe apparently had played numerous gigs in and around York in the last year and every single one seemed to have been commemorated on these walls. I wondered why. Did Ben have some connection (maybe sexual, I thought pruriently) with Zafe? Or did he just have an affection for dayglo posters? Maybe he was colour blind?

I was out in the kitchenette making myself a coffee when the bell went off with a vibration that made the walls tremble and ran down my spine like an electric shock.

'Goody, a customer.' I rubbed my hands and squeezed through the hatch so that I could pop up from behind the till. 'Good morning.'

'You're a woman!' The lightly bearded young man with the stripy hat and earrings took a step back.

'Well done. There are men that have got my clothes off before they discovered that.' I cleared my throat. 'I mean, how may I help you?'

'Is Ben in?'

Ostentatiously I looked around the tiny shop. 'Good Lord, he appears to have sunk through the floor! Never mind, he might be skinny but he'll snag on the foundations. Try again later, we'll spend the rest of the morning winching him up.'

The lad was staring at the ground as though he really did expect to see the top of Ben's head slowly subsiding through the planking. 'I just ... I saw ... thought he might want to know,' he finished. Presumably he charged by the word. 'Will you show him?' Almost coyly he pushed a magazine across the counter. 'Page forty,' he whispered, and by the time I'd picked it up he was gone.

The magazine, contrary to my first impressions and beliefs, wasn't 'Fashion Crimes and Your Part in Them', but the latest edition of *Metal Hammer*, the best-selling music rag for the discerning heavy metal freak and indie-guitar strummer. Page forty was full of news snippets, what's on the grapevine. As the lack of customers continued, I sat back to read through it.

When Ben came back into the shop, carrying the jacket to reveal the surprisingly tight white T that he'd had on underneath, I thought I'd found it.

'A lad brought this in to show you.' I slithered down from where I'd been sitting on the counter swinging my legs and presumably putting off customers in their droves.

'Uh huh. Did you get a name?'

'*Metal Hammer.*'

'Odd name for a lad.' Ben hung up the jacket and opened the till.

'The magazine. And don't worry, I haven't stolen all your cash, in fact I haven't even opened the till while you've been away. I think he wanted you to see this.' I brandished the open page under his nose, my thumb marking the relevant piece. 'They've just brought out a guitar that tunes itself. Like a robot.'

'Cute.' He took the magazine from me and handed me a twenty-pound note. 'Here. Reckon that's enough for an hour and a half spent drinking my coffee and … *no*.

*Please, no!*' He'd looked down at the page of print and dropped the magazine as though it was on fire. He was shaking.

'Ben? Hey ...' Cautiously I touched his arm.

'What?' He flinched, then his eyes searched my face, almost panicked. 'I'm sorry, I'm losing ... I didn't ... hear you.'

'Are you OK?'

He gave a laugh as though something was very unfunny indeed, then slid to sit with his back against the counter. 'Someone walked over my grave,' he said. 'Yes. That's just what happened.'

He had a tattoo at the top of his arm. I could see it where the sleeve of his T shirt had rolled back. It was a curious Celtic design encircling his bicep and again I found myself wondering about him. I had to close my eyes and breathe hard to stop myself. *Don't get involved ...*

'I don't understand.'

He looked up at me. 'Don't even try.' He rested his chin on his drawn-up knees. 'Honestly, Jemima, don't even try.'

'Is there anything I can do?' I was puzzled by his over-reaction. There hadn't been anything on that page that my skim reading had shown up as being a volatile subject. Unless he was truly distraught that Metallica were bringing out a new album.

Again, that laugh. 'I'm afraid not. No.' And now he was staring around at the walls of his shop and I didn't know if he was aware of it but his fingers were moving on his thighs as though he was strumming a tune on an invisible guitar. 'There's nothing anyone can do. And that's official.'

'But ...'

'Go home, Jemima.'

He looked so distraught that it cut through my usual distance. Clenching my teeth I touched his arm again. Traced my finger across the tattooed lines. 'Nice tatt.' Trying to change the subject, to stop the obvious pain.

A hand came up and slapped my fingers away. 'Don't touch me.' It was said wearily, heavily, as though the words were well-used. 'I'm sorry but I can't ...' and then he looked at me again with such pain in his face that I had to look away. 'Just go home.'

I headed for the door and the whole atmosphere was so full of his torment that it was like walking through glass splinters. As I started over the threshold he called me back.

He dropped the magazine. 'Jemima?'

I didn't turn round. 'What?'

'Did you ask your friend?' He was still sitting on the floor with his knees under his chin. His hair hung over his eyes, but I knew he could see me. 'About dinner?'

'Oh. Yes. Thursday. Is that OK?' This was a ridiculous conversation. Ben was sitting there looking as though he wished the world would end, while I, feeling chastised and decidedly shaken, was conversing over my shoulder. And we were discussing dinner-party arrangements? What's wrong with *this* picture?

'Thursday? Fine. Yeah, good.'

'I'll e-mail you. With directions and stuff,' I added quickly. I'd rarely had such a response to someone before. This feeling of sympathy combined with some other emotion that I was never, *never* going to try to identify, had left me breathless. I wanted to get out, to breathe, to reassure myself.

'Thanks.' His voice sounded a little stronger now, a little more sure. Perhaps now he'd established that I wasn't going to make some kind of pass.

'OK. I'll just leave you to … stare at pictures of people wearing real clothes or whatever it is you do.'

This time he laughed and it was a proper laugh. 'Great, thanks. Then afterwards I'll just go off and ignore some proper meals, shall I?'

I half-smiled at him, still over my shoulder. 'You do that, Ben.' And I managed to walk out of the shop, even though every nerve wanted to run.

**24th April**
Did you know? DID YOU? What the FUCK did you think it would do to me, finding out like that?

### I'm
### not
### doing
### this
### any more

'Have you got a *Metal Hammer*? The newest one?' I flung myself into the workshop and confronted Jason, who was eating a sandwich.

'Got a mallet,' he said with his mouth full. 'Any good?'

'The magazine.' I hunted around the office, picking up and discarding various glossy weekly and monthly rags which Jason picked up like he picked up sexually transmitted diseases. 'It's got a picture of a bloke with lots of hair on the cover.'

'Goes with the territory.' Jason stood up and lifted the magazine he'd been sitting on. 'This one?'

'Thank you.' I flicked through to page forty.

'So then, what's the interest? You gonna take up the axe then? Or you looking to be a groupie?' He licked his lips. ' 'Cos I might just be able to help you there. Basic training an' all.'

'Jason, I am *not* a virgin.' I didn't even bother to look at him, I knew what he'd be doing.

'So you say.' Jason stuffed the rest of his sandwich into his mouth and came to read over my shoulder. 'So, whatcha lookin' for?'

'I don't know.' I was still skimming the page. 'Anything unusual, anything out of the ordinary.'

'Metallica got a new album comin' out.'

'Not that. I don't think.'

He blew a cheese-and-pickle scented breath. 'Well there's not much else here. Usual bands split, bands reform, some dodgy old codgers doing a come-back tour … nah.'

'There must be something that set him off.'

'Oho! You getting some action, Jemima my love?'

'You sound exactly like Bill Sykes when you talk like that, do you know?'

'Don't he play bass for Radiohead?' Jason kicked my leg.

'As in *Oliver Twist*, you illiterate.' I finished my third re-read. 'Nope. I give in.'

'Well don't look to me for help. I know nothing about the British music scene these days, spent too long being cosmopolitan, me.'

'Spent too long freeloading in the States you mean.' Jason had only recently returned to Britain after two years spent getting his name, his face and his only other significant part known in America. Apparently the American art world had hailed him as the new 'wunderkind'. I wondered if they knew what it meant.

'Gotta get going.' Jason slithered away back to his studio. 'David B won't weld himself you know.'

I headed out of the workshop and across the scrubby corner-plot garden which separated the barn from the cottage. I had loads of work to be doing, all my paperwork, and some new-build jewellery and the website could do with a bit of attention. But I couldn't settle. There had been something in Ben's face this morning, something wounded and wary and it had caused a reaction in me, as if I was recognising a part of myself on display in someone else. Maybe it was time to start packing.

'Hi, Jem!'

Rosie looked good this afternoon, I was glad to see. Neatly dressed, albeit in one of her old maternity frocks, and with a slick of make-up. Harry was kicking his legs, nappyless, on the lawn under a sunshade while Rosie put the finishing touches to another set of cards, working at the kitchen table she'd pulled outside onto the rough patio which surrounded the cottage. 'Hey, Rosie. How's it going?'

'Good thanks. Saskia's coming over in a minute to pick these up. Do you have time to set a tripwire round the front?'

'Snaring animals is illegal,' I answered happily. It was so good to see her back on bantering form.

'It'd be a kindness. Well, for us.' She slipped the last batch of cards into the cardboard carton at her side and taped up the lid. 'How was work?'

'Do you mean the paid kind, or the artistically satisfying and yet strangely unpopular kind?'

'In the shop. Whichever one that is.'

'It was … yeah, it was okay. Um, Rosie, listen …' I was about to start introducing the subject of, maybe, my needing to move on, head for pastures new, *run away*, when Rosie clutched at my arm.

'It's Saskia!'

We heard the engine approach, like the trumpets of doom, and then a huge 4×4 articulated itself around the corner from the road and drew up on the gravel drive outside the cottage gate. 'Uh oh, there goes the neighbourhood,' I muttered to Rosie. She smiled at me, a tight grin. 'Am I allowed to hide?'

'No!' Rosie grabbed my arm. 'You have to be all glossy and welcoming and stuff, but a bit scatty so that I look organised and together in contrast.'

'So glad I'm only here as comic relief,' I sighed.

'Besides you couldn't expect me to cope with Saskia on

my own. She eats people like us for dinner.'

'She doesn't eat anything as common as dinner. She'd have us as a six-course banquet, with fruit and nuts.'

'Sssh! She's coming.' The door to the 4x4 swung open but to my astonishment it wasn't Saskia who made the descent onto the roadside, but her husband Alex. He walked around the bonnet, held the passenger door open for a pair of exquisite shoes to appear, and then went to the back door and held his arms inside. He turned towards us with their son, Oscar, in his grasp.

'Ah, Rosie,' said Saskia. 'Nice to see the baby getting some air. Gosh, he's rather small isn't he? Is he, you know, quite healthy?'

Alex greeted us with his customary weak grin. I'd heard that he was a cut-throat businessman, that property markets would crash and burn without the attentions of Alex Winterington. But put him beside Saskia and he was just a thickset guy with receding chins and hairlines and no charisma to speak of. Or perhaps that was just the Saskia Effect. After all next to her Attila the Hun would have come across as a bit wussy.

'Harry's fine thanks. Oscar's grown, I see.' Rosie tugged her curls into order and smiled at Oscar, who grinned back with a five-year old's blindness to nuance. He was a handsome chap, with blond hair which grew at improbable angles and brown eyes like his father. He was always pleasant-natured too. Saskia's genes must be circling in there somewhere, waiting to stage a take-over, but there was no sign of them emerging yet.

'Yes, well, Oscar is the tallest in his year at school. Actually, talking of schools, we were just on our way to have a look at Blandford. They've offered Oscar a place there in September, so we thought we'd combine the trip with picking up the cards.'

'Isn't he a bit young?' I piped up. Blandford was the area's leading boarding school, strict, religious and, I'd heard from Jason, the local centre for the acquisition of drugs, as the entire sixth form supplemented their trust funds.

Saskia rolled her eyes at me. 'Darling,' she said in a tone that implied I knew nothing, then turned back to Rosie. 'Have you put Harry's name down for anywhere yet? Or aren't you planning on an education for him? After all, it can be *such* a waste of money if they don't turn out to be high-achievers.'

Rosie and Alex rolled their eyes at each other and I warmed towards him a little more. In his arms Oscar was wriggling. 'There's Jason!' he cried. 'Let me go and see Jason!'

On the far side of the lawn where the big converted barn stood with its doors wide, Jason was just visible lurking in the shadow. He was smoking a huge roll-up which he hid behind his back when he saw Oscar leaping across the grass. He must have palmed it or shoved it in the bushes because when he led Oscar into the barn both hands were empty.

Alex bent next to Harry and tickled him, but straightened up when Saskia cleared her throat. 'So, Rosie. Have you finished the consignment?'

Rosie waved a proud hand at the box. 'Taped up and ready to go.'

'Good.' Saskia touched the cardboard with the tip of

a French manicure. 'I'm glad. Because I'd like another hundred, ooh, I was thinking … in time for the re-opening? Say, by next Monday?'

Rosie opened and closed her mouth. 'I'm not sure –' she began.

Saskia clicked her fingers at Alex. 'Money sweetie,' she said in the same tone that I would have used to ask a dog to sit. Alex pulled his wallet from the pocket of his beautifully tailored jacket and handed the whole thing over to Saskia. She didn't even look at him, just closed her fingers around the pigskin and I found myself wondering what the hell the two of them saw in each other. Or I did until I saw what the wallet contained – Saskia definitely admired a man with a large wad. 'Five hundred. And another four hundred if you get me the second batch before Monday.'

Rosie stared at the money.

'You can get a lot of outfits for that,' Saskia said, looking at Harry. 'Or at least, you can in those high-street places you shop at. And this young man is going to start needing things, stimulating equipment, you know the kind of toy. I'd pass you some of Oscar's old things but we're still hoping that we might have another little one ourselves.'

I was sure I saw Alex give a shudder when she said that, but I could have been imagining it.

'Trouble is, you see, Saskia,' Rosie was holding the five hundred pounds in a clenched fist, 'I've also got to supply a few other shops. Not in such quantity, obviously, a dozen cards here and there but, you see, if I'm doing all these for you I won't have time!'

'Can't Jemima help?' Saskia flicked her hair. 'I mean, she's at a loose end now, isn't she?'

'Actually no, I'm supplying another shop in York. Busy, busy, you know.' Carefully not mentioning that the shop owner had panicked me into thoughts of leaving altogether. Saskia would have offered to help me pack.

Saskia's reaction to my statement was startling. She whirled around and stared into my face. 'What? Which shop? Where? They're not a member of the Board of Trade are they?'

Having for once gained an upper hand I wasn't about to let it go, and just smiled. She turned back to Rosie.

'Well, you'll have to make your choice, Rosie. A hundred cards by Monday or I'll have to rethink using you as a supplier.' Saskia did the clicky-finger thing again at Alex. 'Fetch Oscar, darling, will you? He really mustn't hang around with Jason quite so much.'

But there was no need for Alex to go trotting off because Jason was heading our way, with Oscar holding his hand, pulling and tugging on his fingers like a Labrador. 'Mum! Dad! Jason's got this huge picture of David Beckham and there's nearly a whole train in his barn, with all the controls and everything. He says I can come and see next time he goes and buys one and maybe get to drive it!' Oscar's eyes were shining with hero-worship. Jason's were glazed, probably with dope. 'Can I?'

'You mustn't disturb Jason, darling.' Saskia motioned to Alex to take their son back to the car. 'He's a very famous artist. But it will be nice for your friends, when you start at Blandford, if you tell them that your family is on such good terms with Jason Finch-Beaumont. Talking of which, Jason, may I have a quick word with you? Rosie, could you carry the box to the Hummer for me? My doctor says that I mustn't try to lift large things.'

'She didn't have a problem lifting Alex's wallet,' I whispered to Rosie as I helped her to lift the carton of cards into the back of the vehicle.

'She's not allowed to lift lower-class things,' Rosie whispered back. 'I bet if this box was made of diamonds she'd be hefting it around like a wrestler.'

We sniggered at this image of Saskia until the car's exhaust filled our faces. 'So. What are you going to do? Make her some more cards?'

Rosie sighed and went to pick up Harry. 'Well, I have to, don't I? I mean, she's my biggest sales point and – forgive me, Jem, but I don't want her to do to me what she's done to you.'

'She wouldn't drop you, would she?'

'You've seen her new style. How long do you think my cards will last in that place if she decides on another *refit*? Anyway –' Rosie wiggled her bundle of cash under my nose, Harry tried to grab it. 'How about we use this to go shopping for the ingredients for Thursday night's little get-together?'

'Saskia wants me to open her shop.' Jason's voice sounded a little strained. It also sounded a lot slurred.

'She never gave you a set of keys, did she? You'll have the place full of one of your crankcase installations and dubious friends before she can blink.' Rosie cradled Harry and began putting a nappy on him, one-handed.

'On Monday. She's asked me to be her celebrity.' Jason sat down. 'Me! I know nuffin' about opening things.

'Cept for bottles.'

Rosie and I looked at one another. 'God, she must be desperate.'

'Well he is a celebrity.' I looked down at the bewildered and befuddled celebrity in question. 'I don't think there's much to it, Jase, you just have to cut a ribbon and socialise. It's only Saskia showing you off.'

'I don't want to be shown off!' Jason nearly wailed.

'Tough, sunshine.' I hauled him to his feet by one pathetic elbow. 'Fame is a bitch. Well, no, Saskia is a bitch, you're just the approachable face of fame as far as she's concerned. Now, can I borrow your car keys? Rosie and I are going shopping.'

We left Jason flopping back onto the lawn and went to town in style.

# Chapter Eight

Thursday evening arrived and I was still trying to decide what to wear. Because of the stupendous coincidence of both Rosie and me getting paid in the same week (spending two days paying each other back the money we owed and then finding it about equalled out anyway) we were actually planning quite a posh do. Well, as posh as any do could be which had Jason as a guest.

I'd bought a lovely dress in a curious frosty green colour which made my hair look blonder than normal, but in a good way. So many colours made me look as though I'd gone prematurely grey, but this one made me look all Viking.

I tried the dress on in front of the mirror and couldn't believe it was me I was looking at. Where was that skinny, scared girl now, the one with the bruise-stained cheeks and the gaze that could never quite meet anyone's eye? The quiet say-nothing girl from the prison, head down and flinching as she walked? She'd been overlaid by the new me; Jemima. Poised, strong, confident. I squared my shoulders at my reflection. I could do this. I could stay living here, selling my stuff through eBay and Ben's shop. I was doing it. I was making a life.

But then I went to straighten the hem, caught my own eye and saw straight through the mirror image to the horror beneath. The veneer peeled away and I was left staring at the real me, feeling sick. How could I possibly think I was coping? Had I forgotten so quickly what my life consisted of? And how *dare* I even relish the thought of talking to Ben Davies like a real woman might talk to a man, honest-to-God 'flicky dress and glass of wine' talk, lowered eyes and secretive smiles – didn't I *know* what would happen?

I took the dress off and put my jeans on. But then of course Rosie would want to know why I wasn't wearing my party dress so I was forced to put it on again. How could I tell Rosie that I didn't want Ben to think I'd even considered the possibility of dressing up for him without her asking awkward questions about why I hadn't? Or, even worse, after a couple of drinks asking him why he didn't ask me out – oh God. I took the dress off again.

My tiny bedroom was full of clothes. My one nice trouser suit lay across the bed and it looked as though someone had skinned a corporate lawyer. There were skirts and tops everywhere else, but nothing suitable. I gave up and put the green dress back on.

'Phwoooarrr! Top totty! Oh, it's you, Jem.' Jason was sprawled along the sofa, Harry perched on his stomach. 'Nearly din't recognise you.'

'Thank you,' I said. 'You look very nice too actually. Did it need surgery to remove those overalls?'

'Ha!' Jason tugged at the lapels of his suit. He did look very glamorous in his tuxedo, I had to admit. 'Rosie insisted I dress up. Hey Rosie!' he yelled into the kitchen. 'You want me to put Harry to bed yet?'

Rosie appeared in the kitchen doorway, pink in the face and slightly flustered. 'Oh, would you, Jase? That'd be lovely. I'm just finishing off the starters in here. God, Jem, that's the door – will you get it?' She wiped her hands distractedly down the front of her appropriately Rosie-pink dress and vanished back into the steamy depths.

I squeezed past Jason, who was on his way up the stairs with Harry, and opened the front door to Ben. He was carrying a bottle of wine, wearing a suit minus the jacket and with the top shirt button undone. He had his hair loose but sort of swept back. It suited him.

'Hello.' We faced each other across the crumbling front step.

'You found us all right then?' I took the bottle he held out.

'Your instructions were great. The taxi driver never knew this place existed before now, it's a lovely village.'

'Thank you,' I replied without thinking.

'Build it yourself then, did you?'

'Ah, I see Mister Polite has released control of your body. Come in.'

Ben followed me into the living room and then we stood, side by side, silent. He was wearing the nice aftershave again. 'This is fun,' he said finally.

'Yes. Not a bit awkward or anything.' I could see him eyeing up the dress, and to forestall any difficult questions I grabbed the bottle from the dining table and poured him a glass of white wine. 'So. Sit down.'

'Yes! Ma'am!'

'I didn't mean – ' I took a giant sip of my wine. 'Please. Sit down. If you can bear to soil yourself with our petty furniture that is.'

'I'll try.' Ben sat. I perched on the arm of the saggy but comfortable chair opposite and carried on drinking. 'So, is it just yourself here or–?'

'Oh, no, I share the place with Rosie. She's my friend, the one I told you about.'

'The baby's mum?'

'Yes. And the baby's called Harry.'

'Right.' Ben took a sip of his wine and looked around at the walls. They were plain stone, whitewashed and hung with several of Rosie's pictures, but even so they didn't merit quite the scrutiny he was giving them. The silence stretched.

'Dinner will only be a minute!' Rosie stuck her head into the room again and I seized on the distraction.

'Ben, this is Rosie. Rosie, this is, obviously, Ben.'

Ben stood up and smiled. 'Hello.'

Rosie came out of the doorway towards us, grinning a grin which slowly left her face. She turned to stare at me.

'Jemima?' she asked.

'What? You told me to invite Ben, so I did. That's still all right, isn't it?'

Rosie looked from me to Ben and back again. 'Well, yes, of course. Sorry, I'm just – distracted. Um. Nice to meet you – Ben. Jem, could you come and give me a quick hand, the chilli is playing up out here.'

'All right.' I followed her into the tiny kitchen which was full of bubbling noises and steam, accounting for the frantic nature of her curls. She shut the door behind us.

'Jemima!'

'What?' I was genuinely puzzled by her reaction. 'I know he's a bit skinny but he's OK, honestly. Well mostly OK. Especially when he's not wearing Lycra.'

Rosie dropped her voice so that it was barely audible over the sound of the boiling. 'Don't you know who he *is*?'

'Yes, I already said. It's Ben.'

Rosie ran her hands through her curls. She now looked as though she'd been attacked by an evil hairdresser. 'Jemima,' she said very evenly. 'I know I've never asked questions about your past or anything but tell me this. Did you spend the last five years on *the moon*? That man, in there.' Rosie put both hands on my shoulders. 'That man is *Baz Davies*.'

'His name's Ben.'

'No!' Rosie shook me now. 'Baz Davies! *The* Baz Davies. Lead singer and guitarist in *the* biggest band to come out of Yorkshire in the last ten years and I am *including* the Arctic Monkeys in that. Haven't you ever heard of Willow Down?' She sighed. 'Listen. Willow Down. Huge. Sensation. Made Coldplay look like some outfit touting round Working Men's Clubs. Went to the States. Huge in States. Baz Davies …' She flung out an arm towards the living room. '… dropped out. Went to ground. Band fell apart.'

Benedict Arthur Zacchary Davies.

'Oh,' I said.

'He's been off the radar for five years. No-one knows what happened, they were in the middle of a tour of the States that was, apparently, phenomenal. I saw them once.' Rosie's eyes suddenly went misty. 'Fibbers, that club in York. They played *Foolish Words*, my favourite, I got drunk and went home with a bloke who turned out to be hung like a mule. Ah, happy days.'

I walked out of the kitchen and back into the living room. Ben was still perched on the edge of the sofa, rolling his now empty glass between his fingers.

'We subdued the chilli but I'm afraid the rice might go for your throat,' I said.

Ben looked at me. 'You know.'

'What? That you used to be in a band? Yes. Rosie recognised you. Saw you play Fibbers, apparently.'

He gave a short laugh, then shook his head. 'That's gone, not me any more. This is who I am.'

I felt a little tremble down my spine. 'Yes.'

'I'm not that person now.' Ben stood up.

'I understand.'

'I'd better go.' Ben handed me the glass. 'I'm sorry. I thought it would be all right, but people keep – it's like they won't let it go.' He turned and headed for the front door, but I followed, catching him in the doorway.

'Ben, wait.' I grabbed his arm and he went suddenly still, like a cat picked up by the scruff. Then he turned in my grasp. 'Look, I don't care who you are. I don't even know who you *were*, I never heard of Willow Down before tonight. All I know is you're Ben Davies and you've got a shop in York. That's all I want to know.'

'It's not as simple as that. Really, Jemima. You're best off staying clear of it all. You're a nice girl and I was getting used to being Ben with you, but–' he tailed off, eyes clouding.

'But it's like being haunted by your former self?'

A sudden, surprised smile rose on his face. 'Yeah. Pretty much. Whatever I do, wherever I am, someone will recognise me. Oh, it's less than it used to be, now it only happens once, twice a year and they get fed up with waiting for a sound-bite from me on why I quit, how could I do that to the band, all that shit. My customers stopped bothering to recognise me ages ago. But it's there, always, there in the background with the looks and the whispers.' The smile was gone now, replaced by a hunted look. 'Sometimes – Christ, I can't believe I'm saying this – sometimes I wish that Baz Davies had died.'

'Oh, Ben.' I patted his arm and he let me. 'Look. Stay and have dinner. Rosie's all right, just ask about Harry and she'll forget anyone else in the world exists let alone some ex-guitarist.'

'And you?' There was an expression which might have been hope in his eyes.

'Oh, I don't give a stuff who you were. Right now you're the only person willing to sell my buckles so if you told me you wanted to be known as Mary Jane I'd go along with it.'

Ben leaned back against the wall. 'I don't know.'

'Sooner or later people are going to forget, you know. You're just going to be this bloke who used to play in a band, like millions of others. Come on, Ben. Stop hiding. Get on with your life.' I felt myself cringing inside – I could talk the talk like no other, but when it came to walking the walk – .

'I can't. I can't take the questions, Jemima.'

'Then why don't you give a press conference and tell them what they want to know?'

'No.'

'Oh come on, people will forgive almost anything these days! What was it, drugs? Booze? Drugs and booze? Are you gay?'

For a second his eyes were full of the dusk. 'Why can't you just let it be? Why can't anyone?'

I looked over my shoulder into the cottage. Jason was standing watching us, half-hidden in the entrance to the living room. He raised his eyebrows at me.

'Ben?' Ben had his head down, hair covering his face. I touched him again, finger to shoulder and he shuddered like a nervous horse. 'Come on. Rosie's made one of her Mexican specials. You wouldn't want to disappoint a woman who can cook like she can, trust me. Your stomach will love you for it.'

Every word he'd said had slit through my skin and run into my veins. Every word I'd said to him had been loaded with hypocrisy and I wished I could tell him so. But I couldn't.

'Just promise me one thing.' Ben looked up at me eventually. 'Before I go back in there, before I have to start pretending all over again.' His eyes were very dark. 'Promise me that it won't make a difference. Now you know who I am, who I *was* – that everything will go on the same.'

'What, that we'll still snap and snipe at each other like a couple of prize bitches? Oh, I think that's without question.'

A small smile tinted his face. It took away some of the pallor of his skin and gave his eyes a bit of sparkle. 'Oh, good. I think.'

'Although I have to say that you're the first famous person I've ever met who was glad that I *didn't* know who they were.'

'You've met a lot, have you?' Ben let me lead him back into the living room. The hunched, scared expression was mostly gone.

'Oh, yeah.' Well, I'd been locked up with a woman who'd stalked Robbie Williams. That probably counted.

# Chapter Nine

Rosie, Ben and Jason got on surprisingly well. OK, maybe not so surprising, when you're five bottles and a Mexican Chilli special in, almost anyone you can focus on begins to look like a friend. But it helped that Jason, like me, hadn't the faintest idea who Willow Down had been. Ben finally relaxed and only occasionally betrayed how he was feeling by twisting at the cuffs of his shirt.

'So, you coming to Saskia's grand opening?' Rosie shoved another portion of chilli onto Ben's plate. The bloke looked as if he only weighed about eight stone but he could eat like a man who's been in training. Jason poured Ben another glass of wine and furtively drank the dregs of the bottle.

'Who's Saskia?'

'Well,' I brandished my knife. In my defence I was also more than a little bit pissed. 'You see this pointy thing? Imagine this, in the mouth of a Rottweiler that's covered in pins.'

'With a bellyful of wasps,' added Rosie helpfully.

'That's Saskia. And she's opening her shop – well, re-opening it. Jason's doing it, aren't you?'

Jason jumped guiltily. 'What? What'm I doin' now? Come on, Jem, y' can see both me hands!'

'He's her sleb.' Then I went a bit quiet because we were all painfully aware that Ben's celebrity status could have knocked Jase's into a pond. 'Anyway. It's next week. We're all going.'

'Things like that aren't really my – well, thing,' Ben

said. ignoring Jason. 'I'm not much one for crowds. And I don't know her.'

'That's all right, we all wish we didn't know her and we're still going!'

Ben gave us all an old-fashioned look, which I think was meant to be disapproving but his head was wobbling so it gave him more of an air of a slightly pissed-off glove-puppet. 'You three are horrible, aren't you?'

'And proud of it.' I held out my glass for Jason who'd popped the cork on the last bottle, the one Ben had brought.

There was a flare of lights as a car turned into the driveway and stopped, followed by a momentary blaring of a horn. Ben covered his glass with his hand. 'That'll be my taxi,' he said. 'Need to get up early. Got another appointment tomorrow at eleven. Don't want to be hungover for it. Will you be all right to come over and mind the shop for me, Jemima?'

I nodded. Ben got up and I was suddenly overwhelmed with an urge to grab his arm and ask him not to go. To stay here, shooting the breeze into the small hours and getting giggly over Jason's ridiculous world view, as we had been doing. It was as though we'd been in a bubble for the last few hours, one in which I didn't have to think about anything other than this life I'd made for myself. Me. Here and now. With Rosie and Jason playing host and hostess and this skinny rock-guy with the big secrets.

'Jem?' Ben laid a hand on my shoulder. 'You all right? You looked like you were on another planet there for a minute.'

Some of the stress was gone from his face. I felt a

tiny flutter inside me, somewhere round my heart. Yes, Ben was a good-looking guy. I could see it but I daren't acknowledge it. Even the knowing caused a little acid burn at the base of my stomach.

'Nah, I'm fine. Just tired. I'll see you tomorrow.'

To my surprise he moved a tendril of hair away from my face. 'Yes. Another day of insults and misunderstandings.'

'I'll look forward to it.'

When Ben had left, Jason collapsed onto the sofa and farted hugely. 'It's those frigging beans, Jem,' he said not apologetically. 'An' I reckon you and our Mr Davies could get a very nice thing going, if you know what I mean.'

'Don't be silly.' I helped Rosie clear the table.

'Honest. I saw you and him giving each other the old googie-eye treatment. He's gotcha goin', admit it.'

'He's screwed up.'

'Yeah! *Gorgeous* an' screwed up. Thass what you girls all love, isn't it? Bit of the old tormented genius thing. All the secrets, all the mystery. Hey, you could get it out of him, why he quit that band, sell your story to the rock papers! You'd make a mint!'

'Immoral, even for you. Besides, old news. No-one's going to pay a fortune for that.' Yawning enormously I scraped the last of the food into a freezer container. 'Are we washing up tonight, Rosie?'

'Nope. I'm off to bed before Harry wakes up. Night, Jase.'

Jason looked a little bit deflated. 'What, not even a snog?'

'Sorry.'

'An' I put me suit on an' everything! I dunno, what's it

take to get a shag round here?' But he grinned to show he was joking, or if not, at least not annoyed to be cast out into the cool night, still carrying the bottle.

Rosie looked at me. 'What is it with you and Baz – sorry, Ben? I've never seen you so – I dunno what it is. It's like you're both scared of each other somehow.'

'He's way too sharp. Talk to him for long enough and you'll feel like you've been juggling razor blades.'

'Yeah, well. He's bound to be a bit spiky, look at what he's been through. And now he's running a poky little shop in the back end of York with no customers and, by the look of it, no friends. I think he needs you, Jem.'

'Oh, rubbish! He's fine. I think he likes his life the way it is now.'

Rosie gave me a very hard look. 'But what about you? I was watching you two all through the meal, tiptoeing around each other, never asking the right questions. Him I understand. But you? Why are you so scared to get involved, Jemima? You say talking to him is like juggling razor blades, well sometimes talking to you is like juggling soap bubbles. What exactly is your problem?'

My mouth opened and then closed again. I literally could not think of anything to say. I'd never been so glad to hear Harry begin one of his chugging cries upstairs in his cot. 'Harry's awake,' I said unnecessarily.

Rosie cast her eyes wearily at the ceiling. 'And so another day dawns,' she said. 'Goodnight.'

I watched her head up the stairs. She'd been on top form all evening, sparky and witty and much more like the Rosie she'd been before giving birth. I hoped she'd turned a corner. She clearly adored Harry but it was as if she'd never been prepared for the fundamental life change that having a baby would bring and now she was fighting it. A kind of tussle between her love for her child and the restrictions that he placed on her life.

I sighed and stared at the wall, much as Ben had done earlier. Ben. With his guilt and his fear and his awful confusion, all because he'd walked away from his life. And I knew deep in my heart that I could help him to feel better. All I had to do was talk to him. Tell him. Say those words that I found it impossible even to think, *I know how it feels, because I did it, too.*

Don't think about it. Don't think about his expression – that helpless turmoil in the face of discovery. Don't think about the occasional bone-cold touch of his fingers, his huge eyes so full of disaster …

In fact, go to bed.

### 30th April

Weather. I'm sure there was some. Didn't notice.

I went to dinner with her. Surprised? Yeah, not as much as I was. Last week I was ready to jack it all in, go move to Greenland, somewhere, anywhere no-one would know me. Where nobody would be looking at me, saying 'didn't you used to be in that band? Didn't you used to be somebody?' But really, what did I think? That none of the guys would ever play again, just because I shat on them from a height?

You know something? That's **exactly** what I thought. Willow Down was **my** band. Okay, mine and Zafe's. And now Zafe is out there again, taking over, doing what he thinks is right, but ... what about me, doc? What does that leave me with?

And then. At first I thought she was coming on to me. She's the first person to touch me ... hey, get your mind out of the gutter, man, she's the first person to get inside my head. To look as if she even wants to try to understand what's happening to me. I guess what I mean is, she's the first person to see **me**. Not Baz, not the guy with the lead guitar, but me. Ben.

Thought about standing her up. But, in the end, I couldn't do it. She's got this wounded kind of expression, like she's been kicked in the face and is trying not to show it, the thought of making that expression worse ... nah. Not me. Not cruel. Stupid, yeah, hold my hands up to that one, even a little crazy maybe sometimes. Well, you of all people know what it was like before. And now, shit, I can't find the words to say it ... it's like <u>this</u> is the 'before'. Like something really big is waiting to happen, muscles tense, mind all silver-wire; almost like the coke cutting in, taking it all up to some new level.

No. Before you get that look, reading these words and kinda looking at me over the top of this notebook with that caved-in face like I've disappointed you in some fundamental way. No. Let me say it this once. I DID NOT USE. I am not using. Told you, never again.

I'm tempted though. When she ... when Jemima found out who I was, I thought it was over.

What, though? What could be over? There's nothing to finish. She's a friend and I don't think she'd break over this. But she's getting into me, one tiny little slice at a time. Like a diamond punch.

# Chapter Ten

Ben had left a note pinned to the door of the shop. 'Had to go early. Door's open, see you later. B.' There was a smudge after the initial, almost as though his pen had hovered uncertainly over an 'x' then decided against it, for which I was glad.

I went straight to the computer and hit Ben's guest account. Googled 'Willow Down', 4 million entries. I could be reading through this stuff until I started thinking all rock musicians were long-haired layabouts who should get a proper job. I went for the first, the Official Site. Opened the page and there was Ben staring back at me from the screen. A little younger, a little unfocussed about the eyes, but definitely Ben. Next to him was the heading 'Band to reform without troubled front man Baz Davies'.

Oh.

Well, at least I knew now what he'd seen in *Metal Hammer*. No wonder he'd been so upset, it must be like finding out that all your best mates from school had a reunion and never even invited you. I read on. 'The new line-up with Zafe Rafale moving from bass to lead guitar will be playing dates from next spring. There's been no news on Baz Davies since he walked out on the band in Philadelphia during their world tour in 2005.'

'You only had to ask.'

The voice from over my left shoulder made me leap up and crack my shins against the counter. The pain, in turn, made me angry. 'What the hell are you doing, creeping up on me like that!'

'Creeping? Oh yes, sorry, I was forgetting that this was my shop and that on no account was I to walk in through the front door!' Ben slapped his forehead. 'I just keep on not remembering that.'

I wanted to blank the screen but since I knew he'd already seen what I was looking at, it seemed pointless. Still, the picture of him almost throbbed. 'Why are you back?'

'Appointment was cancelled.' He looked at the computer. 'You Googled me.'

'I …'

Ben shrugged. 'Yeah. Well.' We both stared at different parts of the floor for a moment. Ben had his hands in the pockets of a pair of black jeans which made him look even skinnier than usual. 'I think this is where you apologise?' he said at last.

'Do I?'

'Yeah. Then I make us both a coffee and we forget any of this ever happened.' Those deep brown eyes flickered up to meet mine for a moment. 'Please.'

'I'm sorry,' I started. The wary look stayed in his eyes. 'But you're – you were incredible, it says so here. "Best guitarist of a generation".'

'Things change.'

'Yes but –'

'Jemima.' Ben came very close, standing with his face almost touching mine. 'It hurts. It hurts like hell, what I used to be, all the things I lost. So please don't tell me that I ought to go back to the band or that I should start playing again or any of the other crap that people have spouted at me. If I could, I would. But I can't. All right?'

'You're hiding.'

'Yes, I'm hiding!' Ben turned away from me.

'But what is there to hide from?'

He didn't seem to hear me. Instead he stared at the posters which papered the shop walls so colourfully. 'Zafe Rafale was my best friend,' he half-whispered. 'My mate. We did everything together after we left school, started the band, got drunk, got stoned. Shared everything. Then I let him down big time.' Now he faced me. 'Things got fucked up so royally, so spectacularly that I –' Suddenly he stopped talking. His face was a blank mask. 'This isn't your problem.'

I had to knit my fingers together to stop myself reaching out for him. The pain was so manifest that he was hunched slightly beneath it and I wanted to touch him. To take some of it away. He was standing so close that I'd only have to reach up and I could put my arms around his neck, pull his head down and – hell, what was the matter with me?

'OK, I'm sorry I Googled you. I was curious that's all. But all it is, you were the singer in a band I've never heard of, and now you're not.'

Ben smiled and the mood lifted. 'That's it,' he said. 'That's precisely it. Mr Nobody, me.'

We grinned at each other and, for one tiny moment, the sheet which hung between me and the real world lifted a fraction and I caught a glimpse of the life I could have, if I could only stop walking away from the possibility. A man, maybe not *this* man, but one like him. A baby, a Harry of my own, if I wanted one. A career rather than makeweight jobs to earn money. I could have any of those things, *all* of them, perhaps, if I wanted it enough, and all I had to do was stop running.

'Shall we go out?'

The barrier slammed down again as I stepped back and banged myself again, my hip this time. 'What? Out? Like as in *out* out?'

'I meant shall we go out for a coffee rather than drink it here? There's a snazzy café round the corner and I feel like celebrating the cancellation of my appointment with a hazelnut latte and a big bun.'

I breathed again. Why had I thought that he was asking me to go out with him, as in a date? When I already knew that he didn't. And I wouldn't, anyway? Oh, this was not good, this was not good at all. 'All right. But it better be a very big bun.'

'Oh, and I got some flowers. Would you take them to Rosie? To say thank you for dinner last night?'

I surprised myself with the fierce hot burn of jealousy. 'If you want.'

'She's a lovely girl. And Jason's a nice whatever it is that Jason is. Artist. A good guy.'

'Yes, they're lovely, both of them.'

Ben went to the kitchenette to get the flowers and then busied himself locking the shop door. 'Are you and Jason …?' He made a kind of wavy motion with his hands. 'Or is Rosie?'

'Good grief, no! He's a friend. In as much as you can befriend a wild animal.'

'Right. And you're all going to this opening thing on Monday?'

'Supposed to be, yes. Rosie's flat out doing some more cards for Saskia. She's going to keep Saskia sweet, I'm only going in the hope that she might change her mind about stocking my jewellery, and Jason's going because he's kicking it all off. So we're not what you might call typical guests.'

Ben steered me into the tiny coffeehouse beside the art gallery. Fountains tinkled outside and made me realise how much I needed the toilet. 'If ... if I went ...?'

I was so shocked I nearly wet myself. 'What? You'd come? What if she recognizes you?'

'Well ...' Ben lowered his voice as the rest of the coffee queue looked up at us. 'Most people don't. It's five years ago and I was quite different then.'

I just gaped.

'And it's not like I'm in hiding or anything. I mean, I walk around, people see me. I just don't – it's not as if I go round introducing myself "Hi, I'm Ben Davies, I used to be in Willow Down", or being on Never Mind the Buzzcocks, or programmes like that. Most people who do recognise me just think they're mistaken.'

Oh, God. I was going to wee. Here, on the spot. I was astonished that the entire crowd in the coffee shop, which seemed to be entirely made up from a SAGA coach trip and some overdressed Goths who'd probably got lost on their way to Whitby, weren't all listening in to our conversation. This man, who'd been a virtual hermit for the last five years, was offering to come to a party. With me.

'I'm sorry, I need to go to the toilet,' I said.

'The sound of the flush helps you think, does it?' Ben

asked, a bit kindly for my liking.

'It's either that or pee on your shoes.'

'So, do you want me to come then?'

Oh, more than anything, Ben Davies, do I want you to come with me. I'll get you to play your guitar to me and you'll realise that you've nothing to fear from the world. I'll tell you my secrets and my fears, and just maybe sharing them will take away their power. 'I'll be back in a second,' was what I said.

I sat on the toilet for far longer than was necessary with my head resting against the cool paintwork of the stall. I couldn't believe that I had so nearly betrayed myself. What the hell was the point of making all those promises, of swearing that I would be my own person, only to have it all wiped out by one man? All right, that man was – come on, say it, Jemima – that man was sexy, but you *swore*, Jemima, on your brothers' lives, that you'd never let yourself get used again. He might not look like a user, but none of them do, do they? Until they have you, and then …

When I came out of the toilet, Ben was sitting opposite a man at a corner table. They were deep in a conversation which involved a lot of hand-waving. 'You don't understand anything about me, do you?' Ben was saying as I approached. 'I'm not giving in to this!'

'It's not a question of "giving in" Ben,' the other man replied quietly. 'It's a question of adjustment.'

Ben was breathing deeply. His skin had the faintest trace of sweat on it and his eyes contained an expression of barely restrained panic. 'Ben?'

He jumped as I touched his arm. 'God! Jemima!'

'Sorry, am I interrupting?' I looked from Ben to his friend. It was the man I'd seen outside Ben's shop the time that Ben had kissed me. This time he was wearing cords and a frayed-looking shirt, but he still had an air of authority. 'I'll just go.'

Ben grabbed my hand. 'I'll come with you,' he said, winding his fingers through mine so tightly that it hurt.

'Ben. You can't keep doing this. I really thought we were making progress, you've been getting on so well. Please don't tell me you're going to give it all up now! For the sake of what?' The man eyeballed me as though it was my fault.

Ben's grasp on my hand was threatening to cut off the circulation. In his other hand the bunch of carnations bobbed as though they too were being throttled. 'I'll come to the next appointment,' he said. 'But I'm not promising anything.'

'That's all I can ask.'

'Fine.' And Ben stood up so quickly that the table rocked, endangering the overfilled salt cellar. Not letting go of my hand he squeezed us between the seats until we reached the door and burst out into the sunlit square beyond.

'Okay,' I said levelly. 'So what was *that* all about?'

Ben shook his head. 'Nothing.'

He still hadn't let go. I could feel the bones of his fingers against mine and the warmth of his body radiating from beneath today's God-awful T shirt. 'I'm beginning to feel like a member of the Scooby-Doo gang, with all this mystery,' I said. 'Shaggy, probably. Not one of the girls, they always find out what's going on within seconds. And anyway, I can't do the socks.'

'It's just … nothing. Look, I'd better go back to the shop.' I waited for him to ask me to come too, but he didn't. Just passed the flowers to me.

'I'll maybe see you on Monday?' I relaxed my hand and his fingers fell away. 'For Saskia's party?'

Ben shrugged, shook his head. 'Yeah. Maybe.'

'Tell you what, I'll come to the shop and we could go on from there. It's only round the corner.'

This time Ben looked at me and smiled. 'Were you the kind of kid who thought your teachers lived in the school?' he asked.

'What?'

'I won't be at the shop. Not in the evening.'

'Oh!' I was embarrassed, but at least he was smiling. He looked so much nicer when he smiled, less moody rock-star. 'You've got a house.'

'Mmm-hmm. Here –.' Ben pulled out a pen from his back pocket, grabbed my arm and wrote an address up my wrist in black biro. 'Come here. Monday, around, what, seven?'

Then almost as if it was he who was embarrassed, he turned with a flick of his hair and vanished into the tourist crowd, leaving me standing a bit stunned. The ink on my skin made my arm feel stiff and I couldn't stop staring at the hieroglyphs he'd scrawled alongside my veins.

'He lives *where*?' Rosie was jiggling Harry on her hip and trying to set out a batch of cards when I got home and spilled my story.

'Wilberforce Crescent.' Almost unconsciously I was tracing the writing with my finger. 'Seventeen.'

'Wow, that's a bit posh isn't it? Oh, now look what I've done! Jem, could you take ... thanks.'

I took the proffered Harry and rested his weight against my shoulder. 'I suppose he must have bought it when he was, you know, famous.'

' "Famous" isn't a dirty word, Jem. Well, only when it's applied to Jason, when suddenly everything becomes dirty. Anyway, it might not be his, maybe he's renting or living with someone. Maybe that's why he doesn't date, because he's not single.' Rosie began brushing chalk over the cards with a goose-feather.

'He came to dinner on his own. And he doesn't behave like a man who's attached.'

Rosie looked up at me, sudden interest flaring in her eyes. 'Oh ho! Did he make a move on you?'

'No! It's just the feeling I get from him. You know how married men just seem – different. More secretive.'

Rosie turned her back to me. 'Do they?' She busied herself in her bag, pulling out stems of grasses and pressed petals.

'I mean I know Ben is secretive, too, but not in the same way. I think he's secretive because he doesn't want to remember stuff.'

'OK, so what's your excuse?'

It was my turn to revolve, using Harry as a shield. 'I'm not secretive.'

Rosie snorted. 'Much! Anyway, is he coming on Monday or are the pair of you so collectively secretive that you didn't tell him where it was and he wouldn't tell you whether he was going?'

'Um. Something like that.' I joggled Harry.

'God, you should get jobs as spies. Oh SOD!' A bunch of the cards slipped from the edge of the table and cascaded to the floor in a jumble of pink chalk and brittle stalks. Instead of bending to pick up the overspill Rosie began to cry.

'Rosie?' I put the arm which wasn't supporting Harry around his mother. 'What's up?'

'Nothing!' wept Rosie. 'Except I keep dropping things and Harry won't go to bed and let me get on and I'm really tired but I've got to get these done before Monday and I just feel so *useless*.'

'Ah, useless. Now there's a feeling I'm right at home with.' I gave her a squeeze. 'Look, I'll take Harry down to the workshop. Jase can help me mind him to give you some space, and if I was you I'd use the time to have a bit of a sleep. I'll give you a hand to catch up with the cards this evening. And in the meantime you can gaze on the flowers that Ben sent over for you and ponder on the fact that despite the fact he's *my* friend, you've got carnations and all I've got is a cheap tattoo.' I brandished my written-on arm.

Rosie gave a snot-ridden smile. 'Yeah, for an expensive address.' But she let me collect Harry's changing bag, bottles and blanket and I even thought I heard her give a small sigh of relief as I lugged him and his paraphernalia out of the door.

'Jason!' I strapped Harry into his bouncy chair and sat him down in the doorway to the office. 'Are you in?'

'Oooof! Ow! Sorry, Hazzer me old mate, didn't see you down there!' Jason barrelled in through the double doors and tripped over Harry, causing him to ping alarmingly up and down for a few moments. 'Woss up?'

'Are you busy?'

Jason looked at me suspiciously. 'Is this one of those, wossname, trick questions? I'm an international artist, babe, course I'm busy.'

'Could you keep an eye on Harry for a few minutes? I've got some research to do.'

Jason stared at me for a second. Then a smutty grin spread over his face, which made him look even more Johnny-Depplike than usual. 'Oh, I see. *That* kind of research is it?' And he picked up Harry, bouncy chair and all. 'Come on little guy. We're not wanted round here, not unless you wants to be drowned in all that oestrogen stuff.'

'What are you talking about?'

Jason just winked and he and Harry went off into the big studio from where I could hear the commentary to a football match issuing from Jason's expensive sound system.

I fired up the computer and called up the Willow Down website. Seeing Ben through pictures made me realise just how good-looking he was. Real life seemed to deaden the impact somehow, or maybe it was something to do with the awfulness of his clothing. Clothing which seemed to be purposefully designed to conceal what these old photographs revealed to be a fantastic body. My God, I had no idea that under those skuzzy T shirts there was this muscular torso, whip-muscled arms and corded shoulders. Or, presumably they still were there, but he didn't pose quite the same way, with his mouth unsmiling, hair carefully tumbled and his hips thrust forward in invitation. I'd certainly never seen him stand like that, but then I wasn't sure any human *could* stand like that, not without invisible support from behind. His fellow band members weren't bad either, a collective of dark eyes and tight jeans, like a sack-full of male models handed guitars and dropped onto a stage.

Zafe Rafale, despite his slightly Greek name, turned out to be an ash-blond beauty. All finely chiselled bone structure and immensely long legs like a palomino stallion; his pictures showed him flinging himself around the stage, arms variously wielding a sunburst-yellow guitar or just a microphone. One shot showed the two men duetting. Ben had his eyes closed, one hand loosely around the neck of his guitar, the other holding the microphone stand. Zafe, hair plastered sweatily to his forehead, was pulling at the neck of his T shirt as though about to remove it. With Ben's dark hair and Zafe's resplendent goldenness, they looked like the rock world's version of Yin and Yang.

'Thought so.' Jason loomed at my elbow. 'Having a touch of the lusty are we, Jemima?'

'It's not like that,' I replied, without turning round. 'I'm interested, that's all.'

'Yeah, interested in pictures of young blokes getting their kit off and wagglin' around a stage.'

'This is Willow Down.' I clicked to enlarge the picture. 'Are you sure you've never heard of them? What with you being such a mover and shaker on the youth scene.'

'Nah. Name rings a bit of a bell. Maybe I heard

something when I was in the States. I'm not really an indie-music kinda guy, Jem.' In the workshop, Harry raised his voice in a squawk of protest at being neglected. 'You're so interested, why doncha just ask?'

I sighed. 'He's not keen to talk about it.' Plus, I wasn't keen to push him. Not for all the reasons that Jason might assume, either. Keeping secrets myself made me hyper aware of how an enquiring conversation could turn. One moment you're asking simple questions about someone's family – the next they've spun it all round and they're asking you about yours.

'Man of mystery. Ah, go on, Jem, you love it really. Maybe I should try it, being all cool and inscrutable and stuff.'

'Jason, people only have to ask you what time it is and you've given them your life story.'

'I know. I'm easily scruted, I am.'

'That's not a word.'

'Ha. Harry and I are gonna head up to the village for some more paint-mix stuff. You coming?'

'No thanks, I'm going back to the cottage to make sure Rosie's having a snooze. And I've got some work to do, some orders to parcel up and stuff.'

'Have it ya own way. I notice you're not losing the picture of your boy there.'

Exaggeratedly I pressed the buttons to wipe Ben's face from the computer screen and hoped that Jason hadn't noticed me bookmarking the page.

## 1st May

Weather – Night.

It's like I'm feeling a chord I hit years ago. The music won't let me go, it's here in the back of my head all the time, playing itself out over and over, getting to the chorus, until I feel all I have to do is lean in and Zafe will be there with the refrain, grinning at me from across the stage.

Okay, yeah, before I go any further, I'm sorry I cut the appointment. I should have called you, let you know but … I was going to come. Was nearly at your office before I caught myself thinking about her, standing in the shop, wondering about me. And, for the record, I was right, she'd Googled the band. Was standing there with the DVD screenshot from 'All the rain is broken glass', staring at it like she'd never seen me before.

God, it hurts. Seeing the website, seeing the pics, seeing how we were. But what surprised me was that it hurt more seeing it through her eyes, comparing what I used to be and what I am now. Like … like when she's not looking at me then I'm still Baz Davies, still the guitar-king, screwing all day, playing all night and then sitting up writing songs. Hanging off the roof of the tour bus with a groupie astride my cock and my head full of buzz. And then her eyes fall on me and I'm back to being Ben, back to the shop with no business and all the music locked inside my head.

But I think … I dunno, but maybe she likes me. The **real** me, the me that isn't coked-up Baz or screwed up Ben, but the me that lies underneath it all. The one I think I can be. And, oh, I so nearly told her. I could feel the words, taste the shape of them, knew all I had to do was say them, put them into the air and then she'd know me. Know me right through to my bones. Fuck, I wanted that.

And then I couldn't face up to making it all real. You were right, what you said, I do have to adjust, I'm sorry I blew you out and, no, I was not holding her hand, it was just contact. Right then I needed to touch something that wasn't a part of the shit. You were facing me down and I knew, in my blood, that you were right but I couldn't … I can't make the step. I can't stop pretending.

I'm so scared.

# *Chapter Eleven*

'Wow, Jem, you look great!'

Monday had arrived and I'd spent a lot of the day involved in trivial things. Painting my nails, shaping my eyebrows, stuff that I hardly ever bothered with these days, when there was only Jason to tell me that my legs were so woolly I was in danger of being shot as a runaway llama.

'Thanks.' I pulled at my skirt. It was a little tighter and a lot shorter than I usually wore. 'Thank God for internet shopping.'

Rosie came closer and sniffed. 'Ooh, Lacoste. Yum. But hang on a minute ...' She reached out and carefully undid the top two buttons of my pintucked shirt. 'That's better.'

'Hey, I'm not going to a fancy dress as Little Miss Slutty you know.'

'Yes, but that skirt is all daring and raunchy. Your top half was a bit shop assistant but it looks terrific now.' She gave me a wink. 'Ben's going to love it.'

'I'm not wearing it for Ben. I'm wearing it to show Saskia that I might be down but I'm not out.'

'Hmmm.' Rosie herself looked professional and cool. I looked, I thought, a bit like a walking blowjob in comparison.

'Right. I'm off to Ben's, I'll see you at the – whatever it is we're calling it. The Grand Opening of Saskia?'

Rosie snorted. 'She's been open for business for years,

the ho. Can we pretend it's a party? A real, proper party, where we get to drink drinks we'd normally sneer at and circulate with people we've never met before? After all, I've got a girl who advertised on the village noticeboard coming in to babysit Harry and I really don't want to have gone to all the trouble of squinting at those postcards just to go to the opening of a shop!' She wrinkled her nose. 'Some of those adverts are really *strange*.'

'All right. I'll see you at the party.'

I got the bus to York, which seemed ignominious. All got up like I was I should at least have been travelling in a white stretch limo and carrying a tiny dog in a bag. Ben's house was impressive, a four-storey Georgian townhouse with black-painted railings outlining the steps up to the front door. I clopped up in my high heels and rang the bell. As I waited I stared down; there were windows below street level for what would have been basement kitchens in the house's heyday. Now they were prime sites at which to sit and look up the skirts of passing girls. I hoped Ben wasn't down there gazing up at my gusset.

I knew he wasn't when I heard the sound of someone galloping down a staircase and hurtling to the front door. 'Hey.'

'Hello.' I peered through the crack that he'd opened the door. He still had the chain on, even though he must have known it was me because the door had a spyhole. 'Are you coming tonight then?'

'Oh, God, is it tonight?'

My heart sank and I found that I was pulling down the hem of my skirt. Now I was going to have to walk into Le Petit Lapin alone and Saskia would surely notice. 'Yes.

But never mind. I'll see you another time.'

I'd started to clop back down the steps to the pavement when I heard the chain come off and the door open. 'So, you don't want me to come?'

I turned. There was Ben looking absolutely *gorgeous* in a bow-tie and dress suit. 'You are evil,' I said.

'Yep. Come in a sec and have a drink. If even half of what you've said about Saskia is true, I think we might need to prime ourselves.'

I followed him inside. The front door gave onto a massive hallway, pale wooden floors and tiled walls, with a decorative black-and-white frieze pattern. 'Wow.'

'Did you say wow?'

'This place. Mind you –' I looked around. 'It is a bit like being in a huge gents' toilet.'

'You should see my bedroom.'

There was a moment of silence while we digested that sentence, both realising it sounded as though he'd meant something he clearly didn't mean, and then another moment of flustered consternation while Ben pretended he didn't realise he could have been misconstrued and I tried to over-ride my brain.

'Full of graffiti and smells of wee?' I got there first.

'No, that's my car.'

'You have a *car*?' My voice went so squeaky that Alsatians in Milan could probably hear me.

'Mmm-hmmm.' Ben seemed to be enjoying my astonishment.

'Are you sure?'

In answer he grasped me around the wrist and pulled me over to the huge window which let daylight into the hall. It was high and arched and almost as big as a door. 'Does that look like something I might be a little uncertain about?' He pointed with his free hand at the silver car parked on the roadside beyond the black railings. 'Or does it look more like an Audi R8?'

'That is one sexy car,' I said, a concise, if not exactly Top Gear-level critique.

Ben opened his mouth then obviously thought better of it and began to lead the way down the sleek hallway. Another archway gave onto a huge, high-ceilinged room, still with wooden floors, which contained a few sofas clustered in a corner like furniture playing Sardines. 'Sit down and I'll get you a drink. White wine?'

He wandered over to a cabinet while I gingerly sat on one of the sofas. It was extremely comfortable, squashy and yet firm at the same time. From here I could see the enormous speakers along the walls. 'Is this your music room then?'

He didn't answer, rummaging around and opening doors, then emerging with two glasses of golden-yellow wine. 'So, tell me about Saskia.'

'Nothing to tell. She's stopped selling my things, but she's got Rosie working like a demon.'

'Are she and Jason …?'

'What is your obsession with Jason's sex life? No, as far as I know, Saskia is not having any kind of thing with Jase. She may be an evil harpy with a hole where her heart should be, but she's happily married to Alex. Well, she's happily married to his wallet anyway. Mm, this wine's nice.'

'I'm still not clear why you and Rosie hang around with

her. If she's such a witch. Don't you have other friends?'

There was a pause. 'She was the first person who actually believed in my jewellery,' I said, thinking fast. I couldn't tell him that it was only supplying Saskia that had kept me from having to sleep in a box under a bridge after I'd arrived in York. 'I met Jason in a bar, he introduced me to Saskia when he found out what I did, then I met Rosie and moved in.'

Ben looked at me levelly. 'Okay, not asking for your life story, Jemima.'

*And you're not going to get it. I've seen enough people turn away in disgust and I couldn't bear – I don't want to see that look in your eyes, that look that says 'I pity you.' The look that tells me, what happened made me less than you. A no-one.*

'No.'

'But she's not stocking you now, so surely you don't have to feel obliged to go to this do tonight?'

'I keep hoping she'll change her mind. And if she meets you and finds out that you are willing to sell my buckles – well, she might be so overwhelmed with competitive spirit that she'll try to buy me back.'

Ben looked at me over his glass. 'So, I'm coming to try to provoke her jealousy, am I? Oh, it's okay, I don't mind, just as long as I know.'

I drained my glass quickly. The dryness of the wine made my throat shrink. 'We'd better go.' I stood up and managed to get the heel of my ridiculous shoes caught in the wiring from the speakers. As I bent to sort myself out I could see that none of the speaker wires were plugged in. Either to the mains or to the back of the speakers.

They were all rigged up right, just not connected. 'Ben –'

'Are you coming then?' He'd collected a large bunch of keys, dropped what looked like his mobile on a table and was waiting in the doorway. Seeing him standing there looking really quite beautiful in his bow tie and loose jacket I completely forgot about the wiring.

'I'm ready as I'll ever be, I guess. Are we driving?' All right I admit it, I'm a car slut. I could have sat in that Audi all night without even starting the engine, just for the experience.

'It's only down the road, isn't it? Besides, now I've had a glass of wine.'

'Oh. Right.' Saskia's face, seeing me turning up in an Audi R8 was going to have to remain a figment of my imagination.

In the event, when we reached Le Petit Lapin, Saskia was inside, deep in the throng; she wouldn't have noticed if I'd arrived by donkey. The shop was *packed*. There were skinny women in chiffon frocks everywhere, like tissue-wrapped sticks, and a clash of perfume and aftershave strong enough to knock your nose off-kilter for a week. Ben hesitated.

'Bloody hell.' He began fidgeting with his hair. 'There's a lot of people.'

I looked up at the golden front of the shop. Even the first-floor windows had people in them, holding glasses and trying to look enthralled at being pressed against an unrelated armpit. 'More than I expected,' I replied. 'Maybe it was "Buy One Get One Free" down at RentaCrowd.'

Ben gave me a ghost of a smile. 'I've just lost the knack

of circulating. Still, it'll be nice and noisy in there, I guess.'

I grinned back at him. 'Yep. You won't have to talk to anyone and even if you do they won't hear what you say.' I grabbed his elbow and we forced our way through some of the more decorative members of the throng into the shop.

Inside the temperature was about a hundred bodies and rising. I found that I was clutching at Ben's arm in order not to lose him in the currents and eddies of moving and shaking that was going on. Saskia had invited some of the owners of the larger (and therefore more socially and profitably acceptable) shops which surrounded Le Petit Lapin and everyone seemed to be discussing how well their businesses were going at full volume. A uniformed waiter carrying a superciliously high tray whirled past us and Ben managed to pluck two glasses from it, handing one down to me.

'Aw Roah an Juhu nyer yeh?'

'What?' I yelled at him over the noise.

'Aw Roah an Juhu nyer yeh?' Ben said again.

'I can't hear!'

'I said, are Rosie and Jason here yet?' Ben bellowed into my ear, causing me to step sideways and bump into a large woman who was peering into the display cabinet in the corner.

'Can't see them. That's Saskia over there.' I pointed to the bottom of the spiral staircase where Saskia had set up court, leaning against the wrought iron. She was wearing pink chiffon (it must be some kind of uniform) with matching pink stilettos and her hair up under a fine pink net with jewels studded around it. 'Looks like she got her head caught under a gay trawler,' I muttered.

'That's no way to go about getting re-stocked,' Ben said. He didn't seem to have any problems hearing me above the babble. 'Drink your wine.' He was twisting his glass around in his hands and I noticed it was empty.

'Are you all right?'

He stopped scanning the crowd and looked down at me. 'I'm just a bit, you know, on edge. This is the first big do I've been to since – well, since.'

'No-one seems to recognise you.' I didn't know whether to be happy about this for Ben's sake, or cross for mine.

'I look a bit different these days.'

'Yes. You were quite something in Willow Down.' I spoke without thinking. Ben looked at me steadily, as though we were the only two people in the room.

'You think?'

Oh, God. I started to blush round about my ankles which made my feet slippery inside the angular heels. The blush rose, peppered my spine and finally scalded its way up my face to my eyelids. Ben was still looking at me. 'I mean – err – you, um, you were very hard. I mean – you looked hard. That's hard as in unapproachable, sort of a bit of a nutcase, not hard as in … Excuse me a sec I think that's Rosie and Jason. I'll just let them know we're over here.' I fled to the safety of the doorway.

'Jem? Woss up with you girl? Look like you swallowed somethin' the wrong way,' and Jason let out a filthy snigger that made people turn round to find the cause.

'I've been coughing.' I cleared my throat to add veracity.

'Bin drinking more like. Where's Sass then, better do the honours before I starts necking 'em.' Jason took himself off to find Saskia and Rosie frowned at me.

'Are you all right? You look horribly hot.'

I confessed my *faux pas* whilst trying to rebalance myself, leaning against a tree-trunk which, against all probability and artistic integrity, was being used as a doorstop. 'I don't think he noticed,' I finished. 'But I feel such an idiot.'

Rosie was offered a glass by the same waiter who had ignored me. I wondered how she did it. But then she did look – and this was the only word that applied – stunning. Her black curls were swept up into a style from which they cascaded down her neck in individual strands, her dress was vanilla-coloured silk which hid the post-baby bulge like a dream and she was made-up like a film star. 'He is pretty sexy though, Jem, you have to admit it.'

I gave a half-laugh. 'D'you think so?'

Rosie looked over in Ben's direction. He was leaning against a wall with his head cocked, while a woman in a mesh dress talked at him. 'Oh, yes. He's got *something*. I don't know what it is, presence or glamour, one of those show biz things. The women are all looking at him. Bet that's bugging Jason, he's used to being the centre of attention in crowds like this.'

She was right. Women would glance Ben's way, look somewhere else for a second, then look back as if to check their first impressions had been right. Then their eyes would stay on him while they unconsciously fussed their hair or licked their lips. 'He's okay,' I said grudgingly.

Rosie gave me a stern look. 'Now come on, Jem, this is me you're talking to.'

I looked at Ben again. He'd fiddled his bow tie undone

and folded his arms as if to ward off the roomful of people. 'All right yes, he's sexy and funny and bitchy and beautiful and all that. But I don't intend to do anything about it, neither does he. So you can cut the scheming looks.' A thought struck me. 'Unless you want him?'

Ben was looking at us now. He gave me a smile and I managed a blush-free grin.

'Me? God, no. I've got enough trouble. Look, Saskia's wheeling out Jase, this should be fun.' Without elaborating on what her trouble might be Rosie headed into the crowd in order to be in hearing distance of Jason's opening speech. I went back to Ben.

'I was just telling Rosie about your car. She's always wanted an R8.'

Ben straightened away from the wall and unfolded his arms. 'Yeah. It's sexy and beautiful all right.'

By biting hard on the inside of my cheek, I managed not to react. The bloke must have ears like a bat. 'Come on, Jason's doing his thing now and you don't want to miss it. Jason's "thing" is the talk of five continents.'

'Okay, now I'm jealous.'

Jason gave his speech while I looked around the room. A photographer was busily snapping away, taking pictures of Jason, Saskia, the items on sale, everything. I watched Ben quietly getting out of the way of the camera and then it was all over and Saskia was motioning to the waiters to bring new trays of tasty morsels into the crowd. I snaffled a couple of tiny crêpes and found a quiet corner to start eating them. Unfortunately Saskia found the corner, too.

'Nice to see someone with a healthy appetite. Most people here are watching their weight.'

'I'm a size ten, Saskia. I've got no desire to be completely invisible.'

Saskia raised an eyebrow. 'Size ten? Really? The chain stores clothes are so forgiving, aren't they?'

I looked daggers at her and threw the second crêpe into my mouth. It was filled with a banana-toffee concoction which would have been absolutely wonderful if it hadn't been accompanied by Saskia making little chewy-mouth faces of disgust. 'Yum,' I said to annoy her. 'Are there any more of these?'

'They go straight to your hips, you know.' Saskia looked down at my thighs, very visible under the tight skirt. 'Although in your case I shouldn't think you'd notice.'

I opened my mouth to mention the HobNobs which she stole every time she found herself in Rosie's kitchen, and seemed to believe were negatively calorific, but thankfully, just then Ben came lolloping along carrying a plate onto which he'd rescued a selection of delicacies. Saskia's eyes opened wide. 'Hello,' she purred. 'I haven't had the pleasure of being introduced to you. I'm Saskia Winterington, but then, you'll know that of course.'

Saskia held out her hand at arm's length, limp wristed. I wasn't sure if she wanted to fend Ben off (although that seemed laughably unlikely), or have her hand kissed. Ben juggled the plate for a moment then passed it to me. 'I'm Ben Davies.' He took Saskia's hand and shook it very definitely. 'I'm stocking some of Jemima's jewellery.'

'Hmm.' Saskia retook her hand and looked Ben up and down. 'Well, you're clearly not a member of the Board of Trade, I'd certainly remember *you* at meetings!' She gave a little laugh, but her eyes stayed fixed on his face. Slowly she reached across and brushed a hair from the collar of his jacket, pausing her hand on his shoulder for far longer than was necessary. 'Do come and tell me what you think of *my* collection,' she said, still gazing into his eyes. 'I'll give you the names of some of my suppliers if you like.' Pressing her body into his, Saskia hooked her arm through Ben's and tugged him towards the back of the shop, pausing on her way through to make sure everyone noticed her in the company of the good-looking stranger.

I burned. The taste of toffee-banana had gone from my mouth, replaced by a sourness that etched into my teeth as I watched him walk away. Was this jealousy, this bitter raging which seemed to reach up from my stomach and pull my skin hotly around me? But Ben and I were – what, friends? Business partners? He was nothing to me that should provoke this upwelling, this sense that I was about to vomit bricks. I watched them cross the shop, Saskia bending to talk into Ben's ear and familiarly hug him against her in the crowd, and I wanted to kill someone.

Across the room Rosie was laughing, engrossed in conversation with three men she'd been introduced to by Alex, who looked very dashing tonight in a slightly colonial way. There was no sign of Jason but a tight knot of women in a corner were whooping and giggling in a way that indicated he was somewhere in their midst. No-one came to speak to me, well-clad elbows poked at me and shoes so pointed that their wearers must have had flippers for feet clipped my toes and ankles. There was a muzzy haze of noise and wine-breath filling the air and I began to feel claustrophobic.

This was not my life. I felt as though I'd fallen through a hole into some kind of alter-existence where someone like me had no business being.

The back of the shop was cooler. A small door led into the office and store rooms. It wasn't locked so I slipped through into the fresh air beyond. Apart from a couple engaged in a frantic snogging session on Saskia's leather sofa-ette, the space was empty and I felt the tension begin to ease from my shoulders. Alone, I could cope with alone. I carefully avoided the kissing couple's eyes and went through into the little stock room beyond the office. Through here the noise was muffled, the smell of several hundred perfumed bodies gave way to the York night air and an open window somewhere in the building let a cool draught fan my hot face. I sat down on the corner of a big box and took off my shoes to let my feet have a rest, flapping my shirt free. I was wearing a belt with one of my own buckles, a small piece made from gold wire leaves and acorns. Saskia's entire guest list seemed to be made up of people who already had so much jewellery it was a wonder they could stand up. I sighed. At least Ben seemed to be breaking out of his reclusive habits. I wondered where he was, and then hated myself for even thinking it. This was his natural habitat, his rock-star milieu. It was me who was the pretender here. I was almost swamped for a second by the knowledge I was simply acting. Playing a role, chameleon-like, that let me fit in to the background unnoticed. Wondered, just for a moment, what Ben would think if he knew just how much of me I kept hidden.

The edges of the box I was sitting on began to dig into the back of my legs and I stood up. It was one of several all stacked up on the store room floor, gathering dust. Well, not dust exactly, Saskia had all dust caught and shot, but that faded kind of brownness that boxes take on. I wondered what was in it, what example of art that Saskia was going to sell to some unsuspecting tourist that they would spend the rest of their lives explaining to visitors as ' "Femininity". Not a twig. Honestly.'

The box lid was loose. I lifted it up to peer inside and frowned, my self-loathing temporarily forgotten. The contents looked very much like Rosie's cards. At least the last two consignments that she'd produced for Saskia, maybe more. Puzzled, I slid the box off the one underneath and opened that. It, too, was full of stacks of Rosie's hand-made cards. And the box on the bottom, although that had fewer cards inside. I recognised that batch as the last ones Rosie had done before Harry was born.

Why the hell was Saskia getting Rosie to produce more and more cards when she wasn't selling them? Wasn't even putting them on display? I looked around the room. Yes, there was the box of cards that Rosie had delivered on Sunday evening, shoved into a corner under a shelving unit. I recognised the slightly ragged tape that we'd used to seal the carton. Maybe Saskia was going to put the cards out for sale later? But that didn't explain why they were still stacked into the boxes as they had been when we'd brought them over – they'd never even been taken out. There were *loads*. Saskia wouldn't sell this many in *years*.

I restacked the boxes and went out of the store room, carrying my shoes by a strap. The crowd had thinned, or at least some of the larger people had gone and the skinny girls in the wafty dresses were doing duty filling space like air pockets in soil. My brain had seized on the problem of the boxes with an eagerness that felt like gratitude. I couldn't stop to ponder my relationship with Ben, not when there was something that needed solving.

'Rosie?' I broke in on a conversation that Rosie was having with Alex. He was telling her how Oscar was born with blue eyes but that they'd turned brown by the time he was three months old – I guess you needed to be a parent to appreciate that particular chat. 'Have you seen Ben?'

Alex answered. 'I think my wife took him to show him the display upstairs.' He pointed to the staircase, still littered with people. 'But it was a while ago so maybe he's gone.'

'I'll go and see,' I said but I doubted either of them heard me; they were back into heavy discussions about whether babies look like their parents from birth. I started up the iron staircase, which meant negotiating groups of people with carefully balanced wine glasses, who tutted as I pushed my way between them and carried on their well-bred conversations around my body, leaning to exclude me from any kind of contribution.

In the upper room glass display cases stood against the walls. In the centre of the floor there was a huge square leather stool large enough to seat four comfortably, but at the moment it was only seating two. Ben was sitting in the middle and beside him was Saskia. She was kneeling, face level with his, talking earnestly into his eyes; as I watched she caught his chin as though she was about to kiss him, lowering her body at the same time until she was almost sitting on his lap. Ben hadn't seen me come up the stairs and Saskia had her back to me. Thanking God for my bare feet, I tiptoed across the floor and tapped Saskia on the shoulder.

'I think Alex might want you,' I said as her head flipped up in shock. I indicated the staircase, just *possibly* giving her the impression that Alex had been right behind me. Saskia's heels tore a neat hole in the leather as she snapped her legs back and leaped away, straightening her skirt as she stood up. She fixed me with her best imperious expression, which was only slightly ruined by her smudged lipstick.

'Ben and I were talking,' she said in a voice full of self-justification. 'Business.'

'I could tell,' I said drily.

Saskia pulled herself back to her feet with impressive speed and touched the back of her hand to her eyes. 'God, don't you just *hate* mascara?' she said. 'The way it smudges at the slightest thing? Oh, of course you're obviously used to it, darling, cheap make-up never stays put, does it? You might want –.' She made lipstick motions at me. 'Just a little touch up.' And she was gone, vanishing into the staff toilets.

I stared at Ben.

'What?' he finally said.

'Well, (a) you don't date, (b) she's married and the guy is downstairs, and (c) – Christ on a bike, man, she's *evil*!'

'(a) I wasn't dating her, (b) *she* forced herself onto *me* and (c) yes, you're right she's awful but – Jeez –.' A wicked smile spread over his face. 'She's good,' he finished. 'In an awful way, obviously.'

'You're a slut. A man-slut.'

'Probably. But –'

I stopped him with a raised hand. 'No, don't tell me. It wasn't what it looked like?'

Ben was still smiling the wicked smile. 'Oh, well, I wouldn't say that.'

There was a clinging heat at the base of my neck and a deep feeling in my stomach. 'So, you two were about to go off somewhere more "comfortable"?'

The smile disappeared. 'Jemima, listen.'

'Oh, yeah, right, I'm going to stand here and listen to a man who's just been caught nearly shagging a woman who makes Genghis Khan look like a rank amateur!' I tried to spin on my heel and huff away, but spinning in bare feet on a wooden floor doesn't work. There was a pathetic squeaky sound.

'Jem.' Ben grabbed me by my shoulders and turned me to face him. Because I'd got no shoes on he was suddenly a lot taller than me. 'This is important. As soon as she knew I was the only person in York stocking your stuff she was absolutely *crippling* herself to get to me. She offered me her suppliers, she even offered to help pay to buy in some new stuff "as a trial offer". She kept telling me you were always letting her down; she even told me you still owed her nearly ten thousand pounds for pieces you'd not delivered.' Ben shook his head.

'That is a complete and utter lie!' I tried to pull back but the pressure of his fingers increased until I could feel each individual digit digging through my shirt. 'I've never not delivered!'

'Okay. But she's got the Board of Trade members blackballing you from their shops. She's absolutely serious. In fact I was quite scared at one point.'

'That point being just before I arrived, then.'

'I wanted to see how far she would go.'

I snorted. 'All the way, by the look of the two of you!'

'Jem.' Ben let go of my shoulders and let his hands fall by his sides. 'I thought I was doing you a favour. She was the one pulling the all-over body approach, not me. I don't do that. So I'm sorry if you – But we're just friends, you and me.'

He smelled spicy. Warm and green and slightly of leather. His bow tie was hanging loose around his collar and he'd undone the top button of his shirt where his hair kept getting caught. I wasn't sure whether to be glad of his words or whether to stab him with one of the nicely sharp items on display.

'It's OK,' I said at last, to somewhere over his shoulder.

'I didn't want you to get the wrong … I mean, it's nothing personal, it's me.'

'You don't have to say anything.' I was still talking to the shop wall. Couldn't meet his eyes. Didn't know whether to laugh or cry. Didn't know whether I was misreading the situation or not. Didn't even know why I was so angry.

'I'm not going to. This is it, end of conversation.'

There was a flurry on the stairs and Rosie appeared looking breathless. 'Oh, Jem, there you are! Shall we get a taxi back, only I don't want to keep the babysitter past midnight and I think Jason's taking someone home.' Then she looked at both of us. 'Sorry, did I interrupt something?'

'No!' Ben and I spoke together.

I turned to him. 'I'd better go.'

'Yeah, me too.' There was a pause. 'I've … I have another appointment tomorrow. Would you be free to come and mind the shop in the afternoon? About three?'

'I'm not sure.' I couldn't avoid looking at him any longer but was surprised when I did. He looked closed in, as though he was in pain. As he had the first time we'd met. 'I'll e-mail you in the morning.'

We all went down together. In the main shop Saskia was the centre of attention again. She was standing with her arms around Alex, holding forth on how having Oscar had been the single most enriching experience of her life.

'I thought marrying Alex was her most enriching experience,' muttered Rosie as we headed out of the door. 'Although I suppose there's always the Child Benefit. Harry's enriched me to the tune of twenty quid a week, bless him.'

Ben waved a hand in goodbye and set off towards Wilberforce Crescent without looking back.

'Did you piss him off?' Rosie asked as we went in search of a taxi. She turned around to watch Ben walk out of sight. 'You really shouldn't piss off men with backsides like that. Roooooaaawwww!'

I couldn't answer her. My mind was too full of questions. Why on earth was Saskia lying to Ben about me not delivering? To stop him taking my buckles? Which begged the next question – why was Saskia trying to stop anyone stocking my stuff? And why was she buying in so much of Rosie's output that her entire back room was packed with it? Consistency might not be Saskia's middle name, but this was ridiculous!

And what did I *really* want from Ben Davies?

**4th May**

Tonight. Where do I start? You were right (again, shit man, all those degrees weren't wasted after all) writing it down does help. Gets my head straight. Though I still hate knowing you read it.

Jemima and I were at this party, nothing special, local kinda thing. She looked – oh, so good. Preppy; white shirt and a skirt, with real hot heels, she has fantastic legs – I'm, like, **so** fired up. She's talking to her friend (about me!) and she's looking at me across the room, and her eyes ... there are no words for it. Not in English, anyway.

She's changed somehow. It's like she had this shell, something she'd crawled inside to keep her safe, and now it's got this crack which is scaring her stupid but she's glad of it, in a kind of way. Does that make sense? Like she almost wants me to see through, to put my eye to the fissure and see the real woman inside.

And I ... I want to. But to do that, to let her open up to me, then I have to give something back, don't I? So tonight ... I was going to tell her. After the party I was going to take her home, sit her down and talk. Really talk, like I've not done in ... how many years now? And then, maybe ...

when she knew, then she'd have the confidence to tell me what it is that's got her so terrified. Or maybe she'd want to run. Either way, her choice. Only, I wrecked it.

Oh, my intentions were good, at least I think they were … or did I do it on purpose? Did I know that Jem would come looking for me tonight? A little part of me in the back of my head says yeah, course I did – what was she going to do, leave without me? So. Okay. Yeah. I talked my way into being invited upstairs, then kept talking.

And this is the hard bit. Come on, do it, come out, say it. I did it because I was scared.

At first it was legit, wanted to find out what was going on. Some dirty dealings going down, doc, nothing for you to ask questions about. Nothing to do with you, or me. But I was curious, and it was screwing Jem up so I …

And Jem saw. Feel a bit sorry for the other girl, I led her on maybe more than I should, but hey, she's married, neither of us was going to do anything. I just wanted some info from her. And.. . yeah part of me wanted Jem to know that other women still want me – make her jealous. Isn't that pathetic? Very Year 9. I thought she'd just laugh.

But she didn't.

That scared me worse than anything, even that time the mic went live at Sheffield Arena and nearly killed us all. I dunno if you can understand, doc … <u>she didn't laugh.</u> Suddenly whatever's going on between me and Jem, it's not a game any more, and if I thought I was scared before … what I saw in her face … She looked hurt. I didn't think she was close enough to hurt like that. We were mates, friends, yeah and even that scared me, brought a whole new level to things but … if she got hurt just seeing me with someone else – shit, how much more is she going to get hurt if she finds out about me? So I ran. Blew her out, and ran.

And now the music in my head is playing those two falling notes, like something is on its way.

I am **so** screwed.

Two weeks went by achingly slowly. After the excitement of Saskia's party there was nothing to look forward to. Not that we'd looked forward to it, as such, but at least it had been a communal bitching point. Now everything felt flat and listless. Rosie continued to work hard. Saskia had ordered an enormous batch of winter-themed cards ostensibly for the Christmas market. Jason dumped the skinny blonde he'd met at Le Petit Lapin and started crafting his next exhibition, if crafting is the right word. I made a few pieces and sold some necklaces on line, but was so full of the ennui that pervaded everything I could hardly work up any enthusiasm, even when the cheques arrived.

I didn't mention the boxes in the office or what Ben had said. Rosie was too emotionally fragile to take on board the fact that Saskia didn't seem to want to sell her stuff. And, as she quite rightly would have said, Saskia was paying for the cards. Who cared if she was putting them on shelves or up her bottom? Saskia's attempts to have my name expunged from the vocabularies of York residents didn't stand up in the face of Ben's resistance. Plus, I still had my website and sales through that were ongoing. So, if she wanted to starve me out she had quite a way to go. Not as far as I might like, but I was doing it. I was holding things together.

Occasionally I helped Ben out in the shop, but I mostly managed to arrive as he was leaving and go as soon as he got back. We exchanged a few generalities and he asked after Rosie and Harry, but that was all. Nothing even approaching personal conversation took place and we edged around each other in the confines of the shop as though I was strapped with dynamite and he was Detonator-Man.

He got thinner, too. If that were possible. There was a tightness in his face which sometimes made him look ill and sometimes just made him look wretched but in the spirit of the talk he'd given me I didn't get involved. I kept busy, kept moving and kept out of his affairs. If it baffled me how a man who'd been such a talented musician, such a performer, could be happy running a little back-street shop or why a man who looked like Ben should refuse to have anything to do with women, I smothered the questions.

Then one day I came in from the workshop to find Rosie crying on the sofa. She'd been intermittently tearful lately, but I had thought the worst was over. I minded Harry so that she could work, and his sleeping patterns were becoming a lot more regular, so she wasn't losing as many hours as she had when he'd been tiny.

'What's up?' I sat next to her. Harry waved his chunky arms in acknowledgement and grinned at me from her lap.

'I'm such a failure, Jem.' Rosie clutched Harry round his middle. 'I'm no kind of mother for Harry. You and

Jason, you're more his parents than I am – look at the way he's so pleased to see you! He's never like that with me.' She dissolved into more heaving sobs, squeezing Harry until his expression changed.

'That's rubbish. You're his mum and he knows it.' I patted Rosie's back.

'And Saskia's just sent back that last lot of cards, says they're not wintery enough so I've got to redo them all. And I've been so busy with her stuff that two other customers have withdrawn their orders, so I've *got* to turn in her cards or there won't be enough money ...' She gulped. 'I've even stopped feeding Harry.'

'You've what?' I looked at Harry, who was showing no real signs of malnourishment. He blew a bubble at me.

'I've started him on formula. It's so much easier, not having to spend hours expressing milk, sitting in that grotty little bathroom with all the mould and that black stuff that we can't identify, with that stupid pump that doesn't work! And all the books say that you're supposed to breast feed for at least nine months and I didn't even manage four! I'm crap, Jem, and it's only a matter of time before Harry realises it.'

I put my arms around the two of them, despite Harry's muffled protest. 'You're working too hard, that's all. How about a day out? Something to look forward to.'

'I *can't*. That's the whole point. I've got all these cards to do. I've barely got time to do the laundry, let alone take time off.'

She had got it bad. 'Do you want me to take Harry today?' I'd had him every day for the last week and today was supposed to be Rosie's bonding day with him. She'd started off so well, playing with him in his doorway-hung swing, but it looked as though things had gone downhill. 'I don't mind.'

'I already asked Jason if he'd have him,' Rosie snottily admitted. 'But he's too busy as well. He's off to London in the morning to see some consortium or other. I don't want to ask you again, Jem, you have him so much –'

'I don't mind,' I said. It was a bit of a lie. I'd been hoping to take Harry to the workshop where Jason would amuse him by letting him watch as he prepared his raw materials. I was beginning to worry that Harry was going to grow up a trainspotter. 'I'll take him out.'

'Oh, if you're going out we need some more nappies. And some sterilising tablets.'

'OK, I'll shove him in his buggy and we'll walk up to the shop. He likes stopping off to see the cows in the top field on the way.'

Wrong thing to say, Jemima. Rosie's eyes clouded with tears again. 'You see! You see! I'm his *mum* and I don't even know that. I never get to see him liking cows …' And she set off crying again, wiping her eyes on her sleeve.

'Things will get better. Now, parcel him up and I'll strap him in.'

Rosie pulled Harry's jacket on him. 'It looks like rain. And the wind is chilly. If it gets too cold you will bring him back, won't you?'

'It's the middle of summer and he's got a raincover for the buggy.'

'You think I fuss too much, don't you? Oh God, I'm turning into one of those horrible mothers who won't let the kids out on their own until they're forty and brush their adult son's hair for them and choose their clothes and –'

'Bye, Rosie.' I determinedly set off down the path with Harry cooing and gurgling his appreciation.

We stopped, as promised, to watch the huge Friesians mooching around their field. One of them came and blew gentle breaths over the gate at Harry and, when I lifted him from his seat, ran a rough tongue over the top of his head, making him chuckle. I couldn't help but smile myself, it was one of those moments when I could think of my own mother without tears. Although I allowed nothing to come through but the memory of a sweetness in the air synaesthetically linked to a stroked cheek, I knew she'd loved us. I just *knew* it. It was something I'd held like a security blanket when everything had gone so wrong, the knowledge that we'd been loved. I gave Harry a little hug around his bulky middle as the cow puffed milk-scented air down at us, feeling a wave of something that must approach maternal love for the little boy, and wondered again how she'd felt in those last few moments. Had she worried about me and the boys as much as Rosie worried about Harry? Was she worried then? Did she know what was happening, or did it all come so quickly she didn't even have time to think of us?

I strapped Harry back in and pushed the buggy down to the crossroads and into the main village street. Little Gillmoor only had one shop, a grocers-cum-newsagent, where I bought the nappies and steriliser tablets as requested and partook in a minor discussion about the weather. It looked dodgy so I put the cover over the buggy. Good move. Just as we'd started our walk home the rain came.

Typical summer rain. It didn't float in like a mist, it dumped like an excavator. A tonne of water hit me on the head and went straight through to my bones. Harry, snug under his waterproof coating, giggled. I shivered and thought about heading back into the shop when a car pulled up behind me.

'You're wet.'

'No, no, I'm fine. I like dripping.'

It was Ben and I wouldn't turn round.

'Would you like to get in?' He cranked something up inside and the car made a purring sound. 'I've got heating.'

I stomped back to the Audi, pushing Harry in front of me like a Roman shield. 'What are you doing round here?' I asked as Ben opened the passenger door to let me in. 'Trying to pick up schoolgirls?'

Ben looked a little less rough today. He'd only got a couple of days' worth of stubble on his face and his hair looked clean. 'I came to see you. To apologise. Things have been a bit shitty lately and I haven't been coping very well. I've taken it out on you.'

'Huh.' I wasn't feeling very polite. Outside in his buggy Harry began to grumble about the conditions.

'Do you want to bring him in here? I could drive you both home.'

'No car seat. Rosie would dismember me.'

There was a difficult silence. Ben stared out of the windscreen and drummed his fingers on the wheel, while I kept one eye on Harry and merely squinted at Ben. He definitely looked better. Less strung-out.

'I've thought a lot about what you said at Rosie's

dinner party.' He didn't take his eyes off the rain rolling down the glass.

'Oh? Anything in particular or are all my words etched on your brain?' Okay, so it was unnecessarily sarcastic, but I had wet pants and all this moody staring and silence was beginning to get on my nerves.

'About getting on with my life.'

I stared at him. 'What's this, the Prozac kicking in?'

'Just common sense. Yours, before you make some cynical remark. I'm thirty years old, Jemima, and I'm living like some kind of medieval monk! Going with you to Saskia's, it made me realise what I'm missing out on.'

'Oh,' I said. Wasn't sure what he meant, was this some kind of step-down from his untouchable position? Was that a step I wanted him to take?

'Anyway. Part of the getting on with life thing. I wondered if I might come round to yours one evening, cook you and Rosie a meal. If you had to come to mine then you'd be worrying about babysitters and taxis and stuff all evening. This way it's only me that has to get home.'

A pause. Could I hear the words 'or I could stay over'? Were they echoing in some parallel universe?

'That sounds nice.' There was the sofa, wasn't there? Or the workshop? He could bring a sleeping bag – 'When?'

'How about tomorrow? You don't need to worry, I'll bring everything. You two can just relax, all you need to do is tell me how the kitchen works.'

'Hmm. Big white cold box in corner is fridge, big white hot box in other corner is oven. That's it.'

This time he laughed. 'I think I can manage that. Look,

the rain's lessening up, do you want to get his Lordship back before it starts again?'

Reluctantly I peeled myself off the heated seat, which left me with clammy buttocks. It also left Ben with a damp double-imprint where I'd been sitting. 'Sorry. I told you I was wet.'

'I shall treasure it. Six o'clock tomorrow then, yeah?'

'I suppose. If you insist.'

'I'm overwhelmed by your gratitude.' But he was smiling – no, *grinning*. A proper grin which creased his eyes and relaxed his face and made me swallow hard.

'Six o'clock. Yes, then.' And I watched as he dropped the clutch and expertly manoeuvred the car down the twisty lane back towards the main road. I was going to address a pithy remark to Harry but he'd fallen asleep inside his condensation-filled buggy, like a boil-in-the-bag human. 'Great. Leave me alone with my thoughts, why don't you?' I spoke to him anyway. 'Just when the last thing I want is time to stand around thinking, you go to sleep. Typical man.'

The rain lifted and the sun began slipping through starling-coloured clouds like a spotlight. I started pushing for home. I tried to distract myself with thoughts of the work I had to do: there were two wristbands in silver that I had to pack up for dispatch, a buckle waiting to be built. But this time I failed to lose myself in detail; all I could think of was Ben's eyes, the feel of him when I'd touched his arm. That tattoo over his bicep. The careless way he'd drag his hair back out of his face while he talked, as if he was unaware that haircuts existed. It was disturbing.

What did I think of him? All right, I admired those long

legs, that finely-tuned body. I liked the way his fingers kinked in at the knuckle. His face was pleasant to look at and there was something about the way he moved that made something inside me feel as though I was answering a long-ago call. He didn't frighten me. His slight build wasn't overpowering or threatening, he'd never done anything or said anything which in any way panicked me.

And yet. The way my skin gravitated towards his – that was just biological imperative. Just my hormones trying to force me into something unwanted by both Ben and me. Nothing that was going to make me break the promises I'd made to myself. He was a friend. That was all.

When I got back to the barn, Harry was still asleep. Jason was packing his car for the London trip so I went through to the office and on to the computer. Back to the Willow Down site.

What had intrigued me was Ben's hint that he'd done something to throw the band into disarray. Something that had had repercussions for their tour of the States. I went into the part of the website dedicated to write-ups of each gig they'd played and called up the review.

'Striding onstage like they were aware of their following, Zafe Rafale and Baz Davies came on burning, tearing straight into their biggest hit "Once It was You". The rest of the band joined them and they played all the usual hits plus most of the stuff on the new album *Rent-A-Tee*. The only duff note played all evening was in the final number, "About a Girl". It looked as though inadequate rehearsals told here when Baz Davies set off into another number altogether, getting half way through to the evident puzzlement of the rest of the band before switching lyrics.'

Only that fragment about a misplayed song gave any hint that anything untoward had happened that night. Then, being a suspicious type, I checked out the internet scuttlebut on the topic. There were whole forums devoted to why Baz Davies quit Willow Down. Consensus seemed to be that Ben had had some kind of breakdown. There were wild stories on the net regarding his drug habit, his rumoured stays in just about any rehab clinic you could name, his bizarre behaviour. He'd had an affair with Zafe – no, he'd run off with Zafe's girlfriend. No, Zafe had run off with *his* girlfriend. When it got to the stage that I was reading how Baz had been contacted by aliens and had left music to dedicate his life to Venusian peace-bringers I gave up.

I closed down the computer. Harry was stirring, curling and uncurling his hands around his blanket, and out in the yard I could hear Jason swearing at his car for not being large enough to accommodate one of his canvasses.

'Jase? You've been to more gigs than me.' Carrying a still-sleepy Harry I cornered Jason as he tried to stuff a dead-man's handle on top of a pile of other things on the back seat.

'Jem, there's *nuns* been to more gigs than you. What about it?' He straightened up to look at me.

'If a band was playing a song but someone made a mistake, what would happen?'

Jason stared at me, leaning his long body against the car. '*What*? You mean, like, got the lyrics wrong or hit a bum note, that kinda thing? Nothing. Half the time your audience is so pissed that they don't care if you plays "God Save the Queen", they just likes to look atcha.'

'I mean seriously. Would there be any repercussions?'

'That's like the drums, innit?'

I gave him a hard stare. 'You know perfectly well what I mean.' Harry snuffled into my shoulder and Jason switched his attention.

'Yeah. It happens. If a band don't practise or if they're playing a set for the first time, someone cocks up. Who cares? 'S all part of the experience.'

'Not a big deal then?'

'Not really.' Jason stroked Harry's head. 'This still about your man, is it? He's bleeding bonkers he is. Nice guy an' all but really –' He thrust his pelvis suggestively. 'Crackers.'

'Yes, Jason.' I sighed and took Harry off in search of Rosie.

## 19th May

I did it. Okay, here I'm going to claim all the credit and you can look at me over those shitty half-glasses all you want (they are really crappy, man, make you look like a grandad). Between her telling me I should get a life, and me feeling guilty about how I behaved at that party, and you telling me to come to terms with the life I'd made for myself ... somewhere, between all that, I started to think, you know?

Seeing her with those big eyes looking so ... fragile, so scared of what I might say or do ... And I was feeling so sorry for myself, so dead inside, and all because of what fear had brought me to. Scared to talk, scared not to. So much to say, so much pain, all going round and round in my head, no way of letting it out.

Scored some coke last week off a backstreet hustler who couldn't look me in the face, then I sat in the shop all day and just stared at it lying there. All innocent, pure-looking. And I knew, **knew** that it would make everything feel better, even if only for a while, but a while was all I wanted, to make this screaming confusion and the self-hate go away. Some peace, you know? And I was going to, I was really going to. After all, being clean, where has it got me?

Truth again? I wanted to be dead. In that second I wanted out. It's never been as bad as that before, even in the early days.

Jemima walked in. I'd forgotten she was coming, forgotten I had an appointment, forgotten everything except the choice that I had. All she said was 'you okay?' or something banal like that, didn't even sound like she cared, it was just something to say, something to banish that sick kind of quiet that was hanging round us. And in that second I knew I'd never do it. I flushed eighty quid's worth of snow, and came to see you.

So yeah. A life. I can do it, I can make something out of this shitpile that I've found myself in, something that isn't dependent on what I used to have, what I used to do. I can't be what I was, but I can be something else, something true to who I am. So, I'm starting. Starting to rebuild what I can from the ruins, getting out there, being someone again.

I don't know how far I can take it yet. I want to find out what it is that Jem is hiding from. Why sometimes she looks at me as if she wants me naked and other times she avoids looking at me at all. I'm still too scared to tell her anything, too afraid that she'll get that look, the one that women get when they meet someone who's disabled, or frail; the same one they use for puppies that have been beaten or kittens thrown in the river. That look that dehumanises you, that says you're not a man any more but something soft, something lesser. But I know that, if I want her to talk to me, then I have to talk to her.

I want to pretend just a little longer. But I know its coming.

# Chapter Twelve

Half way through my attempts to tame my hair into something sleek, the phone rang. 'I've got it!' Rosie shouted up the stairs.

'Good! Because if I have to stop now I'm going to look like an explosion in a wig shop.' I carried on straightening my hair. Thanks to an afternoon in the bathroom with a bottle of peroxide my roots were now back to their usual blonde and I was battling my ever-present, but hardly ever seen, curls. Harry was in bed, Rosie was glammed up to the eyeballs, and we were both starving. Ben had better be a whizz in the kitchen because if he produced three cheese omelettes we might just eat each other.

'Who is it?' I went onto the landing but Rosie had taken the phone to the extent of its cord into the living room. 'It's not Ben cancelling, is it?'

Ben's new-found perkiness made me suspicious. Why had he suddenly taken it upon himself to start cooking meals for women? It all seemed to be some kind of backlash to his self-imposed exile and the one thing I know about backlashes is, sometimes they lash right back to the beginning again. I wouldn't have been surprised to hear that Ben was hiding in his basement with a cushion over his head.

Rosie called back something I couldn't hear and appeared at the bottom of the stairs. 'Can you apologise to Ben for me?' She was pulling on a jacket. 'Something's come up. I'll be back in a bit but ... there's something I have to do first.'

'Rosie?' I started down the stairs but she was already on her way out of the front door, calling over her shoulder, 'Harry shouldn't wake up, if he does there's a bottle in the fridge all made up. Thanks, Jem!'

'Like I have a choice,' I muttered mutinously. The door slammed. 'I presume the wicked Saskia is behind this,' I said to the straighteners. 'Probably wants to open a sweat-shop.' There was an ominous smell of singeing. My hair got more and more resistant to being straightened every week. Added to the all-pervading lingering peroxide, I smelled like some kind of chemical reaction. I gave a couple of squirts of perfume to offset it and hoped that Ben wouldn't think I smelled nice just for him.

God I was hungry. Could I get away with a cheese sandwich before he arrived? I'd got the loaf out and had a furtive gnaw at the crust when I heard a car pull up. 'Hello?'

I went outside to be greeted by the sight of Ben loaded down with boxes of pots and pans and ingredients. 'Blimey. Looks like Jamie Oliver's tour bus,' I said, peering into the car. 'What the hell are you making, a seven-course banquet?'

'I can do.' Ben carried several crates through into the kitchen. 'Are you going to help?'

'I thought this was a relaxing evening where you did all the work and I sat around?'

'Ha! Come on, you can whisk egg-whites. Where's Rosie?'

'She's just popped out for a little while.'

'Damn. I had her down for sauce-making duties. Never

mind we can cover. Now, wash your hands.' Ben bounced into the middle of our tiny kitchen and began to sort through his boxes. 'Pans, butter, eggs, cream. I'll get the rest from the car as I need it.'

I watched him as he began measuring by eye. There was something different about him, something sparky and energetic. 'So. Bit of a turnaround for you, isn't it?'

There was a momentary pause before he tipped butter into a pan. 'Yeah. I'm sorry, Jem. Life got a bit out of perspective for a while. I need to get my head around the fact that just because I'll never play guitar again doesn't mean –'

'Who says you'll never play guitar again? You haven't lost the use of your hands, have you?'

The pause was longer this time. 'No. But I just can't.'

I had my back to him as I began separating the eggs. 'So, why not?' I tried to sound casual. There was no answer. Ben had his head down, putting a pan on the stove and concentrating on its contents. 'Is it something to do with what happened in Philadelphia?'

His head jerked up suddenly. 'Where are you from, Jemima?'

As a diversionary tactic it worked. 'It – I – lots of places, you know.'

'No, I don't know.' His eyes were on my face. 'I returned your favour yesterday. Googled you. I thought you'd have a website.'

'I have!'

'Yeah. I found it. Jemima Hutton Jewellery. What puzzled me about it was the date it was set up.'

My heart was beating fast and my palms were too

slippery to hold the whisk. 'What?'

'You've only had the website for eighteen months. Before that, nothing.'

Adrenaline flooded through me like a dam had burst. 'Well, that's all there is. The website, for marketing and selling.'

Ben turned from the pan. In the little galley kitchen he was only a breath away from me. I found I'd got my fingers around the milk-pan in a defensive hold. 'But you've been making the jewellery for years, you told me so, when you gave me your spiel the first time we met. How come you only just set up a website?'

I'd had time to recover. 'Eighteen months ago was the first time I could afford to set one up.' I made my tone light, amused. 'We don't all have bank loads of cash sitting around, you know.'

I felt as though his eyes were scanning me, reading me. Like there was a barcode printed somewhere on my head. 'Then how did you do your marketing? Where were you based? Most people who have websites run at least a Facebook page. A blog maybe. Or they're registered on Friends Reunited, or have a piece in the local paper – they show up *somewhere*. You there's no trace of.' He went back to unpacking food from a freezer box, but kept looking at me. 'So I'd guess you've got secrets, things you'd rather people didn't know about you. Like the fact you aren't really Jemima Hutton at all.'

I dropped the whisk. 'I don't know what you're talking about.'

'Sorry?' His eyes flicked over my face, quickly. Almost as if I'd frightened him.

'Really, I don't know what you mean.'

Ben inclined his head. 'Okay, maybe you don't. I'm just guessing here. All I'm saying is, you know what it's like not to want people pushing and prying into your life.'

I took a deep breath. 'So keep out of yours? Is that what all that was really about? You trying to warn me off? *Blackmail?*'

The look Ben gave me was level and steady. *Damn!* 'It can't be blackmail if there's nothing to hide, can it?' Then he'd flipped away and was tying his hair back. 'Right. Thought I'd start with melon ...' He pulled an alarmingly green melon from the cold box. '... with Parma ham. Then Lemon Sole in a Béarnaise sauce followed by Baked Alaska.'

The kitchen was too small. I felt suddenly huge, as though I was trying to hide myself behind matchboxes, naked and exposed. 'I – it all sounds very – um.'

He turned to me and his expression was a mixture of sympathy and warning. 'This is how it feels to be me, Jemima. Like – like I'm made of holes. People just want to keep poking, see how deep they can get before I flinch. I'm sorry if I've made you uncomfortable, but maybe now you can understand how it is for me *every fucking day*.'

'Then why don't you open up?' Was that a little sob there, just at the end, as though my voice caught on my teeth?

'For the same reason you don't.' Ben weighed the melon in his hand, fingers playing over its rough surface, as though there was still a guitar lodged in his subconscious. 'We're both scared shitless of what the world can do to us, so we never talk.' He took a step towards me. 'I wish

I could. I wish I could get involved, fall in love, really … really *touch* someone because it's pretty lonely where I am.' The hand not cradling the melon reached out, twisted a strand of my hair. 'But it's like this wall, you know? Between me and everyone else.'

'And you daren't let it down,' I whispered. I was giving him ammunition. I knew it but I didn't care. Now, here, with the kitchen getting hotter by the second, and not just because of the melting butter, my guard was splitting infinitesimally.

'For fear of what might come through,' Ben finished, and kissed me.

And, oh God, I let him. Dropped the shields and pressed myself into him, catching at his arms to balance myself, then winding my hands around his neck to pull myself closer against his warmth. I closed my eyes and felt the pressure of his tongue on my lips, opened my mouth and relaxed as his guitar-player's muscles took my weight and rolled me so that I was squeezed between the corner cupboard and him. It was a long, long way from that kiss he'd given me outside his shop to avoid talking to his visitor. Now his kisses were so hard that I couldn't breathe, he kissed like a drowning man given a Scuba mask. Like he literally couldn't get enough. When I felt his hands travel over my thighs, rucking my skirt until his fingers touched skin, I touched his face. Ran my fingers over his cheekbones, down his stubbled cheeks then on to his shoulders. His belt buckle, ironically one of mine, dug into my stomach but even with that distraction I could feel the rigidity of him.

And *it felt so good*. To forget all the promises I'd made

to myself, to forget all the awfulness, all the terror that had gone before. To free myself momentarily from the fear that being close to a man would wipe my personality away and replace it with that of a kicked dog.

And then he shuddered. Moaned in his throat, a cry of – what? grief? frustration? and let me go. Closed his eyes and rested his forehead against the glass-fronted cabinet above the fridge, arms wrapped around his torso and his fists clenched.

I was left gasping. For air and for sense. My brain was scrambled by the onslaught of emotion, both his and mine. And then the heat of desire suddenly drained away, leaving me chilled with the horror of what I'd so nearly done. And with a sadness, an awful, overwhelming ache.

'It's okay,' I found I was saying. 'It's okay, Ben.' Like the aftermath of a crash while the metal is still ticking itself cool, I was forcing myself to be calm. 'Really.'

He was still huddled over himself, eyes shut. Rocking.

My heart was trying to escape. The room seemed to wheel and split and I grabbed at the washing machine to steady myself. 'Ben.' I put a hand on his shoulder.

He jumped. As if he'd forgotten I was there, or hadn't heard my reassurances. '*Christ.*' I'd never heard anyone sound so regretful, so empty, so *lost*.

'It's okay.' It seemed to be all I could say. I wanted him to echo it, to tell *me* that everything would be all right, too. That nothing had broken that couldn't be fixed, that he didn't think of me any differently now. That we could forget this had ever happened.

And then like the call of sanity from the living room, the phone began to ring. Ben opened his eyes and stared at me as though he'd never seen me before.

'*Christ.*'

He was actually shaking.

'The butter is burning.' It was all I could think of. What do you say to a man who's just kissed you like that? What do you say when the memories come back to haunt you and all you want to do is run?

'Where are you going?' His eyes were wide, his pupils huge, they seemed to swallow up his face until all I could see were those holes in his soul. 'Jemima?'

'It's *okay*. I'm just going to answer the phone, it might be important.' And I needed to get out of that room where the smell of burning butter was beginning to take on a brimstone tinge.

It was Jason. 'You sound rough. What's up?'

'Nothing. Ben's here cooking a meal.'

'Yeah, *right*. Cookin'. I getcha. You want to get back in there and show 'im that trick with the ice cubes ...'

'Jason, why are you ringing?' I had to interrupt otherwise Jason would be on the line all night giving me his favourite sex tips. And I so – *so* – did not want to think about sex right now.

'Ah. Well, thing is, luv, I think I might have left the welding iron on down at the studio. Any chance you can pop over and turn it off? I mean, it's not like the place'll burn down or nothing but ... you know, safe side an' all.'

'Can't it wait until the morning?' Or any other time when I don't have a possibly suicidal guitarist in my kitchen?

'How much do you care about your stuff in the workshop? On a scale of one to ten where one is Terry

Wogan and ten is his gorgeousness out there?'

'All right, I'll go over now. Just to set your mind at rest.'

'Thanks. Oh, and Jem –?'

'What?' There was a sound of saucepans clanking from the kitchen.

'The ice-cube thing. Honest. Every time.'

'Shut up, Jason.' And I put the phone down.

Ben had scoured out the burned pan, remelted the butter and was stirring it with careful, close attention. His eyes, when they met mine, were slightly desperate. 'Everything all right?'

'Just Jason wanting me to run over to the workshop, check he hasn't left the welding stuff switched on. Are you –?'

'You'd better do it then. I'll get the starters prepped while you're gone. This is nearly done, so we'll be ready to eat by the time you get back. Rosie will just have to have hers later.'

The heat was making his skin flush and his eyes were vast through the steam. I wanted to fall into them, I wanted to run. How could one person feel so much conflict? My mind was tearing itself apart. And now, thanks to Jason, all I could think about was the ice-cube trick and how Ben would have reacted to it. 'I'll be quick.'

'Maybe sometime you could show me your workshop? It would be cool to find out how you actually make the buckles.'

Had I fallen into a parallel universe? One in which Ben and I hadn't been on the verge of ripping one another's clothes off but had instead spent a decorous evening discussing art and improving literature? 'Yes. But not now, unless you want to burn the bottom out of another pan.'

He smiled, and it was only the touch of wildness at the edge of his expression which gave the lie to his words. 'I'll be fine here.'

The coolness of the night air spread like a lotion over my hot skin. Already the events of the evening were beginning to seem a distant memory, or a dream. Maybe I'd over-reacted, maybe his kiss had been simply an affectionate peck that went wrong. But my thighs jumped and twitched under the remembrance of his touch, the sureness of his fingers against the gap between my hold-up stockings and my knickers. No-one makes that kind of mistake – even if the kiss had been a figment of my imagination it would have taken a work of creative genius to explain away those hands.

Ben had wanted me. And I'd wanted him. *And then with a flash of horror my mind opened and let the memories in. The huge emptiness where our parents had been. Randall, trying to keep us together, Christian falling apart. And Gray. Love that wasn't love but fear turned on its head. And then the running, always the running ...*

I shook my head, letting the air circulate around the back of my neck. It was just one of those things, I had to keep telling myself. It didn't mean anything. Ben was lonely, hurting, wanting reassurance and happened to be there. Meaningless. *So why was my skin burning where he'd touched it?*

The welding gear was standing in the centre of Jason's workspace. I couldn't see any indications that it might still be connected to a power supply but I switched off the plugs, just in case. It was typical of Jason – a man who could quite happily leave bacon grilling for hours but when it came to professional equipment was a worrier.

I made my way back towards the cottage. As I crossed the lawn, I saw the shadow of a vehicle pull up. It was too far away for me to tell what it was, or where it had come from, but the headlights breezed past my feet momentarily then carried on a little way down the drive, past the cottage. I heard the stealthy sound of a door opening then voices whispering. There was a short break, another whisper, the expensive clunk of a large car door closing and then the engine raced the vehicle away, towards the village.

Rosie came through the gate. She and I caught sight of one another and both clutched at our hearts in mock fright.

'What the hell are you doing out here?' she asked. Her voice was a little shaky, maybe I'd genuinely scared her, looming across the grass out of the night. 'I thought you'd be cosy with Ben by now.'

'I might almost suspect you of arranging to go out this evening simply to get that to happen.' I might have sounded a bit shaky, too. 'I keep telling you, Ben and I – it's nothing.'

'That why you've got stubble burn that I can even see out here in the DARK, is it?'

'No, I'm blushing, that's all.'

'Yeah, right.' Then Rosie paused, cocking her head. 'Is that Harry?'

'He was fine when I left, fast asleep.'

'He's not fast asleep now.' She increased her pace and thankfully stopped interrogating me. 'He sounds really upset.'

'I'm sure Ben will have gone to him,' I said. 'Don't worry.'

But when we got into the cottage Ben was cooking madly, grilling fish with one hand and whisking meringue with the other. A tea towel was draped over his shoulder and his hair had come down over his face.

'Ah, there you are. Food is just about ready. Good timing, Rosie.' But Rosie pushed past him without even stopping to exchange pleasantries, heading for the stairs. I followed her, anxious not to be left in those close confines with Ben again.

'Harry?' Rosie rounded the corner into her bedroom. 'What ...'

I could hardly hear her above the sounds of Harry screaming. He'd somehow managed to flip the carry-cot over on top of himself, trapping his body under its weight. Rosie released him and picked him up. She was trembling all over.

'Oh, my God,' she kept saying. 'Oh, my God.' Harry's little red face was streaked with tears and one arm looked slightly blue. 'Oh, God. Should his arm be that colour? Oh, God, Jem, what am I going to do?' She hugged the baby tightly against her chest, rocking him until his screams subsided into a more general grizzle. 'Oh God.' She carried Harry downstairs and sat on the sofa with a kind of numb expression.

'Call the doctor. He'll check Harry over for you but I'm sure he's fine.' I dragged the phone to her and left her dialling, whilst still trying to reassure a hiccupping Harry that he was all right.

Ben had stopped cooking and the steam had died from the kitchen. He was peering through into the living room, watching Rosie and the stricken Harry; he looked pale.

'What kind of sicko leaves a baby to scream like that?' I launched myself at him. 'And don't give me some pathetic story, because you were cooking away and obviously not taking a blind bit of notice. How long had he been crying?'

'I can't – '

'You *bastard*!' And before I even knew I'd done it I'd pulled my arm back and smacked him right across his perfect cheekbones. It was a full-powered, open-handed strike that knocked his head to one side with its force.

Ben froze completely. His whole body seemed to fold in upon itself and his face was made up entirely of eyes. A tear trembled on his eyelashes but the immobility of his expression meant that it couldn't fall. Something inside me tore apart. 'Ben?'

A sudden movement as he swiped a hand across his eyes and then he was gone. Out of the door, fleeing through the garden and down to the road. A pause, surely not long enough for key to meet ignition system, and then the noise of a powerful car being driven at reckless speed down the lane.

Rosie was convinced she was such a bad mother that Social Services would be along any day to take Harry away.

'I can't believe I went out! What was I thinking, Jem?

Anything could have happened!' Rosie was so caught up in her own feelings of inadequacy that she hadn't thought to blame me or Ben. 'I mean, what if he'd got himself trapped under the wardrobe or got his face stuck in something – he'd have suffocated! And I wouldn't have been there!' Another fresh burst of tears. Harry picked up on her misery and began wailing again, despite the fact that the doctor had looked him over and pronounced him to be 'one of the healthiest specimens I've seen in a while.'

'You weren't to know. And we'll make sure it never happens again, so stop fretting.' Half my mind was trying to follow Ben's actions in all of this, wondering what had been going through his head. 'Harry, there's nothing wrong with you and that's official.'

I could feel my own lip trembling in sympathy with the weeping pair. Why hadn't Ben stayed and explained himself? Was all this tied up with his fear of – yes, exactly *what* was Ben so scared of? Physical contact? He hadn't felt scared, not for those few moments holding me in the kitchen. Turned on, yes. Desperate, yes. But not afraid, not until afterwards. I tried to think back over those moments when I'd seen that look of panic appear in his eyes but it all seemed so unrelated. He'd been frightened of going to Saskia's opening, when I'd found out about his being in Willow Down, when I'd asked him to come for dinner – perhaps he was just plain *weird*.

I picked at the melon Ben had left and put the rest away in the fridge. Neither of us had much appetite, although Harry gulped down his bottle and then fell asleep. 'Honestly, Harry, you're such a *bloke*,' I said, watching him settle drunkenly in Rosie's arms. 'No sympathy with emotional turmoil at all.'

I left her cuddling her son and went up to my room. Most of my gear was bagged; shirts oozed over the lip of my rucksack and my toiletries scattered like a puzzle over the jutting window ledge. I stared at it all. I'd never hung anything up or made use of the tiny cupboard. Even though I'd thought I was settled, my subconscious had known and told me not to bother, not to unpack.

I started to sweep loose items back into my bag. Panic was floating somewhere in my chest, unhooked from its perpetual moorings by this turn of events. *Time to go, time to run.* My mind raked back over Ben's behaviour, his desperation for contact and then his ultimate rejection of it, but I didn't kid myself that it was because of the way he'd let his guard down that I was going. It was *my* lowering of the barrier that had frightened me the most. The sudden rise of a desire that I thought I'd killed, the desire to be held, to be loved. An emotion that I could not allow. One I couldn't afford. To let myself desire was to risk falling in love, and to love was to trust. To trust was to hand over control and no man was ever going to control me again. Never. *Especially* not that bony freak with the messed-up hair and even more messed-up mind.

A sudden, unbidden vision of his expression when Rosie had come down the stairs carrying the screaming Harry. It had been a mixture of fear and an almost unbearable resignation, as though he was coming to terms with something that he'd never wanted in the first place. A hungry longing mixed with such pain that his eyes had blackened with it and his face had fallen into stark lines. My heart twitched like a kick.

**20th May**

I'm sorry. I can't go on with this. I wanted her, wanted the life I thought I could have, and now I know I can't. All that happens is that I can see what I've lost.

There's nothing left.

I have to go.

# Chapter Thirteen

The next day I left Rosie lying in, whistled a cheery 'see ya' through her door and hoisted my rucksack onto my shoulder. I'd written her a note of farewell and left it on the pillow of my bed, stripped the sheets and duvet and put them in the washing machine. Wiped all the surfaces clear of any trace of my occupation. She would forget me in no time as lots of people had done before her. Just because I'd felt more at home here, more settled than I ever had anywhere since I was fifteen, it gave me no rights to call the place home. I *had* no rights. No beliefs, nothing to pin myself to. I was a ghost, living on another plane of existence, one not even suspected by any of the people who called me their friend.

A pang of remorse shot through me so fast I had to stop and catch my breath. I was walking towards the bus stop, past the gateway to the opulence that was Saskia and Alex's enormous converted farmhouse. Now I'd never get to show Saskia how wrong she'd been to turn me away from her shop, to carry on this stupid vendetta that she'd got going, for whatever pointless reasons. Never get to rub her nose in my future success. Another dart of loss pierced a hole in my gut, but this time I straightened up, faced forwards and ignored it. The bus was coming. The past didn't matter – I had to keep telling myself that. Recent past, long past, it made no difference. It was all gone. I could forget.

The shop was closed. The main window was obscured

by a huge metal cover locked in place and the door had bars down on the inside. It didn't look as though Ben had been there all day.

I breathed hard, as though I'd run, and wiped my arm across my eyes. What was I *doing*? I never cried, not ever. I'd shed my last tears five years ago, that had been another promise. I was tired surely, that was all. And a little disappointed to find the place locked up and silent. I'd wanted – what *had* I wanted? To talk? To find out what his problem was? Or just to confront him, to ask him how he dared to unsettle my well-being with his sudden insights and his equally sudden turnaround, which had allowed me inside his head while he kissed me senseless? *Stupid. Stupid.*

My path to the station took me past Wilberforce Crescent. The extra half-mile of walking got my feelings under control and I was well able to convince myself that I needed to let him know I was leaving. Just – and this was important – *just* so he could have a chance to find someone else to work in the shop.

I rang the bell. There was no response so I tiptoed down the basement steps and squinted through the blinds covering those windows which lay below street level. Between the vertical slats I could just make out a set of musical instruments laid on the floor as though a band had broken off mid-practice. A guitar rested against a keyboard, casually angled, and a drum kit had the sticks crossed over it. A bright cherry-red guitar had been dropped and lay on its face looking oddly forlorn. And everything was covered in dust.

There was something naked about those unused

instruments closed away in that basement rehearsal room, something bitter in the positioning. As though Ben had been there, trying to play, trying to recreate Willow Down. Or was I reading too much into it, was it just a room that had been closed off and forgotten?

I sat on the step and chewed my lip, a tiny fantasy about breaking in quickly running to the inevitable conclusion. I'd probably end up being hauled out by six armed-response units.

A car beeped from the road. I jumped to my feet, eyes scanning for the smooth lines of the silver Audi but alighting instead on the sassy lines of Jason's sports runabout.

'Hoi, Jem! You'll get piles sitting on them steps! Wotcha doin'?'

'I thought you were in London.' I wandered over to where he was holding up the traffic.

'Yeah. Consortium seen. Back now. Bin looking for ya.' Jason tweaked open the door for me to get in, pulling aside a crate containing a huge quantity of cogs and wheels plus a large square metal box. It looked like he'd dismembered Robbie the Robot. I hesitated and he raised an eyebrow. 'You running out on us, girl?'

'I ...'

'Wanna tell me about it?'

'Nothing to tell.' I got in the car.

Jason looked up at the house. 'This your man's place then? Must be loaded, thass all I'll say.'

'He's not *my man*. And why were you looking for me?'

'Rosie's havin' a bit of a moment. I figured you could help, talk her down, you know that kind of girl stuff. So

I bin driving around trying to head you off at the pass.'

'What are you talking about, you loony?'

Jason gave me a straight look. 'I beat Rosie to it. Read your note. Then I tore it up. Thought I could get to the station before you did and thought I'd come this way. You got it bad, girl.'

'I do not! I just wanted to ... after the way he left last night ... I'm concerned, that's all.'

Jason accelerated into the stream of traffic leaving the city. 'Yeah. So you sit on his doorstep like some kinda lost dog waiting for him to come home, just 'cos you're *concerned*? Pull the other one, darling, it goes ding-a-ling.'

'What's the matter with Rosie?'

'Oho, touch a nerve, did I? Yeah, I reckon our little Jemima's burning the hot stuff for Benny boy. An' for the record, I seen his face, looking atcha like you're gonna pull him from the wreckage.'

'If you could possibly tear yourself away from your rambling imaginings about my love life, what's the matter with Rosie?'

'Social worker. Turned up at the cottage. I just got back from London, clapped out on the couch at the workshop and Rosie comes burstin' in in tears 'cos some nosey old crone came round wanting to know if she's feeding our Hazzer prop'ly. Looking in the cupboards and checking his pram an' stuff.'

'Bloody hell.'

It was Rosie's greatest fear made real. That somehow, someone would begin to suspect what she suspected herself, that she couldn't look after her baby. It was all ridiculous, of course, overwork and guilt making her feel useless; she adored Harry. A social worker on the doorstep was the last thing she needed to make her feel like a capable, coping mother.

'You can talk her round, Jem, she'll listen to you.'

'But –'

Jason gave me a solemn look. 'Luv. Whatever it is, whatever you're running from or to, it'll keep. Honest to God, it will still be there tomorrow. But today – today Rosie needs you. And, just maybe, your man needs you, too. Doncha want to get things sorted there before you takes off to lands unknown? Or is this how you always work, get yourself involved and then run out, so nothing can ever be your responsibility?'

'You know *nothing* about it.'

He inclined his head. 'Anyway, I reckons if I brings you back she might cook us a meal. I'm up to here wiv your fancy London restaurant mush, just give us one of Rosie's Thai green curries an' I'll die a happy man.'

'Jason!' But I had to let out a small laugh. His heart was in the right place, even if it was firmly lodged just above a complaining stomach. 'All right. I'll come back, for now. But first I need some advice.'

'Wot, from me? Wotcha want to know? Nothing I can tell you thatcha don't already know, apart from maybe how to dance the horizontal tango.' He circled his hips suggestively and ended up squeakily crushing himself against the steering wheel.

'How do I go about finding him?'

'Ah, wotcha want him for, when you can have me?' he replied, slightly gasping, trying to rearrange his crotch.

'Like you said, maybe I should talk to him. And don't look at me like that, it's not what you said. I only ... I only want to make sure that he's all right. He behaved like a bastard the last time I saw him and I want an explanation. Yes. To check he's alive and to find out what the hell is wrong with him.'

Jason blew. 'Phooooow. You reckon he's done 'imself in?'

'No! Why, do you?'

'Rosie said 'e were off like a rat out a drainpipe once you got started. Bloke that sensitive, well ... Could of done anything. Driven into a wall, hung himself.'

'You are such a little ray of sunshine, aren't you, Jason? Tell me then, how do I find out?'

Jason looked at me, long and hard. 'Whatcha crying for?'

'I'm not.'

A finger which smelled of embalming fluid brushed my cheek. 'Then your skin's leaking, kid.'

I gave a hiccup, a fighting attempt to keep the tears at bay. I *never* cried. Not ever. 'I'm fine.'

Jason jerked the car into a bus-stop and turned off the ignition. 'Bleeding women! Come 'ere,' and a rough arm dragged me into the surprising comfort of his fleece jacket. 'Any more 'ormones on this coat and it's gonna grow breasts.'

Jason's gruff good nature was almost more than I could bear. Silent tears burned down my face as he held me tight against him. 'I'm just ...' The words came out in half-sobs, further muffled by the generous amount of Jason they were pressed into. 'Ben. He's so ... so *scared* ... all the time. I want to know … what *he's* … running from.'

'He prob'ly wants to know the same 'bout you, Jem,' Jason said quietly, rubbing my back as far as I could tell without lecherous intent. 'We all knows you're running scared too, my girl.'

I struggled upright, tidying my face with the back of my hand. 'What do you mean?'

'Ah, come on. You comes outta no-where, you never talks about what you've left behind and you're terrified of falling in love. That's some serious back-story you're carting around, darling. And I wouldn't worry 'bout him topping 'imself. Guy wiv a face that well known, we'd have heard.' Jason gave me a bone-squeezing hug. 'He's gone to ground somewhere, thass all. Hiding like.'

'Then I've got no idea even where to start looking.' Ideas were slipping through my mind like shadows. Yes. I'd find Ben, find out what he was hiding. Jason couldn't accuse me of running out on anything unfinished. My behaviour would be unimpeachable. *Then* I'd run.

Jason grimaced and re-started the car. 'Sounds like what we got here, my love, is a breakdown in communication. Basic psychological problem, only way round it is for you and your man to get it all out in the open.'

I stared. 'There's more to you than meets the eye, isn't there?'

Jason gave me a sleazy grin and cupped his groin. 'Better believe it, darling.'

Rosie was scrubbing the kitchen when we arrived. A huge

bucket of bleach stood in the middle of the floor and the place smelled like a swimming pool.

'Oh, Jason, you found her!' Rosie clambered to her feet and gave me a moist hug.

'Steady. I can feel myself going blonder just standing here. What are you doing?'

'Making sure that when that stupid woman comes back she can't find anything to complain about.' Rosie peeled off a rubber glove and rubbed a streaming eye. 'She told me I had to clean this place from top to bottom.'

'She *what*?'

Jason, wisely, put the kettle on. Rosie slumped down on the edge of the table. 'She looked everywhere, Jem, it was awful. Even in my wardrobe. She found some old biscuits that I'd left in the cupboard that had gone all soggy – you know I don't like those horrible ones with the coconut in ...and she said ... she said ...'

'She said the place was unfit to house a baby.' Jason had to finish for her.

'Hang on. The social worker said that?' I sat next to Rosie. 'That the place was unfit?'

Rosie just nodded. She seemed numb but that might have been the fumes, the place smelled so strongly of chlorine that we could have used the kitchen to purify water. I put an arm around her.

Upstairs Harry let out a wail. 'I'll go,' Jason said. 'You make the tea, Jem. And there had better be biscuits, I'm warnin' you now.'

I waited until he left then gave Rosie a squeeze. 'Rosie, I don't want to make you feel like an idiot but you did ask for ID, didn't you?'

She paused half-way to pushing her hair up onto her head. 'What?'

'I have never in my life heard of a social worker calling in like this, no prior contact or anything, and telling you to clean your house. I mean there's no problem with Harry is there? Even the doctor said he was extraordinarily healthy –'

'You mean, she might not have been real?' Rosie looked around at the gently steaming bucket and the bleachy condensation running down the walls. 'That I've done all this for nothing?'

'It's just a bit odd, that's all. Social workers are normally pretty laid back about things unless they think a child is in actual danger, which Harry isn't. So I take it you didn't ask for ID?'

'She said she was … oh, Jem, I've been a nutjob again, haven't I?'

Jason, coming back in, met my eye over Rosie's head and mouthed, '*Saskia*'. I nodded.

'I think you've been deliberately fooled. Someone's idea of a sick joke, maybe?' Jason raised his eyebrows.

Rosie let out a huge breath. 'God. You're right of course. She didn't even offer me any ID and she looked a bit – skinny for a social worker.'

'Yeah, well, I don't think they all look like King Kong you know.'

'And I *thought* it was funny, her wanting to look through the cupboards. I – God, Jem, you're brilliant.'

'Just doing my job, ma'am.' I tipped an imaginary hat.

'And look at it this way, you won't have to clean this place again for *years*.' Jason passed Harry over to his mother. 'Think of the time you've saved yourself.'

'It doesn't really work like that, Jason.' Rosie cuddled Harry to her. 'So. In recognition of my being such a total moron I suppose I ought to cook you dinner, Jem.'

Over her head Jason mouthed '*Thank you, God.*' Rosie went on. 'You are such a good friend, Jemima.'

Jason raised an eyebrow behind her back. I felt a wash of such shame that my cheeks must have coloured. How could I have thought that it would be so easy to leave? I looked at the walls, at the hallucinogenic pattern on the old lino, smelled the musty cooked-in smells underlying the bleach. *Why* couldn't I just settle here?

Then Rosie's words hit me. Good friend. Oh, my God. Of course …

# Chapter Fourteen

It wasn't the volume of the music that made my head ring, it was the insistent bass. It echoed through me like a second heart beat and rendered everything in the club dreamlike, although that could have been the barely-there lighting. I bought myself a drink and held it in front of me like a glass wall, lounging awkwardly against a pillar and scanning the dance floor.

Opposite the bar was the DJ booth surrounded by girls looking available. Its glass was tinted and the music was continuous so I couldn't tell if the DJ was there. I wished I'd brought Jason. He might be a complete plonker, but he had the knack of looking at ease anywhere and it might have stopped me looking like a woman in search of a man. Which I was, but it was a particular man, not any of these designer-clad guys, with their smooth taste in shirts and their labels flapping.

I began to sidle around the walls heading for the far side of the club. Hidden speakers vibrated my lungs with volume and the perpetual techno-trance music scraped across my nerve endings. Finally I reached the DJ booth and looked in from behind, at the back of a blond man in a white shirt with the sleeves rolled to the elbows. He swivelled so I could see he had an earpiece in, and his eyes closed and was singing to something that bore no resemblance to the beat that was pumping out onto the dance floor. Two burly black men with radios stood either side and a rope barrier prevented the peasants from gaining entry.

'Excuse me.' I approached one of them, yelling above the music. 'Could I speak to the DJ, please?'

Dark eyes focussed on my face. I gave my winningest smile, lots of teeth and lips.

'Whatcha want?'

'A request?' I had no idea whether DJ's still played requests. I'd been out of circulation too long.

A grunt and the bodyguard folded his arms in front of his body, settling himself further into the floor. 'He dun't do requests.'

Now I really wished I'd brought Jason. He knew the etiquette for situations like this. Well, maybe etiquette was too strong a word, perhaps violence was a better term. 'I only want to have a word with him.'

Another grunt. 'Join the queue.' A vast head nodded towards the girls, still stationary-jogging, although not one breast moved between the lot of them.

This was stupid. I hadn't paid fifteen pounds to come in here and then another seven-fifty for a weak vodka only to be told I had to get behind a bunch of teenagers. I waited until the guard had switched back into resting mode then ducked under the rope and banged on the glass wall. 'Oy, Zafe!'

Three sets of eyes instantly focused my way and two extremely large sets of arms came bearing down on me, grabbed me none too gently and started to drag me backwards, heels skittering out from beneath me. Inside his booth the DJ was already losing interest, sliding back under his music again. I did the only thing a girl down on the floor surrounded by enormous men could do. I lifted the hem of my top and flashed my boobs.

'Oh, bloody hell,' one of the bodyguards exclaimed. 'That's all we need. Put 'em away love, nobody's interested.'

But someone was. Perhaps it was because I'd taken the precaution of writing 'Baz needs your help' in eye pencil right across my breasts, with my nipples standing in for 'e's.

Zafe sat on an empty beer crate while I squatted uncomfortably on a broken stool in a tiny office at the back of the club. He lit a cigarette.

'You do know I've got absolutely no reason to tell you anything?' He blew smoke. 'That bastard dropped us all in the shit back in Philly.'

'Yes, I know. But you were friends once. And honestly, Zafe, you can't feel nearly as badly about him as he does about himself. You should have seen him when he found out the band was reforming.'

Zafe shrugged. His shoulders had filled out considerably since his days in Willow Down, in the pictures he'd looked almost fragile, now he looked like a rugby player. Still as blond, though, and with those same beautiful cat-like eyes. 'Yeah, well.' He sounded almost ashamed. 'I'm still not convinced that's a great move but the management ... hey, not your problem.' Another puff of smoke. 'So, you're what? Baz's new woman?'

'No. Absolutely not.' I cupped my hands around my knees to stop the stool rocking. 'He's a friend, that's all.'

Sapphire eyes slithered across my chest, now properly covered once more. 'Hell of a length to go to for a *friend*, flashing your 36Ds at the whole club,' he said dryly. Another mouthful of smoke threatened to obscure the single bare bulb swinging from the low ceiling. Money clearly all went on front of house. 'Look love, Baz was brilliant back in the day. Best lead I ever played with. But he was – how can I put it? Erratic. Bit fond of the old marching powder, know what I mean? Just before we went to the States on that final tour he took three months out getting his head straight, cleaning up his act, all that kinda thing. But when we got out there – it was like he just lost it. One night he's playing like he's got the devil himself in his soul and the next – pow, he's outta there so fast the band didn't know he'd gone 'til next day. Woke up and he's not on the tour bus, he's not with some girl, he's just ...' Zafe broke off and rubbed at his arms as though something had walked over his skin under his pale jacket. 'Bastard,' he finished.

'Where did he go?'

He pulled a face. 'Dunno. Didn't even know he was back in York until you just told me. He's not been in touch. No calls, nothing. I tried ...' He broke off and sucked hard on the cigarette for a moment. 'I was his friend and he wouldn't talk to me about what was going off in his life. Shut me out. Wouldn't take my calls, nothing. I went everywhere I could think of, hung out in some of our old dives, all his favourite places, no-one knew a thing, no-one had seen him. Knocked on more doors than a Jehovah's Witness that year.'

'Is there anywhere you can think of that he might have

run to?' I was gripping my hands tighter around my knees, could feel my nails digging under my kneecaps.

'You tried the house, right?'

'There was no-one in.'

Zafe shook his hair, clearing his fringe from his eyes. He wore it differently now, long at the front but spiky-short at the back, like he had his expression on the wrong side of his head. 'OK. You know his family?'

'No, like I said, I'm just a friend.' Ben had never talked about his family. Never really talked about anything close to him unless I'd forced him. I shivered. He was more like me than I'd realised.

'Ma and sister live in Vancouver.'

'Canada?' I was horrified by the snatching panic at the thought that Ben might be that far away.

'Well done. Yeah.' Zafe maintained the dry tone in his voice. 'His dad died, they emigrated. All kicked off just as we started up the band so Baz stayed over here. Bought them a place. Put all his earnings into property, all that didn't go up his nose.'

'You think he might be in Canada?'

A considered pause. Zafe narrowed his eyes at me through the smoke. 'You sure you're not some journo after the inside story? Everyone wants to know what happened to the great Baz Davies.' He lowered his head. 'Including me,' he finished quietly. 'Though ... five years, it's a long time, I guess most people wouldn't even recognise him now. And the ones that do ... phht.' He flicked ash onto the floor and stirred at it with a heel. 'No-one cares any more. Old news.'

'So, even if I were a journalist, you'd help me?'

'Nah. If you're a journo you can make it up.' Those blue, blue eyes fixed on me. 'So, can you prove you're not?'

I held up my open hands. 'How do I prove a negative?'

Zafe stood up and ground out the cigarette stub with the toe of his leather boots, forcing it to a smear on the concrete. 'You been in the house?'

'Ben's? Yes, once. But only the hall with all those weird tiles. Oh, and the big room with the sofas. The room with the speakers set up. We went to an opening together and we had a drink in there before we left.' I had to look up at Zafe as he paced around the cheerless cuboid room. He had a loose way of walking, as though his joints were attached by elastic to his body.

'OK then. If you are a journo, you're one Baz trusts. He doesn't let any old hack into his place.' He tapped another cigarette from his pocket and lit it. 'What?'

'You. Chain smoking. Something you picked up on tour?'

'Among other habits.' Zafe Rafale smiled for the first time and I saw why he had all those fans. 'Yeah. So. You're a friend of our Baz's, I believe that now. And he ran out on you. Making a bit of a habit of this, isn't he? Never used to run.' His eyes were inward-looking now, scanning his thoughts. 'Remember this one time, we'd be about fourteen, fifteen. We're at this disco effort, school, youth club, can't remember where. Anyway Baz had his eye on this girl, fancied her for months, he goes up to her and says, "You want to dance?" And this tart she eyes him up and down and kind of sneers, you know, in his face? Then she goes, "I'm not that desperate." And Baz,

cool as Sweden, looks at her and goes, "Nah, but I am."
Amazing. That's Baz. Cool.'

'So what happened between then and now? Why is he
so – broken?'

Zafe blew smoke upwards. The ceiling was almost
invisible now. 'You tell me. I've gone through it all in
my head, over and over; was it the drugs, was it some
girl. Tell you something, it must have been one hell of a
problem, 'cos if you'd asked me before, I'd have said he'd
sooner have eaten the tour bus than quit.' He glanced at
the Rolex on his wrist under a rolled-up shirt cuff. 'Look,
I've got to play a set in ten. Got a pen?' From a pocket
I managed to assemble a biro and a scrap of paper. Zafe
scribbled quickly, an almost incomprehensible series of
squiggles. 'This was always where he went when we had
time off.' He then caught hold of my arm when I went to
slip the paper back into my pocket. 'If you find him tell
him – shit, I don't know. Tell him I miss him. That's all.'

'I think it's a seven.' Rosie spoke more definitely than I'd
heard her speak for weeks. Since she'd had Harry her
edges seemed to have worn thin, as though she blended
with things more. It made her fuzzier, less inclined to say
what she thought, as though she distrusted even her own
opinions. 'Seven, Moor Road.'

'I thought it was a nine. "Nine, Main Road".' I turned
the paper upside down in case a change of perspective
made things clearer.

Jason, who was watching Harry kicking nappy-free

on the lawn, piped up. 'It's Robin Hood's Bay, total population twelve and four fishing boats. It's hardly going to be difficult, is it?'

'Maybe he doesn't want to be found.'

'Then he won't be there, will he?' Jason stooped and picked Harry up. Rosie taped shut the box of cards she'd just filled and removed her son from Jason's slightly sticky grasp.

'I am aware that we usually get more sense from the pig in next-door's field, but Jason's right,' she said. 'All you can do is try. Then maybe you'll feel better.'

I stared at her. 'You're very perky all of a sudden. Yesterday you were half-way to having Harry adopted, today you're like Miss Agony Column.'

'Yeah, Rosie's got a date,' Jason supplied. 'Wiv a *man*. Least I'm guessing it's a bloke, I don't reckon our Rosie swings the same way as you do, Jem, 'less she's like, bi.' He licked his lips. 'And if she is, can I watch?'

I stared at Rosie. 'I wondered about the hair and the frock. So you've got yourself a date have you? You lucky cow.'

Self-consciously Rosie smoothed down the front of her pink dress. It set off her dark curls a treat with the way they slithered onto her silky shoulders. 'It's not ... you know, a bit ... Snow White?'

Jason snorted. 'Snow White? You? More like Mucky Slush.'

Rosie gave a twirl and Harry chuckled in her arms. 'Will you babysit, Jem? I should be back by midnight. If I'm not, there's some bottles made up in the fridge.'

'So there's a chance you might – you know, sleep over?'

Rosie waggled her eyebrows at me. 'You're getting as bad as Jason.'

'Whoa, come *on*. Look at how much experience I've got over our Jem,' Jason complained. 'Anyhow I don't think she's experienced at anything. Know wot I mean?'

I took the proffered Harry. 'Still not a virgin, Jase.' Knowing that he was trying to wind me up, to goad me into talking about myself.

'Will be soon, if you don't get cracking. You wanna borrow the batmobile to go looking for your man tomorrow?' He shook his car keys in my face. 'You can dart him through the window, crate him up, bring him back 'ere, no questions asked. I won't even worry about any stains on the seats.'

'Saskia's coming over to pick up this first batch of cards.' Rosie quite rightly ignored Jason. 'They're all packed up and ready to go. Right, I'm off, I'll see you later.'

Jason and I stared at each other. 'Your man not coming to pick you up?' I asked as Harry wound his chubby little fists into my hair. 'That's a bit mean.'

'No he – he has to work. I'm meeting him in town. Bus leaves in ten minutes. Bye!'

Rosie strode, high-heeled and preened, off towards the stop in the middle of the village and Jason gave me a jab in the arm.

'You know wot? I reckon this bloke ain't on the level. "Working" my arse, only bleeding married, in't he?'

'Rosie's not stupid, Jase.' I headed towards the cottage. 'And she's got Harry to think about. She's not going to go shagging around with married guys with a three-month-old baby waiting at home, is she?'

'She might,' Jason answered, trotting alongside me. 'If it was Harry's dad.'

I stopped dead. 'You think?'

'Come on, Jem, don't tell me you've never wondered? Think about it, if he's available then why ain't Rosie and he all cosied up in some kinda advert-idyll?'

'Maybe they treasure their independence.'

'Wot, like I used to treasure sleeping in the back of me car and dragging the whole of British Rail from place to place when I was trying to get commissioned? Yeah, that'll be right, Jem. Rosie loves living here and working flat out for the Mistress of Pain.'

'Talk of the devil ...'

The huge black 4×4 was back, parking outside the cottage with Saskia in the passenger seat and Alex driving.

'Hello, Jemima. And Harry. Gosh, a bare bottom, well, nappies are *so* expensive these days, aren't they? Of course I used terries for Oscar, so much kinder to the skin.'

'And so much harder on the au-pair. Hello, Saskia, Alex. No Oscar with you today?' I jiggled Harry on my hip, the mere presence of Saskia made him grousy and the absence of his mother didn't help.

'He's having a visiting day at his new school. Bless.' Saskia tippytoed along the path towards Jason and me. 'We've just passed Rosie at the bus stop and I must admit we were a little shocked at her dress sense, weren't we, darling?' As her husband caught up Saskia looped a hand through his arm. 'Of course, I lost all my baby weight within a fortnight and not everyone can be so lucky, can they, but I do think one should dress for one's shape.'

She eyed me up and down. 'Obviously you don't agree, Jemima, but it is important to look one's best at all times. Now, are these the cards? I'm surprised that Rosie can find time to go off gallivanting when I told her I need the rest by the weekend.'

'Surely you can be a *bit* flexible. I mean it's not as if you're even selling them ...'

Whoops.

'What do you mean?' Saskia looked at me from under her eyelashes. Her suspiciously smooth forehead did its best to frown.

'They aren't in Le Petit Lapin, are they?' Unless you count the fact that they're stacked up in cardboard boxes out the back. 'I looked.'

Saskia sighed. 'Oh, but I *did say* I wanted these for the Harrogate shop.'

'I could have sworn Rosie said these were for Le Petit Lapin.' I gave Saskia my best smile.

'No, darling. You're not just the teeniest bit stressed, are you, Jemima? Only, stress can make you forgetful at times and you do look a little ... how can I put it kindly?'

'Unique?'

Saskia gave a chiming little giggle which was like tinfoil on my nerves. 'Unkempt, sweetie. As though you're not taking care of yourself properly. It's *so* important to look after yourself. And how *are* you doing for money, darling?'

Pride cut in and I lied. 'Oh, I'm doing okay. Ben's shifting a fair bit of stuff and I'm selling well on the internet.'

'That's lovely.' A tight smile, as though she was afraid

to grin in case her mouth split. 'Good. Now, we are just a teensy bit pushed for time, darlings, so we'll take these and vamoose. Alex, sweetie, would you put the box in the car for me?' As her husband hefted Rosie's cards into the Hummer Saskia smiled sweetly at me. 'And where's that gorgeous Mr Davies, Jemima? I must say I'm surprised he's not here, you looked so close at the opening.'

'You were a lot closer.' I smiled a saccharine smile back.

'Yes, well, that was business.' Saskia fluffed her hair. 'Do ask him to get in touch, won't you? I've a few little propositions I'd like to put to him. Super.' Saskia turned. 'Alex! I'm ready now. You can drop me off at the house before you go, I've a few phone calls to make.' She turned to wave manicured finger tips at me. 'Ciao, sweetie.' Her voice lowered an octave to take her leave of Jason. 'Goodbye, my darling.' He merited a kiss on the cheek. 'And if you could let Rosie know I'll be by sometime on Sunday for the rest of the consignment?'

The big black car swept away in a spray of gravel. I turned to Jason. 'Can you smell brimstone?'

'I dunno. Whatever perfume Saskia was wearing has made my nose bleed.'

Rosie woke me when she got in at three, wanting an update on Harry's evening. I suppose it was understandable, what with the carrycot-under-the-wardrobe incident, but I suspect I might have been a little less than understanding, being dragged out of sleep to describe nappy contents. The discussion meant I was slightly sleep deprived when I drove off in Jason's car the next morning. Robin Hood's Bay was a tiny village clinging to a rapidly eroding cliffside, all hanging baskets and provisions merchants, like something out of Enid Blyton. I inched the car down to the slipway at the bottom of the village, failing to spot any sign of Ben, his car or any street bearing any name like 'moor' or 'main'. In fact, half of the main road had fallen into the sea a few winters ago. Carefully I turned around, inching the car in reverse because there wasn't much room, and headed back up the slope again past the hotels and guesthouses, past the old railway station and up to where the buildings gave way to fields. I pulled into a gateway, killed the engine and got out.

Far below me on the beach I could hear the sound of children yelling. The sun was brilliantly white, shadows were short and I felt my chest burning with something, some emotion I couldn't name. I leaned against the car and took a deep breath, the heat and light making everything feel slightly unreal, dreamlike, listening to the children playing at the foot of the cliffs, and then I recognised the feeling. It was longing.

Some deeply buried part of me wanted this. To stand in the sun, listening to children – *my children* – play. To have a normal, loving man to go home to, a gentle, smiling man who'd flick his hair out of his eyes and take the baby from me. Ask me how my day had been. Kiss my cheek and then later, in the secret night, draw lines of flame across my body.

*Ben.*

His was the face I saw, the fingers I imagined. His was the body that stepped in to fill the gap in my fantasies. If only I could reach him, talk to him ... if only ... If only I could overcome everything I was. If I could forget all the promises I'd made. If only *things were different.*

I shook my head. Sleep deprivation. That's all it was. Tiredness and unaccustomed driving in a car that smelled of solder and Lynx. As I stood breathing heavily, sun reflected from something very shiny and speared through my eyeball like a migraine. I blinked, turned and caught sight of the road sign. Moor Road it said, with the sun winking and gleaming off it and all but beckoning in a deliberately provocative manner. The feeling that I'd been fooled by some stunt on Zafe's behalf, some way of getting rid of a troublesome groupie, left me and was replaced by a prickle of nerves. Ben was here. Somewhere.

My stomach squeezed and my body turned, so used to running, to getting out of situations before they went bad that it was an automatic response. I was half way into the driving seat with my knuckles white against the doorframe before I managed to tell myself that this was just a stop-off. Just a clearing-the-air pause before I could start again somewhere, clean slate.

Do this, then it's over. It's all over.

Number nine was carved on a weathered bit of elm, nailed to a swinging sign at the end of an overgrown driveway which curved and dipped. The house was a long way from the road. Once I rounded the first bend I could see a car slewed casually across a grassed-over turning circle. It was an Audi but I couldn't be sure it was Ben's. Despite the car the house had a deserted look, curtains pulled across most of the windows and paintwork peeling from the frames. An enormous ash tree flourished alongside and hung its branches down over the guttering. It made the house look like an emo kid trying to hide behind its fringe.

I wasn't brave enough to knock. With the gravel crunching a give-away under my feet, I tried to look as though I had called on unidentifiable business and shuffled around the outer wall of the house down a paved walkway and into the back garden.

Where Ben was sprawled face down on the overgrown lawn.

I gave a moan and dashed over the spongy grass to crouch beside his body. He was half-dressed, barefoot in those painted-on black jeans and the lack of shirt left his tattoo darkly visible, scrawled across his painfully pale skin. I laid a hand against his ribcage to check for movement. He couldn't be dead. He just couldn't.

He wasn't. With a yell that made me leap several feet backwards he jumped to his feet. 'What the ...?'

'I'm sorry, I thought you –'

He cut me off, pulling at the T shirt he'd had cushioning his head. 'What are you doing here? How did you know ...? Why? It's not ... Harry, he's OK, isn't he?'

'Zafe gave me the address.' I watched Ben blinking his way back to wakefulness. 'And Harry's fine. What were you doing out here?' I couldn't keep my eyes off his naked chest. Even though he was clutching his T shirt against himself like a shield enough flesh was available for viewing to show that he had bones and muscles and very little else. He looked like a vertical greyhound.

'What does it look like I was doing? I was lying in the sun.'

My heart had settled. 'It's not working. You still look like half-a-pint of milk.'

An almost-smile. 'And while I wasn't expecting a "hello, gorgeous", I still find myself surprised. So then. Presuming you didn't come just for the insult opportunities?'

'I thought you might –' No, it was too stupid to say, with him standing there looking baffled, still blinking sleep from his eyes. 'I had to show Zafe my boobs before he'd tell me about this place.'

'Sounds like Zafe. He'd make such a rubbish spy.' Rubbing a hand through his already disarrayed hair, Ben moved off towards an open door at the back of the house, not inviting me to follow. Beyond the door I could see a cool, dark room with a table and chairs set on a bare slate floor. The sun scalded my skin as though it was driving me towards the shade but more heavy-headed clouds were building on the horizon, hinting at a coming storm. I shielded my eyes and looked up at the sky.

Ben stopped in the doorway and turned round. 'You've come this far. You might as well see the rest.'

The grass was mossy under my feet like walking on fat green pillows, suddenly becoming cold hard stone as I stepped into the shadow of the kitchen. Between its thick walls and floor hung a pool of cool air and I felt myself relax a little.

Ben, busy plugging in a kettle, ignored me. He'd dumped his T shirt on the table and when he turned to search for coffee I found that my eyes would not move from the middle of his chest. His body hair was as dark as the hair on his head, spiralling from around his nipples to a narrow band running down the centre of his concave stomach. His arms were lean but strong, with the muscles running long and smooth down to his elbows. His ribs pushed the skin of his chest as he breathed, rolling with each exhalation and making the shadows that fell across his body move like snakes.

'Why did you come?' He was wreathed in the gloom at the far side of the room, the kettle sending a shiver of steam between us. He looked like a ghost.

'I was frightened.' I found I'd backed up, the edge of the table was digging into the backs of my thighs and I couldn't go any further without using my bodyweight to force it against the wall.

'Why? Did you think I'd refuse to sell any more of your buckles?'

'That night. With Harry. The way you ran. You were – freaking.'

Ben shook his head slowly. 'And that's it? I lost it and you thought you'd come pry into my secrets? Using Zafe, which, I have to say, is like using a dirty weapon.'

I forced my voice to be calm. 'Ben, the way you took off I didn't know what to think. Zafe was the only person who'd know where you might have gone.'

'Great. Well you found me. Congratulations, go get yourself a gold medal. And then just plain *go*.'

'I only wanted to – talk.' His expression was so dark that I couldn't even bring up the subject of my leaving town.

'Right. So you smacked me round the face that night to – what? Bring me to my senses? Oh, Jemima, you have no idea what you're dealing with here.'

'Then tell me.' I moved across the kitchen until we

stood only one flagstone apart. I stared into his eyes, watching the pupils widen until they almost completely overwhelmed the irises, turning them into ebony discs. 'Go on. Tell me what it is that's screwing you up so totally.'

'Why?' His voice was little more than a whisper and his eyes flickered, taking in all of my face.

Because you need a friend, I wanted to say. You need someone to stop this happening. But my throat was clogged with my own reasons.

'You've talked to Zafe, he'll have told you about the drugs … do you think I'm a junkie? Is that it?'

'Ben, I don't know *what* you are.'

'Oh, God.' The click as the kettle turned itself off was so loud in the sudden silence that it bounced off the walls. Ben was breathing faster now, his ribcage moving under a skin that seemed slick. Was he sweating? 'Jemima.'

'I'm listening.'

He gripped the edges of the sink behind him. 'I feel sick.'

'Do you need me to get you something? Valium?'

Ben's eyes were suddenly intense. 'You seem to know a lot about it. What's your story then, Jemima?'

I shook my head. 'No. That's not what this is about.'

He exhaled. 'All right. Listen. You're wrong. I haven't taken anything since I came out of rehab. It's been a close-run thing, sometimes, but I learned my lesson.' Ben's knuckles were grey against the white enamel. 'I'm better than that, stronger. I found that I don't need a head full of coke to tell me who I am and there's nothing like having been an addict for showing you how shallow it all is. Been

179

there, done that.' And I wasn't sure if he meant the drugs or the fame. 'And now – now everything is different.'

I could see the muscles in his shoulders standing out under the strain. Something was going to give. 'Jemima –' A seething roll of thunder built to a tympanic crescendo and then died to a mumble. Outside the sun was killed by the cloud and a prickle of static electricity made my head tingle. Ben ignored it all, just stared at the floor as though his breakfast was about to reappear. 'Jemima,' he said again, glancing my way and then jumped as a lightning flash speared through the room and was gone.

'Just a storm,' I said. 'Must be nearly overhead, judging by that thunder.'

'Thunder?'

And suddenly I understood. 'Oh, my God. Ben.' The guitars he couldn't play. Harry crying upstairs. *Ben hadn't known he was there.*

He saw the understanding in my face and he broke. The tension in his shoulders transferred to his back and he jolted away from the sink, dropping to the floor with his forehead on his knees, his whole body shaking. Not just crying but sobbing as though everything dear to him had died.

'But how –? I mean –' *The party where he'd known what I was saying on the other side of a crowded room.* 'You lip read.' I went to him, sat beside him. Touched his arm until he raised his head. 'Ben. Oh, God, *Ben.*'

The expression on his face was one I never want to see again. His eyes were black and it hurt to look into them, his hair was stapled across his cheeks with the tears that smeared his skin. He'd been holding this alone for such a long time, carrying it like a private horror. Under my hand I could feel him trembling. 'Tell me,' I said. 'Just tell me. All of it.'

It came in fits and starts and bubbles of speech. His breath sounded as though it came over cogwheels in his throat and his chest heaved with the effort of drawing in air. He'd been diagnosed with a disease that caused a disintegration of the tiny bones of the inner ear, told his condition could stabilise or worsen at any time. Hoped for a miracle and then on stage in Philadelphia suddenly realised he was completely deaf. Ben looked deep into my face as he shared the terror, the isolation. 'It's congenital. My sister has lost part of her hearing, too. That's why I bought them the place in Vancouver, there's a university out there doing research on stabilising hearing and working on rebuilding lost bone. Just because it's too late for me doesn't mean she can't be helped. But there's no cure,' he finished. His skin was chilled under my hand but his breathing was rapid, feverish. 'It's like being completely alone, trapped in here.' He touched my forehead with his nearest finger.

'But hearing aids –?'

'Only work if the bones of the inner ear are intact. Mine ...' He tailed off, making a crumbling gesture with his hands. 'Been through all this with Dr Michaels. Every option. But it's a bastard of a disease, Jem, because once the hearing's gone there's nothing to be done.' He gave a dark smile. 'And, believe it or not, I'm luckier than a lot of sufferers because all the work with the band, being on stage and having to communicate over the music – I learned to lip read a long time ago. Dr Michaels wanted me to learn to sign but that's a fast-track to living a completely separate life. Everyone knowing. I wanted … I wanted to pretend I could still hear.' He shook his head. 'Shit. Thought I'd done all my crying. Sorry.'

'Hey. Don't be sorry. It's … I don't even know what it is. Terrible. Awful.' I didn't know what else to say.

'You want to know what it really is, Jem? It's loneliness. It's being treated as stupid or rude, it's not understanding. And Christ, the *dark* –'

'Dark?'

'When it's night, when I can't see … that's when I really know I'm deaf.' He tried to draw in a breath. I heard it stutter past the tears still in his throat. 'Right. So now you feel sorry for me. Great. I need a friend, what I get is a pity partner.' He dropped his head onto his knees and curled his arms around it, turning himself into a ball, blocking me out. Crying silently.

I left him to let it out. Made two mugs of strong coffee, listening to the rain that had begun pounding down on the outside of the cottage. The little kitchen had been gloomy to start with, now it was like midnight and the rapidly cooling air had dropped the temperature down beyond comfortable.

I took a mug to Ben. Touched his shoulder. 'Hey. Drink this then put something on. You're going to freeze.'

He was watching my mouth. I could see that now. 'Christ, I'm sorry. Jem, I'm so, so sorry. This isn't your problem, it's not your fight. All I ask is that you don't tell anyone else. Please.'

'Ben.' I dropped to sit cross-legged in front of him. 'You need to tell Zafe.'

182

'*How*? For God's sake, how do I tell him something like this?'

'The same way you told me. He deserves to know. At least so he can move forward with reforming the band or whatever. He really cares about you, you know.'

A pale smile. 'Thanks, Oprah.' Another huge, sighing breath. 'Can't believe I lost it like that.'

I threw him his shirt from the table. 'Please. You've got goosebumps so big I can see them from here.' I watched him drag the cotton over his head, loosening his hair from the collar. 'And, for the record, I don't pity you. Don't even feel sorry for you if you want the truth.'

An indrawn breath. 'Okay, guess I asked for *that* one.'

'I've – known people who've lost a lot more than their hearing. And if going deaf is what it took to get you off the drugs then that's a fair trade from where I'm standing.'

Ben's eyes burned through me. 'You want to tell me?'

'No.' I looked around at the dark streaming windows, the ribbons of water dragging down the panes. 'Wow. This place is way, *way* too gothic.'

He laughed. 'I like it that the weather has a sense of the dramatic.'

In my jeans my pocket began to vibrate. I snatched at my mobile. 'And now I know why you never call,' I said. 'I thought you were just being a typical bloke.'

'Hey, I was.' Ben stood up, straightening his legs slowly and stretching. He looked taller and the stretch went on forever. I tried not to look at the way the muscles in his thighs were working under his jeans.

'It's Rosie.' I flipped open the phone. 'Hello, Rosie.'

'Jemima,' Rosie sounded slightly out of breath. 'Have

you found him? Ben, is he with you?'

'Yes to both questions.'

I heard Rosie relaying this information to someone else and then heard Jason's yell of 'ice cubes!' before she came back on.

'It's important. Can you put him on?'

I glanced over at Ben lip reading my half of the conversation. 'Er, he's – he's upstairs at the moment. Tell me and I'll pass it on.' Black eyes regarded me steadily. 'He's busy,' I added in case Rosie was about to insist.

Ben gave a slow, sad smile.

'Okay. But this is important, Jem. Tell him there's been a fire. At the shop. Saskia just rang, apparently the fire engines are out and everything. He might want to get over there.'

'*Saskia* rang?'

'Yeah. Apparently the whole of the street came to a standstill so she sent Mairi out to find out what was going on.'

'What, passing up the chance to ogle a fireman?'

'Maybe she thought Mairi's need was greater. Anyway, tell him, Jem, will you?' And she rang off.

I relayed Rosie's half of the conversation to Ben, leaving out Jason's comment about the ice cubes. Ben grabbed a jacket from its hanging position at the base of the bannisters.

'Come on.' And before I could protest about Jason's car being left half in a hedge, Ben had dragged me out, shoved me in his passenger seat and we were heading at an unwise speed for town.

Ben stared at the steaming timbers of the shopfront. 'There's not much left is there?'

He'd dealt with the firemen while I'd prowled around the site trying to see what had become of my buckles, and now we stood alone in the middle of the tiny square watching ash fall into puddles. Being wooden, most of the outside of the shop had crumbled, leaving the inner plastered walls still standing, fragile and thin, dripping with water. Within the remains, twisted shapes which had once been guitars were tangled on the floor with soaking paper, all swept into one corner by the force of the hoses which had been played on them.

'Oh, Ben.' The air was acrid. 'All your lovely guitars.'

'Yeah.' He sounded tired. Emotionally wrung-out. 'The firemen said there was a lighter and a pile of old newspapers at the top of the steps, looks like kids had been mucking about and then legged it when the place started to go up.'

'Oh, God.' I'd seen the remains of one of my buckles. It lay just inside the doorway between a splintered guitar and spills of brightly coloured paper which had once been Zafe's posters. The heat had warped it out of shape and melted the glue so that it looked like an encrusted metal fist. I went to collect it but Ben grabbed me.

'Don't go in. Insurance people will be all over this place in about an hour, we don't want to have to explain why your footprints are going in and out.' He sighed. 'What a crap day.'

I shuffled through piles of powdery wood where the

firemen had heaped anything they'd rescued from the flames, bending here and there to sieve things between my fingers. Well, at least now I didn't have to worry about leaving any of my jewellery behind when I went.

Ben pressed a finger into a wall support which sagged alarmingly at his touch. 'Insurance are going to have a field day.' A momentary flash in his eyes. 'I *hate* dealing with bureaucracy. Paperwork's okay but the telephone calls are a bitch.'

I kept my hand closed around the object I'd picked up and stared over the smouldering remnants. Ben laid his hand on my arm. The warmth came through my shirt and I found myself very aware of how close he was standing. I shifted my weight and he moved too, a little closer.

'You're shivering.'

'I think I'm in shock.' I looked again at the twisted remains of my buckles in the ruins. 'God. Who's going to stock my stuff now?'

'Is it really that bad?' Carefully, slowly, as though he thought I was going to take offence, Ben slid his jacket off and wrapped it around my shoulders. The warmth was lovely.

I shrugged. There was no way I could tell him. *No way.* I trembled again, feeling trapped.

Ben rubbed a soot-streaked hand over his face, transferring a lot of the soot to his cheeks. 'Times like these I wish I hadn't quit drugs,' he said ruefully.

I punched him on the arm. Quite hard. 'Things are never *that* bad.' I said. 'So your shop's burned down, so what? You're loaded and it's not like the place was exactly heaving with customers, was it?'

'Right, okay, so I'll resign myself to spending my days in some kind of home, shall I, where they can teach me to make ornaments out of raffia to sell to people who haven't carelessly lost their hearing? The shop wasn't there to sell things. It was to give me some point of contact with the human race.'

I glared at him. 'If you're going to come over all self-pitying I am really going to clock you one.'

'Ooh, look who's talking. Little Miss "Nobody wants to buy my things".'

'Yes, but I'm broke!'

'At least you can make money. Deafness doesn't go away.'

'You're *alive*. You got into drugs, you got out with no damage other than your wallet took a big hit. Maybe a few synapses fried – you hardly need a brain to play indie rock, do you?'

In the very back of my head, where no-one could see, I was suddenly aware that this skinny ex-guitarist was so far under my skin that he was inhabiting a region dangerously close to my heart.

Ben made a very rude noise. 'Come on, bitch,' he said. 'Let's go back to mine, have a drink. Oh, I'm sorry, we *have* to go to mine because you don't *have* your own place. Sweet.' He turned around and headed for the alleyway, pausing to add, 'And don't think that because I can't see you I don't know you're muttering under your breath.'

This time Ben took me into the kitchen. It was huge, all Moben and Miele, gleaming chrome and nifty little hanging units. He poured me a glass of wine and watched me clamber up onto one of the tall stools, nudging the wine bottle closer to me. 'So tell me, what am I going to do about those phone calls that the insurers are just going to *love* making?'

'Why don't you tell them you're deaf?'

'Yeah, right, because none of them will know who I am or that I used to be in Willow Down, and absolutely none of them will be straight on to the press.'

'Whoo-hoo, welcome to Mr Arrogance.'

We glowered at each other for a moment, then Ben's face cleared into a smile so gorgeous that I found I was smiling back. He still had the sooty streaks all over his cheeks but his eyes had lost that guarded expression; he looked more relaxed than I'd ever seen him. Also very, very attractive, as though somehow his scruffy bony-ness had grown on me and in an awful lapse of taste I was being drawn to men whose hair points in several directions at once and who look like a well-dressed piece of string.

'You're staring,' he said.

'And you're very cheerful for a man whose shop just burned down.' My eyes were quartering his face, taking in the straight brows, the dark lashes, the way his cheeks looked as though someone had detonated a stubble-bomb under his chin and the fallout had fortuitously highlighted his excellent bone structure.

'You liking what you see?' He dropped his eyes from mine but kept watching my mouth.

'Ben, you said it before, we're friends. That's all.'

'Why?' He leaned back on his stool, resting his back against one of the immaculate cupboards and tilting so that the front legs of the stool rose off the ground. 'Why is that all? What are you so afraid of?'

I looked him in the eye. 'You've fought your demons, got everything off your chest and now you're ready for something else. Well, Mr Davies –' I leaned forward and he let the stool rock back to earth to meet me eye-to-eye over the table. 'Not everyone's demons are so easily subdued.'

Somewhere in the house a phone rang.

'Do you want me to get that?'

'Get what?' Ben's eyes were still flickering over my mouth.

'Oh, for God's sake, Beethoven.' I slithered off the stool and located the telephone in the big room with all the sofas. 'Why do you have a phone, anyway?'

Ben had followed me. 'It was here when I moved in.'

'D' you know, I thought you had a mobile?'

He thought for a second, then pulled from his pocket the slim plastic oblong that I'd seen before. 'This what you mean? It's my vibrator.'

I paused with my hand on the receiver. 'Excuse me?'

'For the door. When the bell goes, it vibrates. So that I know someone is out there. And, incidentally, giving me an exciting little buzz in the pocket region.' He wiggled his eyebrows. 'This baby is why I don't hurry to the front door. And why are you looking at me like that?'

I unpursed my lips. 'I'm surprised you've got room in those jeans. Now, I'm going to answer this call, so please stop making me think about you vibrating in your own pocket.'

He grinned. 'Buzz, buzz. Think about it all you want, Jemima.'

I held a brief conversation with the insurance agents, relaying to Ben. 'I feel like a go-between,' I complained when I finally replaced the receiver. He didn't answer, he was staring at his hands, playing his fingers along the back of one of the white leather armchairs. 'Ben?'

Still nothing. But when he finally looked up his eyes were huge. 'Arson,' he said simply.

'What? The fire brigade said it was an accident, kids playing –'

'Don't you ever read between the lines? What that insurance guy – it was a guy, wasn't it? What he was saying about examining evidence, that means they think it was started deliberately.'

'Ooh, good, it'll be like CSI down there in a couple of days.' I smacked my lips together. 'Blokes in suits rubbing pencils up the walls and stuff.'

'Aren't you even a little bit concerned that someone's burned down my shop on purpose?' Ben began pacing up and down, his trainers making squeaky noises on the polished wood of the floor. 'Who hates me enough to do that?'

'Like I said, my heart refuses to bleed for someone who's got as much cash as you have.' I sat down on the squashy sofa. It was hideously comfortable.

'What is it with you?' Ben squealed his feet round to stand facing me. 'What is your hang up with money? Yeah, okay, I get that you're broke, well, don't start grudging me my money 'cos I worked for it, babe. And I won't have some chippy little cow telling me that I've got it easy, that I shouldn't mind shit happening, just because I've got a few houses and a nice car!' He slumped down on the sofa opposite me, curling his head down so I couldn't see his face. 'That place was my therapy, my salvation. If it hadn't been for the shop, what do you think I would have done? Because I'll tell you, Jemima, I'd have done what I was tempted to do when I realised my hearing had gone for good – headed downtown, scored a few grammes of best Colombian and not given a shit about anything. Buying the shop, setting up the stock, it all gave me something else to concentrate on while my head got round the facts of what was happening to me.' A shiver crept its way down my spine. Ben met my eye. 'But you know how that feels, don't you?'

My hands on the leather were suddenly sweating. 'What are you talking about?' I dug my nails into the seat.

He shook his head. 'Just – this feeling I'm getting from you. I've always been good at faces. Body language, that kind of thing. And you, Jemima, are giving "fuck-off" in clouds. Something bad happened to you, something that means you don't trust, you don't give in. That selling your jewellery is something to do to stop yourself thinking.'

I stood up. 'You spent all this time being a man of mystery, and suddenly there's no shutting you up is there?'

Another one of his sudden, beautiful smiles. 'Better believe it.'

Watching him sitting there, one ridiculously long leg folded over the other in his groin-challengingly tight jeans, I almost weakened. The urge to tell him everything, to let him know me properly, rushed over me. At that point I realised I was dangerously close to loving Ben Davies.

'Can you lend me the money for a taxi so I can go and

get Jason his car back?'

'Are you changing the subject?' His smile had faded and the tightness was back in his eyes.

If it had been anyone but Ben then maybe everything would have come tumbling out, the whole sordid story. But it was Ben. And if I told him – he might not like me any more. But I owed it to him, didn't I, to explain why I wouldn't – *couldn't* – get any closer than this? To tell him that I was leaving, maybe to tell him *why*. And suddenly the thought of being without him made my breathing faster, my palms sweatier. 'No.'

His face relaxed again. I began to realise how much it had cost him to confide in me. 'That's good.' He unfolded himself and stood looking down at me. 'Look, when you're ready – hey, I can recommend telling someone. Telling *me*.' He shook his head slightly. 'Let's go pick Jason up and I'll drop you off at Rosie's to get your stuff together.' I made an old-fashioned face at him. 'What? I need you here to field the phone calls! Where's the problem?'

Quickly I turned my face from him so he couldn't read my expression. *Move in here? With a man I ...* My mouth was dry. But then it would be easier to run from here, and Ben wouldn't be quite so omnipresent as Rosie. I'd be able to pack and go without him suspecting a thing.

'Just promise me if Jason says anything about ice cubes, blank him. Or you can hit him if you like.'

'Ice cubes?'

'Trust me, he'll mention them.' I took a deep breath. I could do this. I really could.

# Chapter Fifteen

Just before he got into the car with Ben, Jason pulled me aside. 'Jem, got something to tell ya.'

'You're not pregnant, are you?' The drive over had contained a lot of silences. Ben was clearly waiting for me to talk, to share my soul with him as he'd shared his with me. *What the hell was I going to do?*

'Nah. Why, you offering to impregnate me? 'Cos I'd give good money for that if I din't think your Mr Davies would rip me head off and shove the mushy end up me shitter.' Jase looked around. 'Where's Rosie?'

'Giving Harry his tea. What is it?'

Jason put his mouth to my ear. 'Took a trip out to Harrogate today. Had a picture to deliver so I took the van –' a head-jerk towards Jason's horrible, fuel-guzzling Landrover. 'Be glad to get the car back, I mean yeah the van's useful, but bloody hell it don't pull nothing but sheep. Anyhoo. While I was over there – yeah, awright mate! Keep yer wig on.' This shouted across to Ben who was leaning his elbow on the horn of the little car and making hurry up motions with both hands. 'Popped around to Saskia's little shop, din't I? And guess what I found? Round the back someone's been having a great big bonfire. There was empty boxes piled all over an' a lovely big mess of burned-up paper.' He arched an eyebrow. 'Three guesses wot it was she'd bin burning? And two of 'em are a waste of time.'

'Rosie's cards?'

'Got it in one, my love.'

'And the staff let you see this?'

Jason looked sideways under his hair. 'Aw, come *on*. This is me you're talking to! What kinda sex symbol would I be if I couldn't charm a few little shop assistants? And, incidentally whilst taking a little peep out in the yard, getting one helluva shag off Saskia's mate, Christine. Now there is one *hungry* lady. And, I may add, one who used to be an actress.'

'What?'

'Do we know anyone who might, possibly, have needed someone to *pretend*, just as a joke you understand, to be – oh, I dunno, a social worker, say? To pop round to someone's house and tell them that their baby wasn't being looked after proper?'

I gawped at him. 'What, and you got this out of her while you were screwing? Your sex talk needs a lot of work.'

He waggled his eyebrows. 'We got chatting, all right?'

'Before or after?'

'Hey, I don't just love 'em and leave 'em, I put the hours in. And a few other things I could mention ...' He rubbed at his crotch.

'I don't know whether to admire you or despise you totally.'

'Just don't tell Rosie, thass all. Saskia's still got her churning those cards out like there's some kinda world shortage. You tell her it's just so that Saskia can warm her chilly tits I reckon she might go into meltdown.' And with a little skipping run Jason took off towards the Audi, where he and Ben could be seen greeting each other with blokey slaps.

I went into the cottage to find Rosie spooning mush into Harry's happily open mouth. 'You look like a mother blackbird.'

'Believe me, worms would be cheaper.' Rosie put down the spoon and turned around. 'But the health visitor said he's such a hungry baby, weaning would be the best thing. Wow, Jem. You look – different.'

'You only saw me this morning.' Self-consciously I raked my hands through my hair and smoothed my cheeks. 'How different?'

'I don't know. Sort of glowy.' She covered her mouth slowly. 'Oh, God. Does this mean you and Ben …? Oh, Jem, is he absolutely fabulous?'

'No, he's a complete pain in the arse,' I retorted, thinking of Ben's irritating attractiveness.

'Pain in the … oh.' Rosie blew out a long breath. 'You mean – anal sex?'

'You spend far too long with Jason, do you know that? Ben and I, we're just friends. He's been –' how to describe what had gone on between Ben and me? – 'unburdening himself in my direction, that's all. And,' I added hastily. 'Not in a wanky way, either. God, we *both* spend too much time with Jase.'

Rosie shrugged and turned back to Harry, loaded spoon back in hand. 'All I'll say is that *something* is making you pink-cheeked like you've been lit up from inside. I'm not going to pry into what's been going on, apart from asking what the hell all that stuff about a fire was.'

I explained about Ben's shop, watching Rosie look more and more distressed as I went on. 'But there's a good side,' I put in quickly, seeing the tears start up in her eyes. 'Ben's asked me to stay at his place for a while. So you could put Harry into his cot in my room. It'd give you a bit more space and you won't have to worry about him rolling himself out of the carry cot any more.'

Harry grabbed at the spoon, annoyed at the slow service. A kind of porridgey slush flicked over Rosie and me, and she began dipping the spoon back into the jar in jerky little movements. 'You aren't telling me everything, are you?' A quick look at my guilty expression. 'If you and Ben aren't screwing fit to bust there must be something else going on. Blokes like him, they don't just ask women to stay. Not without *some* kind of Special Services. Is it something to do with the fire?'

Without saying anything I reached into the pocket of my jeans. Drew out what I'd found lying in the rubble and discarded papers outside Ben's shop. Uncurled my hand and showed it to her.

'Yeah that's one of the seed heads I use for my cards.' Her attention went back to Harry again.

'I found it. Underneath some of the stuff the fire brigade had piled up outside the shop.'

'At Ben's?' Rosie's eyes met mine and I saw understanding slowly dawn. 'What? You think …?' I dropped the pink-sprayed seed head onto the table. 'But that's stupid. Why on *earth* would Saskia set fire to Ben's shop? That's – yes, it's more than stupid, it's ridiculous.' She lifted Harry from his seat.

'I know.' I chucked Harry stickily under the chin. 'It's just circumstantial. And maybe I'm seeing ghosts that don't exist. But, and I hesitate to make this dreadful pun because I'm not Jason, there's no smoke without fire. And now, I'm going to pop over to the workshop to collect some bits and pieces. Thought I might have a crack at making something specific for Saskia's shop. Maybe a tiara?'

Rosie sniggered, falling into step alongside me, Harry winding sticky fingers into her hair. 'Tiara! Mind you I reckon she already thinks she's Victoria Beckham.'

'You've seen the house, she probably does. But Alex is so far off being David Beckham it's amusing.'

The sniggering stopped as we approached the barn. 'You will still keep coming over here, won't you?'

''Course.' I unlocked the main door and went into the office. 'I'll need some sane company anyway and because I'm referring to you and Jason as sane company I hope you'll infer that Ben is not exactly Mr Stability.'

'Yeah, well, stability can be boring as hell.' Rosie's voice vanished into Jason's workshop as she searched for Harry's chair. 'Conventional is over-rated. I reckon a fling with a rock star would set you up nicely.'

'He's not a rock star.'

'He was. He'll still be raking in the royalties. Might be again one day if you can persuade him to pick up a guitar once more. Never know your luck, Jem, you could be looking at a life on the road.'

My heart squeezed. 'Not going to happen.' I opened my e-mail.

'The fling? Come on, wake up and hear the music, the guy is so hot for you that he's going to spontaneously combust if you give him the push.' She saw my expression, tinged blue by the light of the screen. 'What's up?'

197

My throat was burning and I had to whisper. 'Look.' I turned the screen around to face her. 'Someone has reported me for fraud. Repeatedly not delivering goods that have been paid for. eBay are suspending my listing.'

I sobbed into Rosie's ample shoulder. She patted my back as though I was Harry. 'Oh, Jem.'

'*I've done nothing wrong.*' Couldn't tell her that without eBay I had no way of selling anything when I moved on. That I'd been relying on sales from the internet to keep me going while I set up somewhere new. And then it wasn't just that, it was everything. It was Ben and his awful secret, his fragility, and my knowledge that I wanted him so much all I could do was run away. '*Now* what am I going to do?'

'If you need some cash I could lend you –'

'It's not just the money. It's – oh, Rosie, I don't know what I'm doing. Ben is ...' Ben is everything. Everything that I'm afraid of, everything I've ever wanted. All those secret desires that I've hidden for so long underneath so many layers that now even *I* don't recognise them.

'He's told you why he quit the band?'

I could only nod against her shoulder.

'And it's not drugs?'

A head-shake, which spread snot along her dress.

'You could take it to the papers.'

I jerked my head away from her. 'Rosie!'

She smiled. 'Yeah, thought so. For God's sake, just *tell him.* Tell him you're in love with him. Everything else will work itself out.'

'Is that experience talking?'

Another smile, achingly sad this time. 'Afraid so. It's

just that sometimes things take longer to work out.'

'Anyway, who says I'm in love with him?' I wiped my eyes on the back of my hand.

'Jemima, you're broke and you won't sell the most valuable thing you've got. The information about Ben. There's press and music papers and fans, they'd all pay really good money for the inside story on the Philadelphia débâcle. But you won't even think of it.' She shook her head and the section of her hair which wasn't covered in porridge bounced around her face. 'If that ain't love, well.'

'When I wasn't here did you get visited by the Wisdom Fairy?'

'Only Jason, and he's not eligible on the first count. I think the second might be negotiable. Just do it, what have you got to lose?'

*Only my freedom*, I thought. *My ability to run, to get out whenever things got awkward.*

Nothing I could articulate. I looked at Harry jiggling his legs until his bouncy chair rocked on its thin metal suspension. 'You still being hard work for your mum?'

She sighed. 'He's not so bad really. It's just the sheer volume of work I've got. Saskia seems to be cornering the market in hand-made cards, but she pays well and I can't turn her down. Besides, she's got me working so hard I've had to drop all my other customers and my chances of getting them back if she dumps me are remote. I have to keep going.' Another sigh. 'I wanted to start taking Harry to the mother-and-baby group in the village, but there just isn't time. I feel as though I can't enjoy him properly, can't enjoy being a mother.'

Half-heartedly I began collecting all my beads and crystals and wires together. 'It won't go on forever,' I said, thinking about a bonfire behind a shop, all Rosie's hard work going up in flames. Ben's shop burning. Saskia, sitting in the middle of it all like a spider in a web. No, more like a bloated puppeteer, pulling strings and watching us dance. 'Something has to give.'

## 22nd May

She looks at me now and I feel transparent, like my bones, my hair are all invisible and she can see right inside to the fear and the loneliness, almost like she touches me where the blackness hides and makes it all right.

Shut up. Not like that. You are fucking filthy, doctor, you know that? We're not. Not that I don't want it, Christ, waist down I'm like concrete, but she's ... she's not ready. Doesn't push me away but ... it's almost like she's a virgin or something. Scared of what'll happen if we get down to it.

I can wait. I'd wait forever if she asked me to. I just wish she'd feel she could talk to me, wish I knew what it was that frightens her so. Because not knowing means I can't help. And I want to take away that expression she gets sometimes when she thinks I'm not looking. It's part fear and part ... I dunno, a kind of deep sorrow, like she thinks I'm about to chuck her onto the street or something. Like she wants to be with me, wants it to be more than just this kind of flat-share thing we've got going on. Like she's memorising my face, my clothes, as if Crimewatch is reconstructing me next week and I don't know about it yet.

And yet ... she makes me feel like nothing matters. I'm still me, still Baz Davies, still the best <u>fucking</u> lyricist of the twenty-first century (hey, that's NME talking). She pulls me up beyond it all, like she's pulling me out of the shit and the dark and up, back on top of the world, where I used to be. Okay, I don't get what people say – so what? I do pretty well for a guy that's stone deaf. Hey, look, I can say it! I am deaf. Can't hear a note. And it doesn't hurt like it did.

Jemima. I'd give you this whole, messed up, planet if you asked.

# Chapter Sixteen

'Can you see anything?' Ben wiggled underneath me, shifting my weight more evenly across his shoulders.

'Can't you stand still?'

No answer. Of course. No way even Ben could lip read when my head was four feet above him and hanging over three strands of barbed wire. I clung to the top of the wall which ran around the outside of the tiny yard belonging to Le Petit Lapin, desperately trying to steady myself against the brickwork. There was no sign of any burning, just a couple of plastic patio chairs where presumably Mairi and Saskia put their respective feet and hooves up during slack spells.

I slapped Ben's shoulder and he lowered me to earth, sliding me down the wall and gasping in an unflattering way.

'Woah! You've got thighs like steel, woman.' He ruefully rubbed the back of his neck. 'So? Anything doing?'

'Not really. I need to get inside.'

'Come on. It's only in really bad films that the villain leaves incriminating evidence lying around.' Ben looked at my face. 'Oh, please! Tell me you aren't going to break in?'

'There's a little window down in the back office. I reckon I can crack it. In and out and she won't even know.'

'Yeah, right. And how are you going to do that eh? Pop home for your Girls' Book of Breaking and Entering?'

'No, I'm going to thank God for historic cities building regulations not allowing shopowners to replace old latch windows. Bunk me up.'

'Jem?' He was staring at me now. 'You serious?'

'Bunk me up,' I repeated.

'Hang on. This is more than I signed up for. You said you were just going to have a look in the yard –'

'– where there's nothing to see. So now I'm going in.' I looked him in the eye. 'Are you with me?'

'Sheesh. All right, Don Corleone. Don't get your salami in a twist.' Ben bent and formed his hands into a cup. 'But I'm not sure I can bunk you right up there. I mean, Christ, woman, how much do you weigh?'

'You'd better hope I get arrested,' I said, putting one toe into his palm. 'Because if I don't, you are going to pay for that remark.'

I didn't need him to put any effort in. The action came back to me as easily as if I'd done it yesterday. Toe in, spring off the back foot, balance against the wall and – up. Ben straightened, looking surprised.

'Jem?'

I was already taking off my T shirt, wrapping it over the barbed wire. 'Have you got a credit card on you?'

Ben was staring at my chest. At least I was wearing a half-decent bra, although the balconette style made my boobs look fuller and more barely-restrained than should have been the case. 'What? You want me to pay to cop an eyeful?'

'Just hand it over.'

He raked about in pockets, eventually finding a card. 'American Express?'

'That'll do nicely.' I grinned down at him as he stretched up with the card. This was feeling more and more like the old days. I straddled the barbed wire, carefully holding the padding. 'Okay. In and out.'

'What if someone comes?'

'It's three o'clock in the bloody morning. Who do you think is going to come?'

'We're here.'

'Well, if any burglars arrive, tell them this place is spoken for. All right?'

I dropped down into the yard, my hands sweaty, my heart thumping and my chest attempting to escape. All the old feelings, all the old thrills. 'Jem?' I couldn't see him, the wall was a good nine-feet high, so I didn't bother responding. 'Be careful,' I heard him breathe.

I crossed the yard, pulled one of the plastic chairs up to the window and used the credit card to slip the latch. One hop and a wriggle and I was inside, although I left some of my skin on the frame. I nearly called back to Ben but realised it was futile.

I'd become an expert on sussing out a place without going any further than point of entry, I had better eyes than most for the tell-tale signs of advanced alarm systems. Saskia had nothing. The cheapskate. Although, I thought as I circled the shop floor, there was nothing here that even the most desperate of burglars could want. The till was empty with the tray pulled out to show there was no cash and as for the items on sale – well, I guess if you wanted to beat someone to death they might come in handy.

Ben was right. There was nothing here. To corroborate

Jason's story all the boxes of Rosie's cards that I'd seen on the night of the party were gone. I went back into the office and noticed an appointments diary on the desk beside the telephone. Using the tip of one finger I flipped it open.

All right, so I'd hardly expected Saskia to have written 'TODAY MY PLANS COME TO FRUITION' across the pages in lipstick, but I was unprepared for the sheer dullness of the entries. For example under today's date was '4pm, Oscar, Orthodontist'. The poor kid was only five and she was already having him fixed. He hadn't even *got* all his teeth yet.

I flipped back further. Three days ago. The night of Ben's aborted dinner party with Rosie and me. Nothing but a lightly pencilled 'A'. And then a question mark. Further back, and all that seemed to concern Saskia was the coming and going of Alex and Oscar's various appointments. All I managed to learn was that Alex was out a lot and poor little Oscar was undergoing major restructuring work. God, she was a boring woman. I was flicking through dates now, anything that sprung to mind. On my birthday apparently Oscar had a music exam, on Rosie's a book test. On 20 February, the day Harry was born, she'd written 'A out'. As in he was somewhere else, or he'd decided to confess to being gay?

I replaced the diary and went back out through the office window, removing any spare skin from my ribs on the way. I carefully levered it shut with Ben's card; although I couldn't relatch it from this side I could leave the arm lying along the frame so hopefully Saskia would think that it hadn't been properly closed.

I moved the chair up to the wall and used it to get enough of a boost to climb back to the top. As I jumped I gave the chair an almighty kick which sent it right to the far side of the yard, where it tumbled onto its back as though a gust of wind had caught it. I paused by the wire to untangle my shirt then dropped lightly back into the alleyway where I landed beside Ben, who was leaning against the wall trying to look nonchalant.

He jumped. It was disconcerting to have him flinch every time I arrived unexpectedly.

'Hey. Anything?'

'Apart from Saskia conducting a father-and-son time-and-motion study, nope.' I flicked out my T shirt. There were only a couple of snags in it from the wire. God, I was good. I went to slip it on but Ben put a hand on my arm.

'Wait.'

'What?' His hand was warm, his fingers soft. Adrenaline was still burning its way through my synapses and leaving a bitter, dry taste in my mouth. 'Ben?'

Pressure on my forearm until I turned, reluctantly. 'Yeah. I thought so.' Then a finger ran down my spine. 'You've got a gang mark.'

*How the hell did he know?* 'It's just a tattoo,' I said lightly. My skin prickled around the blue stain on my shoulder blade as though it was bursting through my flesh.

'What? I can't see your face.' Ben spun me so that my bare back was pressed against the roughness of the wall. 'Now. Say it again.'

'It's nothing. Just a pattern.'

'Bugger *that*. You've been in a street gang. Where? Why didn't you say? And what the hell *happened* to you?'

Adrenaline drained. I was flat, empty. Goosebumps broke out across my chest and shoulders and my skinned ribcage ached. 'I ... I don't know ... I ...'

Ben let me go and raised both hands to rumple through his hair. 'Jemima.'

And suddenly I wanted him to know. All of it. All of me. 'Take me home,' I said. 'And I'll tell you.'

A half-smile. 'I bet you say that to all the boys.'

I met his eye steadily. 'Only you, Ben. Only you.'

Ben's house was silent and dark. As we went in he turned on lights, flipping switches like a man possessed, room by room until we reached a small study off the kitchen where he only turned on a lamp. There were bookcases against all the walls, a table and sofa, deep carpet on the floor. It was snug.

'Okay.' Ben slumped onto the sofa, reaching for a whisky bottle and glasses from the little side table. 'Go on.'

I hovered uncertainly, finally settled for sitting on the floor in the corner furthest away from him. 'First tell me how you knew.'

'Hang on. *You're* the one with the secrets and *I'm* the one answering the questions? What's wrong with this picture?' The mouth of the bottle jigged against the glasses as he poured us both a generous measure. 'All right. Mark. Drummer in Willow Down.'

I took the glass but didn't move closer to him. Just rested my back against the wall. 'He was in a gang?'

'No, you plank. He's a sociologist.'

'Your *drummer* is a sociologist?'

'They're not all two brain cells and seven pints of sweat. Anyhow. These tattoos were his idea.' Ben rolled up the sleeve of his shirt, revealing his encircling tribal mark. 'He took it from the street gangs where they use them to mark their own, to strengthen the group bond. We all had one, all four of us. Same tatt, same spot, to remind us we were all in it together.' He rubbed the mark thoughtfully.

'So you're not going to believe I got drunk one night and picked it out of a tattoo parlour window?'

He smiled. Leaned forward with his elbows on his knees, slopping whisky unnoticed over the couch. 'Nice try. But I've seen the textbooks.'

I took a deep breath. 'All right. But listen up because this is a once-only story.'

'I'm listening, Jemima.' Then a little grin. 'Figure of speech. But I'm here.'

Where to begin? As someone once said, at the beginning ... With thoughts and memories I'd blocked and denied for so long that even I couldn't be sure how accurate they were. Rewritten and reworked they might be, edited for all those snaggy moments of sibling rivalry and parental arguing, but they were all I had. It was time to own up to them. 'I had a great life. A Mum and Dad who loved all three of us completely. A good school, nice house, I had riding lessons twice a week and the boys did rugby and ... never mind. It was normal, you know?'

Ben didn't move. Kept his eyes fixed on my face.

I lowered the barrier even further, until images came with the emotions, pictures of twisted metal, and I had to work not to let it all come screaming back in full technicolour. 'When I was fifteen there was an accident. A stupid, *stupid* accident, something so random ... Mum was driving Dad to work. She wanted the car because hers was in the garage or something, so she was going to drop him off. I had a competition to go to, show jumping I think, and she didn't want me to miss out so she ... And they crashed. No-one knows what happened, she just lost control and hit a bridge.' I rubbed my chest, trying to ease an ache that would never heal.

Ben hadn't even blinked. 'And they both ...?'

'Yes. We were told it was instantaneous but – you always wonder, don't you? Anyway. There was no family to take us in. Randall was sixteen, but he was told he was too young to be allowed to take charge of us because Christian was only twelve. So they were going to split us up and put us in foster homes.' I looked down at my hands, knitting my fingers in my lap. Only realised what I was doing when Ben reached across very gently and tipped my head back up so he could see my lips. 'We ran away.' A burp-like giggle escaped. 'We were so naïve, you see. Stupid, middle-class kids who thought real life was like some kind of early-evening kids' TV, living in an empty house, taking food from the supermarket to eat. But we were scared. We'd lost our parents, we didn't want to lose each other too, and we thought we'd only have to wait until Ran was eighteen, and then he could adopt us and we'd get a flat and live together and ... Too much TV, as I said.'

Ben sighed. It had a catch in it.

'And then this gang found us. We were hiding out in a disused warehouse, starving because none of us knew how to shoplift, we were all too scared of getting caught, and it turned out we were hiding in a crack den.' I gave a sudden, shocked laugh. 'We didn't even know what a crack den *was*. But these guys, they took us in, me and Ran and Chris and they looked after us. Properly, I mean, they got us a place to live and food and stuff. And okay, so we didn't go to school much or anything but we were together, things were fine. Say what you like about street gangs, but they look after their own.'

'You joined a *gang*?' Ben's surprise was almost comical.

'We talked posh. Well, according to them we did, anyway. And it's surprising what people will believe from someone who talks "posh". The gang used us, con tricks, distraction, that kind of thing.' I took a long, deep breath. 'I got the mark, I went on jobs. I was *good*.' I defied Ben to speak but he stayed silent, watching me.

Breathe, Jemima. Breathe. It's all over now.

'Despite it all, Ran and I stayed clean, it was the only way to be ahead of the game, to be in control. But Chris … he joined a band.' I gave a smile which was like a humour black hole. 'Always loved his guitar, did Christian. Obsessive. Thought he'd make it big, get discovered, that kind of thing. He thought he could handle anything, he was very young, didn't know what he was getting into, he didn't know how hard it would be to get out of, he thought he could drop it any time but –' I stopped.

Ben leaned forward and refilled my glass. 'We're talking about what? Heroin?'

I talked to my drink. 'Have you ever? Tried it, I mean?'

Ben shook his head. 'Nah. Hate needles, hate smoke. I've done most things but not smack. I know Zafe did it once or twice but ...' he shrugged. 'Nothing heavy.'

'It was heavy for Chris. Five years it took but eventually ... he dumped the band, vanished for days, turned up rambling and sick. Even ...' I gave a strangled hiccup of ironic laughter. 'Even sold his guitar. We tried to straighten him out, Ran and I, but –'

'You have to want to stop. I should know. No one can tell you.'

Despite the cosiness of the little room the air felt like a corpse. I should have known Ben wouldn't flinch at this story. I should have trusted him.

'While this was all going on I ... got together with Gray. Ran warned me off him, told me to keep away but, I dunno. He was sexy. Dangerous but sexy. And I was seventeen, thought I was in love, so of course I wouldn't listen to my brother, I mean, what did *he* know –' My voice cracked and I took a deep gulp of the whisky, even though it was bitter and hot in my throat. 'I thought love was meant to be like that.'

I could see Ben open his mouth to ask what it *had* been like, then think better of it. A little shiver ran over his skin and I saw the goosebumps rise.

'Then Chris OD'd. One day, down a back alley in Bristol. He'd been sold some stuff that was pure and we didn't find out for a week.' I tilted my chin up to stop my voice cracking. I could still smell the smoky, foul odour that I'd grown to associate with Christian, still taste the fear at the back of my throat. 'Ran found the guy who'd supplied Chris. It took time to track it all back, but he found him. Killed him.' I licked my lips. There were no tears. Not now.

'Wow.' Ben rubbed the back of his neck. He was about to say more but I leaped in. He had to know it all.

'I was there, I begged Ran to stop but he wouldn't. Just kept on and on …' I half covered my ears as though I expected the echoes still to be sounding. 'I called an ambulance, and I lied, Ben. Told them that there was another gang trying to take over the area, that there'd been a fight. Oh, the police found out I was making it up, of course, it was hardly CSI and I'm not exactly a criminal mastermind. They got hold of Randall, open and shut case. I went to prison as an accessory.' *The cells, the noise, the relentless banging. No peace. Never any peace, not now.*

'But why? Why all this, over something that wasn't your fault?'

'Because the dealer was Gray.' I drained the nearly full glass in one gulp. 'And now you know. My judgement in men is so crappy that I spent nearly five years with a guy who was dealing heroin and I didn't know. He was selling to my own brother *and I didn't know.*'

'Shit.' Ben put down his glass.

I started talking quickly. 'Ran went down for murder. For life. I was only inside six months and while I was there I learned to make jewellery so I took that and I ran away.'

'And you're still running?'

I nodded. Five years of running, of setting up and moving on. Of living in people's spare rooms, in guest houses and squats. Of making just enough money to eat.

'But why? What are you running from?'

'Memories.' I held out my glass for a refill and was proud of the way my hand didn't shake. 'I've blocked this all out. There's some kind of psychologist's word for it, but I'm good at not remembering now, if I don't try it all stays dark. Ran died in prison. Knife fight. And once he was gone there was nothing to hold me, nothing to stay anywhere for. So I've kept on travelling. It keeps ... it keeps the memories from surfacing. That's why I didn't know anything about Willow Down. I was abroad, working anywhere I could get a bed for the night. I'd make a few pieces and sell them to get enough money to move on whenever ...' I tailed off.

'Whenever you felt you were getting settled? Oh, Jemima.'

I drained another glass. 'And my name isn't Jemima. It's Gemma. Gemma Bredon. I chose Hutton off the map one day when I was passing through. York seemed such a nice place. Then I started supplying Saskia regularly. I met Rosie and I thought – I thought it might be different this time.'

Ben's eyes were immense in the lamp light. 'And I thought *I* was damaged,' he said softly.

The whisky was making my head swim. 'I'm pissed,' I announced.

'You wouldn't have told me, not without a bit of Dutch courage.' Ben held out an arm and hauled me to my feet.

'I wanted you to know.' His body was pressed against me, I could feel every bone through his clothes and smell the fresh, clean scent of him. His hair brushed against my neck. 'But I thought you might hate me for it.'

'Jem. What kind of guy do you think I am?'

'It's the fact you're a guy. That's all.'

He frowned. 'What's that supposed to mean?'

I rocked on my feet. 'You know you said you didn't date? Because you were afraid, of rejection, of not being perfect, of –' I gestured rather wildly. 'Of whatever,' I finished. 'I don't date because I don't want to make those mistakes again.'

I felt him flinch he was so close to me. 'Like how?'

'Look. Gray wasn't – he wasn't exactly the perfect boyfriend, you know what I mean?'

'*Jem.*' He breathed it rather than saying it.

'There were other girls. And he'd flaunt it, tell me who he was getting off with, what they did for him that I didn't. And he'd make me … He used me for everything, I was like his toy, you know? Something for him and his friends to play with, something that would take anything, *do* anything. And yeah, I knew deep down that's not how it should be, but – I stayed. And, since then, I've promised myself no men. Nothing. Until I can feel that I'm a person, you know? In my own right, a something. Not just a *thing* bringing nothing to the relationship except my body. *That's* why – I thought I was making it, with Saskia's shop stocking my buckles and my website and everything and now, one by one, it's all going down the pan and I'm right back where I started.' I caught the sob before it escaped. 'And I won't be used again, Ben. I won't.'

He took half a step away. 'You think *I'd* use you? Christ, Jem, it's not like that, not at *all.*'

'I need to know that when ... if ... I walk away, I'm still the person I was. That I'm not losing myself by giving myself to someone. I can't trust and I can't ... *won't* depend on anyone for anything. So you can see, I'm not really girlfriend material.' I stopped, aware of how stupidly close we were to one another.

'Jem, we're friends. You must know that, even with all the shit that you've had before, you must recognise a good thing when you see it?'

Now it was my turn to step back, to widen the physical gap as the psychological one was becoming a chasm. 'You mean that because you've got all this ...' I swept an arm round indicating the house. 'That I'm supposed magically to throw off the memories of everything that's happened to me? Because you've got cash to spare, suddenly the death of my brothers *doesn't matter*?' My voice was icy.

'That's not what I meant at all and I think you know it. You're using your past to stop you from having to make yourself a present.'

'You know nothing about it.'

'Yes, I do.' His voice was low. I had to lean a little closer to hear him. 'What do you think I was doing, Jem? Pushing everyone away, keeping the deafness secret? It was all so that I never had to face up to it. If I never told anyone then maybe it wasn't real, maybe I wouldn't have to live with it forever. That's what you're doing, denying the problem, moving on whenever life starts to get real just so you never have to face it.'

'You know *nothing*,' I repeated and stalked out of the room feeling the weight of his gaze on my back. I looked over my shoulder, just once, to see him raking his hands through his already dishevelled hair and rubbing his tired-looking face and I almost turned. Almost. I wanted him so much that it ached. But why would things be any different here, with him?

# Chapter Seventeen

'Oh, my God.' Rosie's hand shook on my arm. 'Oh, Jem. Can we still call you Jem? Or what? I mean – oh, I don't know *what* I mean. It's awful.'

At our feet Harry sat in his new cushion chair, chuckling and waving a well-gummed elephant rattle. I kept my eyes on him. 'Jem is fine. I was always called Jem anyway. That's one of the reasons I chose Jemima as a name.' One of the other reasons was that Jemima had a ginger-beer and salmon, jolly-hockeysticks ring to it. A name close enough to my original one, and conjuring images of the life I'd lost so *so* long ago. No more than thirteen years in time, but thirteen lifetimes in experience.

'God,' Rosie repeated, pulling me into a strawberry-shampoo-scented hug. 'Jase and I thought you must have left an abusive boyfriend, that's why we didn't push. We thought you'd tell us, when the time was right.'

'I am. And it is.' I straightened away and took another sip of the too-hot coffee. 'And for the record, Gray wasn't exactly going to get "Boyfriend of the Year", so you were pretty nearly right.'

'Jase is going to be *so* smug,' Rosie said thoughtfully. 'Although, actually, I think his first theory was that you were on the run from an international consortium of white-slavers, but he'd been reading Ian Fleming novels. Well, looking at the pictures anyway.'

I still kept my gaze on Harry. If I had to meet Rosie's eye, if I had to see the sympathy there I'd collapse.

'Shouldn't you be –?' I waved at the half-filled box by the table and the stack of cards.

'Sod Saskia, she can wait. This is important.'

'Look.' I took a deep breath. 'The reason I'm telling you now is because I'm going. I didn't want you to feel that something you'd done had driven me away.' Everything here was dangerously familiar, the smell of baby powder and last night's dinner, the worn edges of the sofa cushion, the pictures on the walls. It had been the very ordinariness that had seduced me into staying as long as I had, the way that life had gone on around me and drawn me in. I knew I couldn't outrun my old life, but I'd hoped that by standing still it might have passed me by unnoticed. I should have known that it would double back and creep up behind me.

'I don't see why you have to go!' She was plaintive. 'Sorry, Jem, but it's just stupid. You fancy Ben, he fancies you. Why can't you just throw yourself into it and see what happens?'

I hid my face in my hands. Harry, thinking I was playing peek-a-boo, chuckled even more. When I raised my head he gave a delighted whoop of laughter. 'Ben is – complicated. He's going to need someone who can give him what he needs.'

Rosie looked at me shrewdly. 'You mean you're scared.'

'No. Not of Ben. Maybe of the situation.'

'And you can't tell me what that is?'

I shook my head. 'It's not my secret to tell. And I don't know if Ben's ever going to be able to. But the fact is I've got nothing. Less than nothing, now that eBay has got me under investigation. Okay, I can take a stall at the market but that's going to cost me and what I make is a bit expensive for the market shoppers. I can go down to using ordinary wire and plastic but then the techniques are different and besides, there will always be cheaper stuff from Korea. Basically, Rosie, I need to go. Set up somewhere else, somewhere the shops will stock my things. I was thinking about the South East, Canterbury way. I've heard it's okay down there.'

'Because you feel like a nobody.' She was shaking her head. 'It's so, *so* silly. I mean look at Harry.' She plucked him out of his chair and brandished him at me. 'He loves you, he doesn't care what you've got, what you do for a living, he'll love you whatever. What makes you think that Ben won't be like that?'

'Because Ben isn't three-and-a-half months old.'

Rosie gave me a friendly shove. 'And aren't you glad?'

'Shut up. Yes, all right, I like him. There might even be more to it than that. But. Look at it this way. If Ben and I – started something, what happens to me when it's over? Who am I then, Rosie? I need to *be* someone, to have something to hold on to that's mine. The gang, Ran, Christian – even Gray, I defined myself through them, I was never a person. And I can't let it happen again, not now.'

'Have you told Ben you're going?'

I shook my head. I'd got up mid-morning to find Ben and his keys gone. Ashamed of myself I'd hunted round the kitchen until I'd found a tea tin filled with pound coins and fivers and I'd taken some. Enough for the bus fare to get me to Rosie's. But, in my defence, I had written an IOU and stuffed it into the tin in place of the missing money. I'd also left the tin on the dresser so that Ben would know what I'd done.

'You mean you were going to take off? How do you think he's going to feel when he finds out that the woman he's told – whatever he's told, has run away? Don't you think he might be the tiniest bit *pissed off*?'

Harry squawked, Rosie's grip on him must have tightened. She turned abruptly away from me to quieten him.

I stood up and touched her shoulder. 'Rosie. I don't want it to be like this, I just can't see any other way. It's not the easy option, honestly.'

She whirled around so fast that Harry was still facing the window when she started to speak. 'Jem, *life* isn't the easy option! You seem to think that you're the only person suffering, that that makes it all right if you keep on running. Well, sometimes you *can't* run.' She kissed Harry's forehead. 'Stay. Stay and fight.'

'Fight?'

'For Ben, for your work. Maybe this is the line in the sand. Maybe this is where you say "no more".' She gave me a quick half-armed hug. 'I'm sorry, I don't mean to be so bossy. It's just that I can see you and Ben are so right for one another and I hate to think of you throwing away a chance of being happy because you're worried about what might happen.' The hug intensified. 'Sometimes you have to seize the day.'

'Look. I never said Ben and I can't be friends, I only said that I don't want to end up sleeping with him because I'm confusing like and lust.'

Rosie stepped back, wiping her face with the back of

her hand. 'Okay. So you don't want to sleep with Ben. What *do* you want? Apart from to run away.'

'I didn't say that, I – I don't know. What do you mean?'

'For the first time you've got control. You've got a great guy who wants you, you've got a business –' a raised hand forestalled my immediate come-back on that one. 'Yes, at the moment it's a bit stalled but that's just for now. It's still yours, you can still make your jewellery. Don't you see? Everything is in your hands. You're not dependent on the gang, or your brothers, or anyone, to make you happy. This fear of being with someone, it's all in your head because of what happened to you in the past. All you have to do now is *take* that control.' Her earnest green eyes looked deeply into mine. 'So. I repeat. *What do you want?*'

'Daytime TV is really getting to you, isn't it?'

She cocked an eyebrow.

'All right. What do I want? I want to find out what Saskia is up to. Who she thinks she is, to tell me that I can't sell my things in York and that you – that you should be working like a slave. I want to know whether she had anything to do with Ben's shop burning down.'

'I'd quite like to know where she gets those little power suits she's always wearing,' Rosie chimed in. 'Is there a shop somewhere that sells brimstone-proof clothing?'

'Why is she so awful? She's got everything: rich husband, lovely little boy, great house. So why does she come over like a pantomime villain in couture clothing?'

'Mink the Merciless,' Rosie giggled.

'What does Alex see in her?' I frowned.

'She's not bad looking, I suppose.' Rosie looked down

at her still-voluptuous figure. 'Slim.'

'Her face is entirely drawn-on. Have you looked at her? Lip liner, brow pencil, eye liner – I bet when she takes her makeup off she's just completely blank skin.'

'And two tiny little eyes. Like a couple of marbles on a sheet.' Rosie grinned for a moment, then refocused on me. 'Hey! Nice try, sister, with the badmouthing of Saskia. But we were talking about *you*.'

'I have to go, Rosie. I *have to*.'

'But I thought – all that stuff about finding out what Saskia is up to? I thought you'd changed your mind.'

I shook my head. Tears were threatening again. Every time the curtain shifted and I thought I could see a glimpse of how life could be on the other side, a memory or a thought would cut in and bring me back to reality. *This* was my life. *This* was me. Saskia was just a woman with no sensitivity. No evil agenda. The seed head I'd picked up outside Ben's shop was a coincidence. Ben wanted to sleep with me because I'd listened to his problems. And I was still a street kid loser with a prison record and visible root regrowth.

'I'm sorry,' I sniffled, and ran out of the cottage. As an exit it lacked a certain something and I had to wait a humiliating ten minutes for the bus, crouched behind the bus shelter in case Rosie decided to follow.

# *Chapter Eighteen*

So early the next morning that the birds had hardly cleared their throats I sat in the elaborate guest room and stuffed my belongings into my rucksack.

They'd get over it, they'd *all* get over it. And Ben ... Ben could look after himself. I was closing this chapter and starting a new one. In a different book, preferably one with a whole lot less subtext.

I listened, but there was no sound of Ben stirring up in his attic bedroom, all whitewashed walls and floors cluttered with sheets of half-written music. I had to be quick.

I yanked my last shirt from where it had fallen, shoved it all back in. It wouldn't matter if things were creased and unwashed where I was going, who was there to care? I looked around at the carefully minimalist luxury of the huge house, the sanded floors and the painted walls. Perfect backdrops for Ben, perfect foils for his everywhichway hair and raggy jeans. Showing he could afford better but didn't care.

Stop it. I didn't want to think about him. He was just another one of those passing elements which periodically tried to combine with me, just another thing to be shrugged off, to become a faint sketch in my memory. Okay, so I'd allowed him to get closer, I'd let myself down on that one, lowered my guard. Right, lesson learned there, don't let *anyone* get in, even skanky deaf musicians could worm their way past the defences. From now on I'd keep myself to myself and this would be the experience I'd needed to make sure it never happened again.

I swung my bag up onto my shoulder. Ready.

Oh no, one thing first.

I went to the kitchen and tipped out the jar of cash, pushing fivers deep into all my pockets, filling the pockets of the rucksack with coins until it jingled each time I hefted it. *That would teach him. Trust no-one, Ben Davies. The world is out to get you.*

Then without a backward glance I pulled the front door of Wilberforce Crescent closed and stepped out into a new life. Although never before had my throat felt so swollen, as though I was trying to swallow all the possibilities which could have been mine or my vision so clouded with the futures I could have had. I forced them down. Stowed them away for discarding, just as soon as I reached my new destination.

York shone under the summer sun like an illuminated drawing, the Minster on its slight hill, the pale stone buildings postcard-perfect. I felt a tug somewhere deep inside as though I was attached physically to those medieval streets and gatehouses by some elastic device. I shook my head and walked on. It had been the same before in Prague, hadn't it? Where the bridges and walls had seemed to conspire to hold me? But I'd walked away then and I could walk away now.

I had a sudden image of Ben, waking up. Walking through the house, room by room. Room by room. Searching. I hoisted my bag higher. He'd let go of Willow Down, he could let go of me. Let's face it, I'd been a fleeting moment. I was a passing phase, a *nothing*.

I reached the station and collected enough coins from the pockets of my rucksack to buy a ticket to Glasgow. It took several handfuls and the man in the ticket office looked pained as he bagged them all but a few minutes later I was through and stepping onto the train. Hearing in the rhythm of the departing locomotives the refrain *hesitationisdeath, hesitationisdeath*. This had to be done. Like in the prison, the smells of sweat and reluctance, of fear and loneliness, all things which could be borne, which *had to be* borne. A time which had to be lived through.

The doors slid shut behind me, then there was the no-man's-land pause, when I belonged neither to York nor to Glasgow. Could choose either. Inaction chose for me. The train pulled, leaned to the slight incline and drew its way out of the station.

Nothing could touch me now.

**25th May**

I thought it was all over, that the worst had passed. Jem and I were ... equal. Her life for mine, stories traded like dreams. And now ...

I didn't think there was anything left to hurt me. I thought we could work it out. Now I see that I was just waiting for her to give, like the walls she'd built were paper things that would fall under the weight of ... of what? My desire? Like I am all she needs? How hypocritical, how egocentric can I be? Jesus, doc, why has no-one told me even now, the world as I knew it is gone? No more groupies on their knees, no more yes-men with their wraps of snow. It's not all about me any more.

I let being deaf define me. In my head I'd become this genius, this towering musical prodigy that deafness had levelled, had forced to become human; like I should be given special treatment. But now I know. It wasn't deafness that made me human again, it was Jemima. I misjudged. Screwed up. And now she's gone.

I woke up and found she'd left as though none of it counted. The fears and the secrets we'd exchanged weren't worth the air we breathed to tell them. Fake currency. But I never meant to use those secrets to buy her, never wanted gratitude or sympathy to be the coinage that kept us together, I wanted her to **want** to be with me.

And it's all I can think. She's gone. And the last bit of my ego is screaming and punching the floor, because I want her so much. But my head knows she did what she thought she had to.

And the rest of me knows I have to find her.

# Chapter Nineteen

Glasgow was a hard city, all sharp Scottish corners and accents and from the moment I stepped from the train I knew I'd made a mistake. Even the sunlight was gone, replaced by a damp greyness which seeped through my clothes. The tears which had haunted my journey threatened to reappear, making the outline of the railway buildings blur. I sat heavily on a step. *What was I doing?*

Getting old, that was what. Twenty-eight, and the months of comfort staying put in Rosie's little cottage had blunted my edges. Time to get back into practice, get back on that horse and ride. I shouldered my rucksack and leaned into the straps, heading up the hill towards Sauchiehall Street where the craft shops stood. I put the tears down to tiredness, to the anxieties of relocation. It often hit me this way. Well, not exactly *this* way ... I usually enjoyed the heart-thump of new possibilities in a new location. Especially when scoping out the shops, looking for possibilities. The thrill of a new chase, new conquests.

And then on the other side of the road, I saw a figure. Tall and skinny, in ripped black jeans. Long dark hair tracing its way over the collar of a huge grey coat. Walking away from me, heading down the hill. '*You bastard,*' I thought. '*How dare you follow me? How dare you even think* ...' I swung myself after him, confronted him, hand on shoulder as he was about to turn into a side street.

'Awae, hen, what's the matter?' The broad Glaswegian

vowels spun me out of my self-delusion. Not Ben. Not even really close, this guy was broader, had earrings in both ears and nowhere near the cheekboned glamour of the ex-guitarist. I stammered my apologies and walked away, keen eyes watching me go amid a highly accented attempt to get me to stay.

*Stupid. Stupid.* Seeing what I wanted to see, deep deep down, hidden behind so many layers of self-loathing and fear. As I walked I saw more faces in the crowds that littered the streets. A guy, so much like Randall that my heart went into free-fall, pounding the air from my lungs. Same hair, same quick laugh, passing me by as easily as if I didn't exist. And over there, sitting by the river, dropping beads of bread for uninterested ducks – Christian. Or Christian as he *should* have been; clean, blond. *Older.* Holding a small child by the hand, amused at her efforts to get the bread to land in the water.

I was seriously losing it.

I paid for a week's lodging in a B&B in a road not far from the shopping streets and lay on the bed listening to the sounds of the street outside. I needed to get my things into the shops. Needed to get out there, to start selling, find myself somewhere to set up a workshop. So why was I lying here, a slow string of tears quietly renewing itself on my cheeks? Crying didn't pay the bills. Didn't give you freedom. All it did was tie you to the memories of something you couldn't have. A luxury I didn't want and couldn't pay for.

Stop wasting time, Gemma.

And then another part of me thought, *Why not? Time is one thing I've got plenty of. Why not waste just a little of it mourning for everything that went before?*

And then I cried. Properly for the first time since Randall had died. Bringing all the misery and loneliness and fear out where I could see it, showing myself exactly what I'd lost. My parents, Christian, Gray, Randall. Anyone I had ever cared for. *And Ben*, whispered a little voice. *Rosie, Jason, Harry. But you chose that, didn't you? Chose to throw that affection away.* And I turned into the pillow for fear that my sobs might cause my landlady to come and find out what was the cause of the strange noise in room 14.

I'd forgotten how hard it was, starting over. How had I let myself get like this, soft and unprepared? The first two rejections dug into me like fingernails and tears were never far from the surface. I found myself jerking the straps of my rucksack into my shoulders, using the pain to keep my mind from wandering. *Focus.* And then the third shop said they'd think about it. Took my details. The seventh shop took two buckles on approval and I found a flat to rent on a card in a newsagents. Out of the city and two bus rides from the main shops, but a roof over my head. Paid for with the last of Ben's money, although I kept one coin in the bottom of the inside pocket of my bag, telling myself it was for absolute last-ditch emergencies. Knowing all the time that it was my final link with the world I had left, the last thing I had that Ben had touched. And sometimes, deep in the night, when I woke with my heart scratching at my chest to be released, I would hold the little bronze disc against my cheek as though I could imprint him onto me through it. Waiting for the feelings to burn down to a dull redness before I could sleep again.

And still I kept seeing him on the streets. I'd learned my lesson, though, and stopped accosting innocent strangers who just happened to bear a, sometimes quite embarrassingly slight, resemblance. After two weeks things were back to normal. I was supplying two shops on a regular basis, had made a couple of casual drinking friends and found a workshop space courtesy of the art college. My heart had stopped hurting me every time I caught a glimpse of a rangy dark-haired man and if I found myself twisting my last pound coin in the night, I assured myself it was simply my good-luck charm and nothing to do with the memories it carried.

I spent a lot of time sitting in the park near the river. Most people were afraid of this part of town, muggings were rife, but I had nothing to steal and the cool water flowing through the city reminded me harmlessly of York. There was nothing unexplored about this situation, nothing scary. A measure of control had come back to my life and I was heading for the edgy contentment which was the nearest I felt to happiness these days.

It was nearly three weeks since I'd left York. Now I could flip the pound coin between my fingers almost thoughtlessly; my default activity when my hands weren't occupied with buckle-making. Sitting in the park, feeling the sun on my back and flipping my coin. On this particular evening I felt someone move into the space between me and the park railings and instinctively I put a foot on my rucksack to prevent a casual running theft. But the figure didn't touch my bag. Instead he reached over the top of me and snatched the coin at the top of its arc.

'You could have had everything.'

I turned my head. Ben was standing beside me watching my face with an almost greedy expression. He looked awful, which was how I knew he wasn't an illusion. My illusions nowadays were better dressed. 'Have you been following me?' My heart began to thunder in my throat.

'*Following?* Believe me, following would have been a piece of cake.' He sounded rough, too. Like his throat was sore. 'Why did you do it, Jem?'

I waved an arm. 'New life.'

Ben shook his head. 'Really? What's so new about it? Running, tramping the streets, always moving on, in what way is this a new life? Because it looks exactly like the old one to me. Only with a distinct lack of people who care about you.'

'Maybe that's what I like about it.'

'So it's okay to destroy people's lives then, is it? To wreck people's emotions?' A hand went to reach for me and then dropped, drawing my attention to the fact he was wearing one of my buckles, the one I'd seen him wearing before, in the shop. Decades ago. In another life.

'I thought you sold that one.' I gestured.

'No, bought it myself. I wanted something that you'd made. Yeah, stupid, I know.' His voice was sour. 'To care so much for someone who wants anything but concern for her welfare. But I do.' He coughed. 'Bloody Zafe, he's wrecking my throat with those fags.'

'You went to *Zafe*?'

An inclination of the head. 'I needed to find you and

I needed help to do it. Someone who could hear. Jason's got his work cut out looking after Rosie, and there was no-one else to turn to so I ...' A small shrug. 'It took him hard when I explained. It was weird, you know? He said he thought that I'd ... Christ, stupid sod ... that I'd been diagnosed HIV positive. That I'd taken myself off somewhere to die. So at first the fact that I was as deaf as a brick was, like, a *good* thing. And then he realised – ' Ben closed his eyes briefly. 'He realised it was the death of music for me and that was almost as bad. Worse, in some ways.' He looked me in the eye suddenly, for the first time. 'There was a *lot* of hugging that day.'

My blood was settling down now, rather than heaving and retching through my veins. There was a small, slow burn in my chest that I wasn't familiar with. 'I'm glad.'

He shrugged. 'Why? It's nothing to you, is it? *I'm* nothing to you.'

'Ben I ...' But he interrupted me.

'Just to *leave*? Not a note, no explanation? Jesus, Jem, what were you trying to do? Prove something? I thought ... I thought you *cared*. I saw it in your eyes and don't tell me you were lying because I'm a bit of an expert there and *no-one* can lie with their eyes. Not like that.' He slid down to lie on the crisp-packet strewn grass as though fatigue would no longer let him stand.

'Maybe I can.' Under the bravado my tone wavered, just a bit.

He shook his head. That was all.

'So. How is everyone?'

A shrug. 'Do you really want to know? Rosie is missing you. She said you told her you were going and that you argued about it when she tried to make you stay. She told me that you – never mind. And Harry cries a lot. She blames you for that, too.' Another shrug. 'And who knows what Jason thinks, but his message for you is – now, hang on, let me get this straight – "get your head in gear, babe." Oh, and something about ice cubes, but I'm not sure what that was about.'

A hot blush lit my cheeks. The feeling setting itself like a crystal in my belly acquired a name. Guilt. I looked at him, digging his fingers into the soil and the feelings rushed over me like an incoming tide. I had to breathe slow and deep so as not to drown. 'Ben. I –'

'Yeah, I know. You're not interested.' Now he stood up, dragging himself upright as though his bones were reluctant. 'Sorry. I thought, maybe, I could make a difference. That you might just be able to look inside yourself this once, and see what you're doing to everyone who ever loved you. See that maybe you should stop being so fucking *selfish* all the time.' He put both hands against the railings and looked into my eyes. There was a fire in his intense brown stare that I'd never seen before. 'Yeah, it was shitty what happened to you. But you really think that Randall and Christian would want you to live like this? You think you're doing their memories a *favour* by cutting and running all the time? Okay, yes, I applaud your decision not to get involved until you feel whole, feel like a real person, but don't you ever stop to think that maybe *being involved could make you feel that way*? And you know what *really* makes me mad?' Ben lowered his voice, speaking right into my eyes now. 'You listened to me. You took it all on board, told me it didn't matter my not being perfect, when all the time you were planning to run. You *lied*, Jemima. You fucking *lied*.'

'My name isn't Jemima. I told you.'

'You're Jemima to me. That girl you were, that Gemma, she doesn't exist any more. Jemima is who you've made yourself into, that's who I ...' He stopped. Coughed.

'Ben, before ... it wasn't a lie. I just never knew it would be this hard.'

'Yeah? Well it's not exactly a picnic with the Queen from where I'm standing either. You aren't the only one with problems you know, but you are the only one who runs away.'

Now I stood up too, feeling the strain in my thighs and calves as wobbly muscles tried to take my weight. 'How did you find me?'

He smiled a rather humourless smile. 'Zafe rang around and a guy at the station remembered you.' The smile briefly became warmer. 'Honestly, what were you *thinking*? Over seventy quid in one pound coins – the guy was in serious trauma.' Then his expression became wary again, eyes watchful. 'So we knew you'd come to Glasgow. And I waited for you, Jem. I gave you the benefit of the doubt, thought when you realised what you were doing, what you were making of your life that you'd ... I thought you'd come back to me, you know that? I was that deluded. And then, when I knew you weren't coming, that I wouldn't ever see you again unless I did something, d'you know what? For five seconds I thought, "Why should I? Why should I care?" But there's something, something that wouldn't let me sleep, wouldn't let me rest until I knew you were safe. With me or without me, I wanted you safe. So I drove up four days ago. Been looking for you ever since. And let me tell you, this accent is a bitch to lip read. Half the Glaswegian population thinks I'm Care in the Community now.'

The warmth rose from my stomach to engulf my body and my face and I realised that what I was experiencing was the scalding blush of shame.

This man – *this man* had driven several hundred miles with no guarantee of finding me. He'd left himself at the mercy of a strange city, unable to communicate properly, just for me.

I looked at him standing there, looking sleep-deprived and even skankier than usual. But, and I had to admit it to myself, very sexy. Very cute. And here. Despite what I'd done, despite the awful way I'd betrayed him by running away, he was here. Giving me another chance. And the thoughts didn't send the usual sting of fear through my bloodstream. He wasn't here to possess me, to force me to go with him. He didn't want me to belong to him, he just wanted me safe.

I stared across the water. What did I do now? Back down, return with him? But what would that mean about all those other times when I'd run ... that those hadn't been real? That I just hadn't tried hard enough?

And there, clear and hard as good diamonds, were Chris and Randall. Shouldering their way forward to stare at me across the years. Loading me with the memories of the things we'd had to do back then to survive.

We'd all made our decisions. Chris had turned to heroin, his decision. Ran had killed Gray, his decision and I'd lied for him. My decision. And now I was beginning to understand. The boys had loved me. They wouldn't have wanted me to keep their memories safe at the expense of forming new ones of my own. Our parents had loved us. It hadn't been their *choice* to die, after all. They would have wanted me to have a proper life, a settled life.

And now Ben was giving me the chance to move on. Not forget it, I would never forget any of it. But I could get over it.

'I didn't lie, Ben.' My lips hardly moved. 'But running is what I *do* and I don't know if I can break the habit.'

Wary and huge, his eyes were on my face now. 'You need to …' A finger touched my mouth. 'I can't read if you don't. Please.' As though it hurt him to ask. I repeated myself, feeling a bit ashamed and he stroked my hair very gently. 'Hey, Jem? Clean now for five years, six months and two weeks. If there's one thing I know about it's breaking habits. Break yours, now. Come back with me.'

*Could I? Could it really be that simple? Just … go back?* And then I remembered Rosie's words about the line in the sand. The way I'd felt sitting on the steps of Glasgow station, too old, too tired to keep going. Maybe it really *was* time to face those demons.

'Ben.' I stood up. 'I'll come back with you. But it has to be on my terms. I have to be able to sort myself out, I can't – *won't* – rely on you to do it for me.'

'Understood.'

'I have to find out what Saskia is doing buying all that stuff from Rosie and burning it. Why she's got me blacklisted from here to … well, not from *here*, obviously, even the devil doesn't deal in Glasgow, but why she's got eBay to shut me down.'

Ben raised an eyebrow. 'Okay. We do all that. And then what?'

'Then when I'm back on an equal footing I'll decide what to do. I can't be tied, Ben, I have to feel that I'm free to do what I want. If I stayed ...' My voice tailed off.

'If you stayed you'd want to know you were staying because you wanted to, not because you'd got nowhere else to go. Yeah?' His fingers closed very gently over mine. 'That's what I want too, Jem. I want you with me because you can't bear to be anywhere else, not because you owe me. You've made me realise so much about myself, about the way I've behaved, that I ...'

For a long, long time we just stared at each other. His huge eyes seemed to suck me in until they were all I was aware of. Eyes, and a wisp of hair which blew across to tickle at my cheek. 'Ben ...' He smelled sweet. Indefinable. So much himself that I found it hard to breathe.

'Jem. It's okay.' A small step and he was so close. The panic tried to rise in me but there was simply no room for it, not with the sudden flush of my skin and the racing of my heart. 'It's really okay.' He leaned forward to brush his mouth against mine and suddenly I found myself winding hands in his hair, pulling him down, pulling him closer. Desperate, hungry for the contact, for his tongue searching my mouth and his body pressed tight against me.

I did it in the sure knowledge that, wherever they were, my brothers were cheering and catcalling and probably making hand gestures that Jason would have been proud of.

'I'm afraid, if things start to get difficult I'll run again,'

I whispered. It was as if I had to say the words aloud, even though he had no hope of seeing them. But then he did that disconcerting thing of speaking without knowing what I'd said, yet continuing the conversation.

'You know your past?'

'Yes.'

'It's just that. Past. Instinct might tell you to run but I hope – *God how I hope* – that you'll stop and think. Rationalise. Talk to me. And if things ever get so bad that you can't, well then maybe you'll run somewhere I can find you.'

'You've had a long time to work on that speech, haven't you?'

'Since the day you walked out.'

'Smooth, Mr Davies, very smooth.'

'You have *no* idea.'

# Chapter Twenty

We drove back in Ben's car. It was hard, leaving my stuff in the shops in Glasgow, but they had my mobile number and the sum total of my other belongings didn't even occupy half of the tiny boot. Ben was incredulous.

'You've been in Glasgow for three weeks, with only *this*?' he asked, when we stopped for coffee on the motorway, holding up my rucksack by one strap. 'What did you do for clothes?'

I wrinkled my nose at him. 'This from a bloke who smells like he's been wearing the same jeans for a fortnight.'

'Yeah, but you're a woman.'

'Thanks for noticing.'

A long, dark look. 'Oh, I noticed.' He gave me a glance. 'Saskia's offered me a place in the Shambles. Says she feels sorry for me, with the shop burning down and all. She took the lease of the place but she doesn't know what to do with it, apparently. Thought a music shop might go well over there.'

'Really, the Shambles? That's tourist central, you'd make a mint.'

A pause. 'I think she just wants to control what I stock. After all it's her place, she has ultimate veto. She won't want me bringing her shop into disrepute.'

'You mean she won't want you having my jewellery in there.'

'Well. We'll see about that.'

A companionable silence fell, and we got back into the car. I watched Ben drive, neat sureness of movement, long legs inching the pedals, dramatic fingers wrapped around the wheel and I felt a sudden shudder through me. It rattled my teeth and sent a scalding blast down to my thighs like a damp rush of steam. I leaned back on the leather seat and tried to make sense of it. It felt like ... yes, it felt like physical attraction with knobs on, so to speak. I blew a breath which condensed on the window and pretended to be involved with the scenery but I didn't miss Ben's sidelong glance at me nor his secret half-smile. The way he ran a fingertip over the tiny head of the gear lever *might* have been accidental but I didn't think so.

Two words for this situation. Uh and oh.

It was dark when we parked outside Wilberforce Crescent. Ben stood aside to let me through the front door and I found I was relaxing ever so slightly as we went into the kitchen. As though this place was home.

He'd left the empty money jar on the table.

'I'll pay it back.'

'Cool.' He opened the fridge and took out some yoghurt, some fruit and a bottle of something cold from the bottom rack. He put it all on the table. 'Hungry? Help yourself.' There was something about him, something I'd never seen before. A new kind of sureness in his movements, a different confidence. He wasn't watching my face with the same desperation that he usually had, afraid he might miss something.

'Ben?'

No answer. He was groping in the back of the fridge and rattling drawers in and out, finally turning, juggling the makings of a salad, a loaf of bread and a knife. He began cutting slices with an easy motion.

'Why did you come looking? Why couldn't you just let it be?' A sudden jolt of the memories I wouldn't let myself have. I hadn't seen anyone cut bread like that since I was a child.

Ben stopped. Leaned on the knife handle. 'I thought you might want to come back but that maybe you didn't know how to give yourself permission.'

'You and your drummer must have done a lot of talking.'

'Yeah, over the years we talked a lot. On a tour bus there's not a lot else to do when you're in transit. It's amazing what you can pick up.' He put two thick slices of granary bread, a bowl of salad and dressing in front of me. 'But you're pretty good yourself, you know. All that stuff you told me about getting in touch with Zafe? Well, you were right, he did deserve to know. I was a coward, running off without telling him anything. He was my best mate. I should have handled it better.'

I bit into the crusty bread. 'And now? Are you and he …?'

He shrugged. 'He's working on forgiving me. But hey, sometimes when you really care about someone you *have* to forgive. Do you understand that? And then we spent a lot of time talking about you.'

I nearly choked. '*Me?* What is wrong with you two? You've got five years of history to catch up on and you talk about me?'

'Just returning the favour. Apparently when you met him all you did was talk about *me*.' Carefully Ben laid the knife down on the table. There was something in the way he was looking at me. Something in the air, as though it was thickening. 'You were scared something had happened to me, Zafe said. You said I was broken.'

I swallowed. The bread was proving difficult to get down and the way Ben was looking at me wasn't helping at all. 'I didn't mean ...'

He cut me off. 'You were right. It wasn't just *me* that was broken, Jem, it was my soul. When my dad died it made me different. Forced me to be someone I wasn't even sure I liked. And the deafness made me more human, but isolated me so much that I couldn't make contact with anyone.' I was still sitting at the table. Ben came round it and I had to swivel on the stool to keep watching him. The look on his face was so intense I didn't know what he had in mind. 'And then I met you.'

I forced myself to laugh. 'Just when you thought it couldn't get worse, eh?'

He was leaning now to look down into my eyes. 'Oh, no,' he said. 'Things got very, very, *very* much better.' And he was so close now that his hair flowed across my throat. 'No pressure, Jem. No pressure.'

His lips met mine and I was astonished at the force inside me which sprang me up off the stool to rest against him, hands pushing his hair back. He tasted of honey and mint from the salad dressing he'd licked off his fingers. He leaned further forward and before I knew it I was half-sitting on the edge of the table, Ben's mouth travelling down to my throat, my hands dragging at his shirt, trying to yank it off over his head so I could touch skin.

This was something total, something so unexplored in

me that I didn't know how to handle or channel it, all I could do was go with it and try to ride it out. It felt as if I was some kind of conduit for feelings from another, unknown universe as I met his mouth again, whispering into it. 'Ben ... please ...' without even knowing what I pleaded for.

He freed my lips so he could look into my eyes. 'Are you sure? Really, *really* sure?'

How could I be sure? I'd never known anything like this. In lieu of an answer I slid a hand down to his belt, began working the buckle free whilst keeping my eyes on his face, slipping the keeper away from the tongue until I could pull it loose. Laid a finger on the top of his zipper, feeling how aroused he was.

Suddenly his hand came onto mine, not to help but stopping my fingers from moving any further. 'Jem.' His voice was steady. 'I want to know. I need you to say it. *Do you want this?*' And I knew he didn't just mean this, sex. He meant everything else it would bring: him, a relationship, the complications and the ties.

My breath caught in my throat. 'I want ...' Desire tried to overrule and my hand moved on his fly again but his grip was firm. 'I want to be *safe*.' The words nearly choked me, but as I said them I realised they were true. I wanted safety. Security. Something that was mine after all these years of running and hiding.

Ben moved back half a step. 'And do you think I'm safe? You feel that, with me?'

'I can try.'

'No. I want more than that.' Ben took the other half-step away and straightened his T shirt, combed his hair with his fingers and took a shaky deep breath. 'I know you think I'm in this for a fuck, Jemima, but it is so much more than that it's almost funny. C'mere.' Fingers closed around my wrist and I found I was being pulled out of the kitchen and along a hallway to a small door. Ben unlocked the door with a tiny key and drew me onto a narrow dark staircase. 'This is the old servants' quarters,' he said conversationally, and not at all as though we'd just come within moments of ripping one another's clothes off.

Still with his fingers cuffing my wrist he led me down the shallow steps and into the room below. It was the one I'd seen from the street, the old basement. Dust had collected into every depression and the instruments were covered in a shallow layer of it. Ben stood in the middle of it all and let go of me.

'I haven't been in here for years,' he said. 'Couldn't. This was our practice room. The guys never tried to get their stuff back, at least, I don't think they did. I was too busy hiding to know.' He turned, picked up a drumstick and experimentally tapped a cymbal. 'Mark's kit.' The bass guitar was leaning against a silver keyboard. Ben picked it up and strummed the strings. 'Zafe's.' A small puff of dust blew out and he laid it back down again to run a finger along the black and white keys. 'This was Si's.'

Nothing was amped up so there were just dull, tinny notes, like ghosts of what should be. Finally Ben picked up the cherry-red guitar which had fallen face down onto the rush matting flooring. Like a man touching an old love, he reverentially stroked its back, leaving finger streaks in the dust, then turned it against his body and threw the strap over his neck. 'This was me, Jem,' he said softly. 'It was fantastic.' With the weight of the guitar pulling down his shoulder he turned to look at the collected instruments. 'Willow Down. The most brilliant thing ever to happen to me.'

There he stood for a second as he'd once been, head back and eyes glowing. I could almost hear him addressing the crowd, almost see him posturing his way across the invisible stage. Then his shoulders dropped, he unslung the guitar and placed it carefully back on the dusty floor. 'And now there's you.' I stared at him. My heart was beating so fast that I had spots in front of my eyes. 'This was before. My old life. None of it is coming back and I've come to terms with that now. The good stuff, the bad stuff – and believe me there was a lot of bad stuff, whole gigs I don't remember, coke paranoia, the works – over. I'm leaving it behind.' He was watching me carefully, standing angled in that odd dusty room. His hair was smooth over his shoulders, his face lit by the streetlights beyond the barred window, throwing curious shadows which rippled as he moved. 'And I want you to do the same.'

'I have!' The soundproofing that lined the walls made my voice sound dead, toneless. Without real meaning.

'No, really. What nearly happened just now ...' Ben drew a huge breath. 'That was *wrong*. Was that how Gray told you to do it?' He put both hands on my shoulders. 'Because that was just sex. Disposable bump and grind.' His fingers worked on my muscles and gradually I could feel myself relaxing a little. 'What I want is to make love with you, Jemima. Not fucking. *Loving*.'

I must have stared because his hands were suddenly painful, digging in to muscles hard as rock. 'I don't ... I can't ...'

'I love you. It's not easy, it's not simple and God knows, it's far from making the world go round at the moment but, hey.' There he was again, right in my face. 'Now. Shall we see how it's really meant to go?'

All I could feel was the insistent pulse in the background as though the world was breathing. 'Yes.'

Then Ben kissed me. Properly. And I realised that all the other times he'd kissed me had been mere preparation, he'd been holding back. This kiss was dynamic. It sent all the little hairs on the back of my neck shooting straight up, made my skin wrinkle into goosepimples against his fingers. It sent the breath from my lungs and took the strength from my legs until I nearly buckled against him.

'Now,' he said. 'Now you know.'

'Ben.' It was all I could say; a plea, a warning, a promise. My body was limp with desire for him. And for once I was surrendering control *and I didn't care.*

'Yes.' He answered me. 'Oh, Jem, yes.'

He kissed my mouth and my neck. Looked deep into my eyes and slowly ... *too slowly surely* ... began to unbutton my shirt. 'Don't rush it,' he whispered as I tried to move, tried to pull at his T shirt and draw it over his head. 'We've got all night.'

A button at a time, with his mouth following his fingers, dipping inside the fabric as it fell away. And then he let me touch him, tracing the line of him outside his clothes and then as I grew braver, underneath to feel the tension of his muscles and the leanness of his flesh.

Slowly, still slowly, we undressed each other, pausing every other moment to kiss and wonder at the miraculousness of one another's flesh. I tugged his shirt, inching it over his head and then stepped back to appreciate the sight of his pale skin tinted an unearthly blue by the streetlamps. 'There's nothing to you.' I ran a finger over his ribcage. 'Skin and bone.'

A wicked grin. 'You reckon?'

And, oh, there was a good deal more to him than that. I uncovered him, inch by inch, as he drew my jeans down over my hips, until we both stood naked.

He looked me in the eyes, drew me down to the floor. 'Okay?' he asked.

'Oh, yes. Very, very okay.'

But he didn't immediately enter me. Restrained and gentle, he teased me with his mouth, moving from nipple to bellybutton and then lower. I was almost exploding with heat.

'Christ, Ben.' I was gasping, couldn't get enough air, enough words, enough … enough. A riotous shudder broke through me, a sensation of absolute rightness and I whispered his name. Too quietly to hear, but he was watching my face, saw my lips move and then with a small smile he was in me.

There was no pain, no forcing, just delicious delightful friction and wetness and the dust balling under my back as Ben moved, so, so gently at first, until he was sure. Then he finally gave it all he had and I was surprised again by the bursting feelings tearing through me, his sudden whisper of 'Oh God,' and then the feeling that my thighs had just exploded as he shook, holding me, eyes on mine so it felt as though he was inside my head.

We lay back on the dust-covered floor, breathing fast. Where our bodies were sticky with sweat little bunches of grey fluff collected, Ben's shoulders were covered. I raised myself up on an elbow and looked at him. Naked he was a lot better looking, long and lean with muscles in all the right places, lightly covered in dark hair which whirled from between his nipples, swept past a below-navel-level mole to become an eyebrow-thin line down his body to his groin. He looked strong. He looked gorgeous.

He had his eyes closed, dark lashes netted on his cheeks like an image of Rock God perfection. I knew it was pointless speaking until he opened his eyes so I lay back, resting against his shoulder and breathing in the scent of sex and closed rooms. My thighs kept trembling with the aftermath of the explosions which had racked through me, feelings and sensations I'd never known existed.

'You all right?' Ben finally opened one eye and regarded me slightly blearily.

'That was –' I stopped. Couldn't think of the words. 'But I guess you've had plenty of practice, all those groupies and everything.'

His fingers played a refrain against my ribcage. 'You're missing the basic point of groupies, my love. There to please me, not the other way round.'

'Chauvinist.'

'Look. I've had my cock sucked seven ways to Christmas but nothing compares to what we just did. That, my dear Jemima, was making love, the way it should be.' He slowly sat up and leaned his back against the wall. 'You were expecting me to hurt you, weren't you? I felt you flinch.'

'I'm sorry.'

Ben burst out laughing. '*Sorry?* Jem, it's not your fault.' And then the laughter died and he shook his head, reaching out his arms to encompass me. 'This is now, Jemima. For both of us. Forget what was, we make ourselves now.'

As I lay against his chest and felt his breathing slow, dropping into sleep, I wondered if it could really be that easy.

**15th June**

I love her. Christ, it feels like ... I'm just totally ...

This feeling, it's like a brain-wipe. Like a reset button putting me back to who I was before, with this fantastic, wonderful, gorgeous babe, who wants me for what I am now, not what I used to be. And when I'm lying holding her, nothing that went before matters. Wouldn't have it back as a gift. I never liked myself then. I only realise it now, now that Jem knows the core me, the real me, that what I was then was some kind of fake. All the posturing and the drugs, that was me trying to make myself into something I liked. With a head full of coke and E I could be anyone, anything. And that's just what I was. Anyone.

When Dad died I felt I had to look after Mum and Emmie, had to be someone, and I had the band and they only had each other; it was all crazy stupid and I reckon I rebuilt myself into someone that could cope. Which is what Jemima did. She turned herself into something that was hard enough to take what was happening, but only on the outside. Inside, she was like me, hiding and scared. Lost.

And now we're found. I'm found. Willow Down is going on without me and I don't mind. Zafe will make a fine lead. I've got Jem and I will do anything in my power to make her happy. Because she's saved me in some way I can't even start to define.

I'm not saying it's all over. Not yet. She looks at me sometimes as though she thinks I'm going to blow it all. I don't think she knows that she's the one with all the power, that she could destroy me, simply by leaving. I'm breathless with the thought that she might, one day, just pack and leave, even while I know I have to give her that freedom. Otherwise I've just caged her, haven't I? And what kind of love would it be, that only came from inside a box?

I want to keep her, but I don't want to tie her. I need her to be able to run, but not to want to. I need her to know that. I need her to feel safe with me. Fuck it, I just need her.

Saskia tapped her toe on the threadbare carpet. 'I'm *positive* I told you I'd be here to pick up the cards today.' She turned a little circle with an expression which made it look as though her upper lip was attached to the ceiling by invisible wires. 'And I can't *believe* you're letting me down.' The wires tightened and the lip curled a little more.

Rosie deftly buttoned Harry back into his rompers. 'Honestly, Saskia. You never said anything about picking them up. I thought I had until next week.' She lifted Harry. 'Anyway I couldn't have done them that fast, you must know that.'

'Hmmm.' Saskia tapped a nail against a tooth. There was an echo of falseness from both. 'It may be that I have to rethink our contract, Rosie. If you're going to do this sort of thing.'

'*What* sort of thing?' I waded in on Rosie's behalf. 'Looking after her son? Doing housework? It's not like she's off clubbing all hours, is it? What are you trying to do, confine her to the house?'

Saskia threw me a glance I couldn't have read with a dictionary. 'In business, Jemima, one has to be reliable. Absolutely and without question, one has to be professional.' Another look. 'And, may I point out, this isn't your problem or your concern and I would appreciate you keeping your rather pointy little nose out of things.'

Rosie and I gaped at one another. Saskia must be rattled for her insults to have become so overt.

After a moment's consideration, Saskia looked me over again. 'I know this is just a *tiny* bit personal, darling, but you're not expecting, are you?' My mouth fell so far open that from the side I probably looked like a basking shark. 'You do seem to have put on some weight.' I tried, but I couldn't help myself and glanced down at my stomach. Saskia gave a small smile of triumph. 'But then I shouldn't think that darling Benedict could be responsible, he seems like a man with a rather more, how should I put it, *subtle* taste in women.' Like an unconscious reflex she ran a hand through her hair. 'And he really is the most adorable kisser.'

Did she think I didn't know? Or was this a rather pathetic attempt to make me jealous? Or just paranoid?

'I'm going to make some coffee.' Rosie pressed Harry to me. 'And possibly inhale some kind of glue. Chat amongst yourselves.'

'Chicken,' I hissed at her but she rolled her eyes at me and fled into the kitchen.

'Oh, this *is* a shame, having to leave without the cards.' Saskia pulled her Blackberry from her bag and consulted it. 'Oh, well. And I find myself having to double my order, too. Rosie is certainly in for a busy weekend!' A scythe-like nail pressed a button. 'Please ask Rosie to excuse me, won't you? I am rather pushed for time.' A sideways smile. 'Oscar has his induction today and I need to rush home for my hat.'

'He's *five*, Saskia. He's starting school. For most mothers it's check that his socks are level and that he's got his lunchbox. You make it sound like the winners enclosure at Goodwood.'

This time I got a chilly stare. 'The two have a surprising amount in common, Jemima. Although I do realise that the words "surprising amount" and "common" are used rather differently around you. Now excuse me.' She turned around and lifted the Blackberry again, obviously using it to block me out.

'I don't know what you're playing at,' my voice was cool, my tone level. 'But one day someone's going to stop you, Saskia.'

'*Playing?*' Saskia tapped a couple of keys then snapped the lid down. 'I wasn't aware that life was a game, Jemima.' She stood up, hands smoothing down the sides of her skirt where the silk had creased and ruffled deep gouges like ravines. When she spoke again, it was almost a whisper. 'No. It most certainly is anything but.'

She swivelled so that her hair twisted a circle around her face, pulled a cutely clothes-matching purse from the table and headed for the door. I couldn't put my finger on the emotion I felt when I realised there were tears smudging the edges of her mascara'd eyes.

After a decent interval, Rosie poked her head back through the door. 'Thank God she's gone.' She flung herself down onto the sofa. 'She's trying to make out that I'm bonkers, what with her "I'm sure I told you", and "but we *arranged* …".'

Her emphasised speech was uncannily like Saskia's. 'Very good. Have you been practising?'

'Yeah. I sit up at night doing Saskia impressions and feeding Harry lemons so that he'll grow up associating her with bitterness. He'll thank me for it when he's eighteen and she's trying to get into his trousers.' Rosie took the baby from me. 'Now. You've only apologised for leaving about, what, five hundred times, so I'd like at least another thousand and possibly some Hail-Mary-type penances, stat. Oh, but that's after you tell me what's put such a smile on your face … and if it's anything Glaswegian-related then I'm afraid you can just bugger off back to Kilt-and-Haggis Land, 'cos I've got good money resting on you staying put back here.'

I said nothing but let my half-smile do the work for me.

'Oh God, oh God.' Rosie danced around the room, with Harry nearly making himself sick trying to keep focusing on her face. 'You and Ben. Oh, this is just so *fantastic*!'

'Steady on. We're not exactly choosing curtains you

know. It was only …' I tailed off, realising I didn't *know* what it was. 'I'm not settling down with him. I stand by what I said, what I've *always* said; no men until I'm a person in my own right.' But I could hear the hollowness of my words this time, and my smile had become so broad I was nearly swallowing my own ears. *Ben and me. Yes.*

'But you must think you're nearly there, otherwise you wouldn't have done it, would you?' Rosie twirled her son about in a makeshift waltz. 'Years of no sex, and you broke it with Ben. That's fantastic,' she repeated, whilst Harry made threatening belching noises. 'Am I allowed to tell Jason?'

'Tell me what?' Jason loomed over the threshold like a bad smell. Complete with a bad smell.

'Jem had sex with Ben Davies.'

'Rosie! I didn't say you *could* tell him.'

'Oh right, you try keeping anything from Mr MI5 here, especially if there's sex involved.' Her words were a little sour.

I looked from one to the other. 'Rosie? Jase?'

They both shook heads. 'Nothing. Honestly, Jem, nothing.'

'Now, come on, give us the grief – did he tie you up? Gotta be a bondage kinda guy, trousers like he wears.'

'Jason, you *have* to tie your women up otherwise they'd see sense and go home.'

'Jemima, when they sees what I got in here –' Jason clutched at his groin. 'They don't want to go *nowhere*.'

'Shutupshutup.' Rosie waved us both down with the hand not gripping Harry. 'I want to know all about it. Where, how, why?'

'And what wiv,' Jason added, leeringly.

'I wish I hadn't mentioned it now.' I wandered through to the kitchen to put the kettle on, leaving them bickering. There was a slightly pointed edge to Rosie this morning, I thought. She'd been overjoyed to see me but something wasn't quite right with her. Or, more exactly, not right with her relationship with Jason. There were definite undercurrents, things not said. And given that Jason, Mr Verbal Diarrhoea, was involved, that was something for the *Guinness Book of Records*.

I shook my head and tipped some Crunch Creams onto a plate. Then thought about Jason eating them all and replaced them with Rich Tea biscuits and a couple of soggy digestives I found in the back of the cupboard. This wasn't my home any more. When it had been, there would never have been a chance for digestives to go soggy at the back of the cupboard.

But if this wasn't home, then were was?

A picture rose in my mind like yeast in a warm oven. Ben's body, which I'd originally thought of as scrawny, now revealed in all its glory as lean and perfectly muscled. The way he wore his jeans, slung low on his hips and tight across his thighs. His long, untidy hair and his relentlessly stubbled cheeks.

My hands were shaking so much that I nearly dropped the kettle and slopped boiling water all over the draining board.

'What's taking so long?' Jason appeared in the doorway, preceded only slightly by the stench of formaldehyde. 'People dyin' of thirst in here, girl.' I swallowed hard and tried once more to bring the kettle into conjunction with the mugs. 'You all right?' His hand steadied mine, but his touch just brought more memories of Ben. 'You're not going to run again, are you, babe?'

'No, Jason, I'm not. I think I'm staying around, at least for a while.'

'Well, I don't mind tellin' you, I'm glad to hear it. How long has it been?'

'Last night it averaged about eight inches,' I said just to see his face, and to my gratification Jason actually blushed.

'… okay, my turn. My dream, my ultimate dream, yeah?' Rosie dragged a semi-drunken hand over her head, sending spirals of hair ricocheting off her skull. 'And for the record Jase, I still think yours is pathetic.'

'Hey, there's nothin' wrong in ownin' an island. Plenty of time to paint.'

'If you say so.' Rosie adjusted the weight of Harry who was sleeping in her arms. 'Hmmm. My ultimate dream.' She glanced around the room and I saw her gaze come to rest on the half-finished pile of cards on the table. 'I want to see Saskia lose all her money, and get struck ugly. Oh, and live happily ever after. That's me, not her. Your turn, Jem.'

I pushed my seat back from the table. Rosie had cooked up one of her classic lasagnes and my stomach felt like it might be forming an independent state. Perhaps Jason would like to own it. I opened my mouth to say this and then saw the way Jason was looking at Rosie. 'Thass your ultimate dream, is it? To see the back of Saskia?' His voice was very gentle and I knew neither of them were interested in my ultimate fantasy. Which, I might add, I had no idea about.

Rosie nodded, bending her head to kiss her sleeping son.

'Well,' Jason reached out and stroked her hair. 'Thass one dream won't come true. Two dreams, yours and mine.'

There was such a terrible tenderness in the way he spoke that I suddenly felt like the world's largest gooseberry. 'I ought to go. Ben said he'd be over around tennish to give me a lift back – he's chewing the fat with Zafe this evening. I'll wait out at the bus stop, save him having to turn round in the lane. Thanks for dinner, Rosie.'

'I'll walk with you.'

'No, it's okay, Jase.'

But he was already grabbing a jacket and forcing his arms down the sleeves. 'Aw, come on Jem. I still wants to hear your ultimate dream. I reckon it's gonna be filthy.'

Rosie laughed and stood up. 'And I'd better get this lad to bed.'

'Thass *exactly* what I'm hopin' Jem's gonna say. Her ultimate dream, yeah?' Jason nudged me. 'Can't fight it forever, girl.' But once outside, as we moved through the twilight, he dropped the act. 'We got problems, Jem. Big problems.'

'I knew there was something up. Why is Rosie so off with you tonight? You haven't made another pass, have you?'

But he didn't rise to the humour. Instead, he stared out into the gathering dusk, more focused than I'd ever seen him when he wasn't working. He looked even more Johnny Depp-like than usual. Still didn't fancy him, though.

'I've come to care about you and Rosie like the sisters I never had,' he said at last.

'You've *got* sisters, Jason, you hate them both.'

'Yeah, that's why I care about you two. You're the *nice* sisters I never had.' A brief smile flashed in oncoming headlights. 'An' I am really worried about Rosie. She's told me some stuff – look, she *had to*, all right? It was eatin' her up and you've got your own stuff goin' down an' I found her – doesn't matter. Promised I wouldn't tell ya, so, you know how it goes.'

'Not really. Surely if it's that bad –'

'You're keeping Ben's secrets, aren't you?'

'It's not my secret to tell.'

'There y'go then. But I will tell you this. We gotta get Saskia and Rosie away from each other.'

'I'm all for that. She's ruining Rosie's life with her constant orders. Trouble is Saskia is her only customer now, she's had to drop everyone else but because Saskia pays so well it's all been fine. What would she do if Saskia *did* stop ordering?'

Jason shrugged. 'She'd survive. Maybe the two of you could set up together?'

'Great idea, but you're missing the fact that eBay have still got me banned and the whole of York regards me as marginally less marketable than typhoid.'

'It'll straighten out. Now you've got Ben.'

'I'm not going to be living off him, if that's what you're thinking.' Even the thought of being financially dependent made my breath thicken in my throat. 'I've got plans. Well, sort of. I'm planning to get Saskia to tell the Board of Trade members to start stocking me again and that's a start.'

'Just get Rosie out from under, Jem. Whatever it takes.'

I shook my head in the darkness, forcing my breathing to steady. In, out. Don't panic. 'I'll do what I can.'

'Great.' We walked along elbow to elbow for a bit.

Then Jason broke the silence. 'I'm going back to the States in a couple of weeks. I need to know –.' He cleared his throat. 'I need to know Rosie's okay before I go.'

'Jase, you old dog, do you fancy our Rosie?' I prodded him with a finger. 'Why don't you ask her to go with you? I'm sure she'd love to see New York and it would be great for Harry. Plus it would get her away from Saskia – I mean, her kind can't cross water, can they?'

I stopped teasing suddenly. There was an expression that I'd never seen before on Jason's handsome face. A kind of longing. 'I would *so* love to do that.' Even his voice was different, softer. 'I asked her. But she wouldn't come, Jem. She said, maybe one day, when she's got stuff sorted … but I need to go now. Can't stand around and watch – ach, still not my secret to tell.'

We both focused on the headlights approaching. Even before I could see the big silver car, I recognised its growl. 'Here's Ben.'

'Yeah.'

'Jason …' But he'd already turned away and folded the darkness around himself like a blanket.

I climbed into the Audi but Ben didn't immediately screech away from the kerb. 'It's lovely out here,' he said, buzzing down the driver's window. 'Smells fresh. Like childhood.'

'You are such a romantic, aren't you?'

'Never used to be, but, yeah. Maybe I am now.' He opened the door and slid long legs out onto the kerb, the streetlamps strobing across his face and making him look like a manga character, all limbs, eyes and hair. 'Let's walk, Jem.'

'What, back to York?'

I got a well-worn sort of look for that. 'Romantic, remember? Just, around.'

I reluctantly climbed back out again and stood next to him on the pavement. 'Dead romantic this. I'm sure I can smell tomcat-pee.'

'Probably romantic if you're a lady cat.' An arm looped around my shoulders and he drew me into a slow walk. 'It's so quiet. Perfect place for a studio.'

'A *studio*? What are you going to do, go into pornographic movies?'

'Music studio.' I gave him a look. 'I'm going to write with Zafe. He's the music man now but I've still got a shed-load of tunes in my head. New material for Willow Down, stuff for the new album – I dream it up and Zafe lays the track down. Plays it for the guys and if they like it, they'll record. And they do like my stuff, least, they always used to, me and Zafe wrote most of the tracks on the last two albums.' Ben looked down the street. 'Wonder if that place is for sale?'

I looked at the impeccably raked gravel drive half-hidden behind the carefully trimmed yew hedge. 'That's Saskia's place. You could make her an offer; I think she'd take you up on just about anything.'

'Looks cool. Plenty of space.'

The moon made his eyes glow almost amber and his hair shone a tawny leonine shade. He was so clearly enjoying himself, scouting out locations for his future, I didn't like to say anything which might bring him down, so I just held his hand as he walked closer.

We stood for a while in the shelter of the big hedge and Ben wrapped his arms around me. I had to admit it, it felt good, and I was content just to lean into him, feel him breathe and smell the expensive cologne that he used mingled with the scent of the night. There was a strength to him now, a certainty.

*Could I do it? Could I trust him enough?*

Gradually though I became aware that Ben's attention wasn't on me.

'Hey ... *fuck* ...' His voice was little more than an exhalation.

'Your language has really gone downhill, you know? I used to think you were such a gentleman.'

But he didn't even realise I was speaking. Head up, he was looking over the hedge towards the lit windows at the front of the house. 'So who is he ... what is this *about*?'

'Ben?' I touched his shoulder. Slowly his gaze came down to mine.

'Saskia is ...' He raised his chin again. 'She's talking on the telephone. Over there, in that room to the left.'

I peered through the branches. Ben was a good six inches taller than me and I couldn't follow his eyeline but I could see a dim figure moving around inside the house. Pacing, it looked like.

'She's talking to ... hang on ... someone called Dave. Who's following ... *who*? Turn this way, bitch, oh yeah, following Alex. That's her husband isn't it?'

'Following? Like a fan you mean?'

But Ben couldn't hear me. He was too busy listening in his own way to Saskia.

'She wants photographs. Proof. Jem? Where are you going?'

I turned so that he could read my lips. 'She's got it in for me and Rosie already. I'm not going to let her get started on poor Alex as well. This has all gone far enough.'

He jogged to catch me up. 'What are you going to do?'

'No idea. We'll make it up as we go along, shall we?'

In front of the main door I hesitated for just a second, then raised my hand to the huge bronze knocker which bore more scrollwork than a medieval library.

'Jemima?' Saskia's face peered through the gap that the security chain allowed. 'What on earth are you doing here at this time of night? I didn't realise you were usually up so late.'

'I want to talk to you.'

'Have you been drinking?'

'No. Well, yes, but only a bit. All right, half a bottle. Ish. And it was only 12%, that rosé stuff that they sell in the shop.'

'Ah, yes. Cheap plonk.' Saskia enunciated the words to give them an extra helping of disgust. 'What did you want to talk about? I presume the state of the nation and the environment, the sort of thing people like you rabbit on about when you've had too much alcohol.'

'No. Important stuff.' My palms were sweaty now the initial adrenaline rush had worn off. 'Like, why you're trying to work Rosie into a nervous breakdown and then burning her stuff. Why you've told the York Board of Trade not to touch my things.'

Saskia made a dismissive gesture through the gap. It was truncated by the front door. 'Your paranoia is really *not* attractive.'

'All right. How about, why you're having your own husband followed? By a man called *Dave*? Just what the hell is the *matter* with you? '

The door closed for a second then reopened with the chain off. 'You'd better come inside.'

We walked into the impressive hall with its huge oak staircase winding up to the first floor. The walls dripped with tapestry and hangings, and tiny ornamental tables held *objets d'art*. Saskia's personal taste seemed to run to Hollywood Medieval.

She led us through into an office and sat on an overstuffed sofa, knees together and her hands indicating that Ben should sit beside her. I, evidently, could stand wherever I wanted. 'Now. You might as well get this out of your system, Jemima. Tell me what you're thinking then you can leave and we can both get on with our lives.' She threw a little glance at Ben.

I opened my mouth, but before any words could come out the telephone on the desk started ringing. Saskia gave a little start but sat firm, her eyes watchful, as though the handset might begin to smoulder.

'You'd better get it.' Ben gave her arm a nudge. He must have picked up what was happening from her body language. 'Didn't you tell Dave to ring as soon as he knew anything? He knows you're waiting for his call.'

Her expression seemed to be under some tight control, but she couldn't stop disbelief from seeping through. 'How did you know? Is this room bugged?'

I rolled my eyes at her. 'Yeah, 'cos we're a couple of top professional spies. Just answer the phone.'

Reluctantly she stood and picked up the sleek black handset. 'Hello?' Then she clamped her lips together, pushing the blood from them until they looked like a pair of albino slugs. 'Uhuh,' she said a couple of times. 'I see.' And then. 'She's in his car? Yes, thank you, but you can forget about the pictures. I know who it is now.'

Ben and I looked at each other. Understanding was blooming through my mind, connections being made. I didn't know how far behind Ben's comprehension was running so I took the initiative. I leaned forward and disconnected the call, leaving Saskia standing, a single tear caught in the act of running down her cheek.

'Okay,' I said. 'So. You suspected that Alex was having an affair with Rosie or me, you didn't know which one, so you punished us both. Cutting off my sales outlets, and trying to work Rosie into what? Post-natal depression? You knew she was feeling a bit shaky after Harry was born, so you decided to push her over the edge?' I moved closer, so that I was looking her right in the eye. 'Am I getting warm?'

The tears were beading down her cheeks now. Her throat moved as a sob tried to escape.

'And you burned down Ben's shop, made a false report to eBay, all just to get even with me for something I *wasn't even doing*?'

'You don't understand –' Saskia's voice was thick.

'Too right, I don't. What kind of a lunatic behaves like that? Who puts other people out of business because they *might* be up to something? You are seriously deranged, Saskia.'

Ben gave me a serious look. 'Jem, steady.'

'I am going to repeat this very slowly. She. *Burned. Down. Your. Shop.* All your things, the guitars, everything. Just to stop you selling my buckles. Do the words "call the police" mean anything to you?'

'The insurance people were satisfied it was kids playing with lighters. They're paying up.'

'And I'll make it up to you, I promise.' Saskia sounded earnest. And, for once, honest. 'I'd heard you suspected me, something Rosie said. But you said nothing, *did* nothing. For that, I'm grateful.'

'Wasn't really enough evidence,' I said, grudgingly. Wouldn't want Saskia attributing philanthropy to me. 'Just a seed head. I thought you might have had it stuck to you or something when you went down there.'

'I'm giving you the lease.' Saskia went back to looking at Ben. 'Making it over to you. The shop in the Shambles is yours. You can do what you like with it.' A quick look at me. '*Sell* what you like.'

I breathed hard and clenched my fists. I wanted, *so much*, just to punch her little Pekinese face, but the steady trickle of mascara-laced tears made me stop. It was the first time I'd ever seen Saskia lose control. 'But *why*? Why all this drama? Why not confront Alex? Tell him to go, if he's shagging around?'

'Have you ever been in love, Jemima?' Her voice was a whisper, broken by catches in her breath. 'Truly, utterly in love? And known all the time that you were driving the other person away? And you knew what you were doing but you still couldn't stop yourself – pushing them away when they wanted to be close and then wanting them to touch you but afraid of what would happen if they did ...'

Something made of ice crept down my spine. I refused to look at Ben. 'I can imagine.'

'No, you can't! Look at you with your no make-up and your skinny little jeans and your flimsy tops, all "I'm so beautiful I don't have to try". What do you think it's like to have to try, every day, knowing that it's getting harder and harder and one day it's all going to fall apart? And watching the person that you love most finding other people more attractive –' A sob broke through and she stopped. Forced several deep breaths. 'Even when they weigh the same as a small car and have the dress sense of Judith Chalmers,' she finished, with the old Saskia springing to the fore once again. 'It would have been better if it had been you. At least you're pretty.' She was back to the whisper again.

'Alex was working away such a lot, up until this summer. But he suddenly decided to change his arrangements so he could work from home, with Oscar starting school. So that he could see more of his son ...'

The realisation hit all three of us at once. 'He's Harry's father.' I said it first. 'The bastard.'

A watery smile creased Saskia's mouth. 'Sympathy for the devil, Jemima?'

'No, I meant, all that time when Rosie was frantic trying to look after Harry and get all those cards made for you. Jase and I were looking after Harry, where was Alex?'

'But what could he do?' Ben joined in. 'He couldn't

offer to help without arousing suspicion. And you were quite happy to help, Jem, particularly when you were getting low-rate board-and-lodging at the cottage.'

'I can't believe she didn't tell me.' I sat down hard. 'All that time, she's been sneaking off to see him – I can't believe she didn't give me one hint. I thought Harry's dad had been some one-night-stand. Not this.'

'What am I going to do?' Saskia's wail would have aroused more sympathy in me if she hadn't promptly turned to Ben and thrown herself against his shoulder, continuing to speak muffled into his shirt. 'I love him.'

Panicked, Ben looked at me over her head. 'Is she talking?' His eyes were wide. 'What's she saying?'

I stared at Saskia. The sound of my heartbeat was drowning out my thoughts. *This was love. This was what it brought you to. You loved and you were left.* 'So. We confront them.'

'We?' Saskia raised her head. The mascara streaking her face made her look fragile, like a made-for-TV movie heroine.

'Well, what were you thinking of doing?' I knew my voice was sharp. 'Letting it all go on?'

'I don't know.' Once again Saskia looked humble. 'I think I was afraid. I wanted to know but I didn't want to *know*, if you see what I mean. If I had no proof then I could pretend it was just me, being silly.'

My mouth twisted. Silly? Only little girls were *silly*. Full grown women were stupid or blind.

'But things were getting worse. I'd started writing it down every time he was away, or out, or working late, trying to find a pattern. But it was all so random, just half-an-hour here, an afternoon there, nothing I could pin down. And then a friend of mine recommended this man, this *Dave*, as someone who could make things happen.'

I shrugged off Ben's hand. 'Right, come on Saskia.'

Between us we escorted Saskia to the cottage where Jason was cross-legged but alone in the armchair.

'Rosie's press-ganged me into babysitting the little guy. Said she had something to do.'

I felt the tremor run down Saskia's arm. 'We think we know what that something was.'

Jason looked at Saskia. 'Bloody hell, girl. Looks like you've done ten rounds with Estee Lauder.' He glanced away, down at the carpet. 'I presume you found out then.'

'You *knew*?' Ben, Saskia and I all chorused together.

'She had to tell *someone*, it's been eating her alive.'

'She could have told me.' I was more hurt than I could have thought possible. Rosie was *my friend*. And how many nights had we spent, during the pregnancy and after it, choking down tears of laughter as we speculated on the parentage of her baby together. It had all been lies.

The sound of a big car's engine on the road struck us all dumb. Except for Ben until I mouthed, 'It's Alex. Outside.'

Ben let go of Saskia and headed out of the front door, whilst at the same time Rosie came in the back. Saskia burst out crying again. Proper hard sobbing, not picturesque tears this time. Jason put his arm around her, scruffy but chivalrous.

Rosie stood in the kitchen doorway and stared at us. I watched the expressions cross her face, bewilderment, slow-dawning comprehension, and finally relief. 'Saskia?'

'Don't talk to me, you husband-stealing bitch.'

I put myself between the women. 'We know about Alex.'

Rosie gave a small smile. 'I gathered.'

'Ben's gone to get him.'

'Okay.' Disconcertingly unabashed she turned back into the kitchen and began filling the kettle. I followed her and watched while she got mugs and coffee from the cupboard.

'I don't know what to say to you,' I said. Emotions ran riot around my adrenal glands. 'I thought you might have told me.'

Rosie shrugged. 'Nothing to tell.'

Anger rose again. 'Right. Just say that to Saskia, would you?'

A rising cry from Saskia indicated Alex's arrival in the living room via the front of the cottage. Rose and I reached the doorway in time to see her launch herself at him across the room, ululating as she went, hands raised in fists in front of her face. 'You –'

Alex looked scared. 'Sas?' Then he looked over at Rosie and I was surprised to see the same expression of relief on his face as on hers. 'I guess it's over.'

Saskia's shriek of grief sawed across my nerve endings. It sounded as though her world was ending. 'No! Please, don't say that.' And she stopped the rather pathetic slapping that she had been doing and flung her arms around Alex's not-exactly inadequate torso. 'I'm sorry I've been such a cold bitch, I've just been so scared and it's the way I was brought up. My parents were the same and I don't know how to love you but I'll try, I really will try.' She raised her porcelain face to his. 'We could try counselling?'

'I meant, that the pretence was over.' Alex rested his chin on the top of her head. He had to stand a little bit on tiptoe to do it. 'I'm sorry, Saskia. I should have come clean a long time ago, but ...'

'It was the village May Fair, last spring.' Rosie stood in the doorway wiping her hands on a tea towel. 'We both got very, *very* drunk.'

'I had to carry you home,' I said. 'And you were sick down my blue jumper.'

'I knew I'd had sex with someone but I couldn't remember who. And then Alex came round to apologise. Kept apologising, too. It's all right, Saskia, he thought I was you.'

All of us looked from plump, dark-haired Rosie to blonde, broomhandle Saskia. 'Blind drunk were you?'

'It – look, I really was incredibly smashed.' Alex stared at the worn carpet. 'I mean, almost too drunk to do anything. But Sas had been helping out with the drinks and I went round to the back of the bar tent, saw her bending over to pick up the empties and – well, by the time I realised it wasn't Sas, it was all over.'

'It was terrible sex,' Rosie agreed. 'Really, really shocking.'

'And Rosie and I, we agreed we wouldn't mention it again.'

'Ever,' Rosie put in.

'She didn't even tell me she was expecting until I met her in the shop a couple of weeks before –' His eyes raised ceilingwards. 'Didn't even tell me then, actually, I just, kind of deduced.'

'I was the size of a bungalow. He couldn't have missed it.'

'And then, of course, I offered to pay but Rosie wouldn't have it. Said that I'd hardly been present at the conception, it wasn't really worth my while being present for the baby. But I – well. I love Oscar so much, I didn't want this chap … *Harry* to miss out on a dad, so I – well, I've been getting together with Rosie just for updates and suchlike and also …' Alex tailed off, scuffed a foot on the carpet, looking every inch the prep-school boy he'd no doubt once been.

'He gives me stuff. Food, nappies, that kind of thing. Just to help out.' Rosie shook her head. 'I'd sort of convinced myself that Harry was some kind of immaculate conception. I don't *remember* the sex. But Alex was so keen on doing the right thing. He's even been taking me over to Blandford to look over the place.'

'You were going to send him to the same school as Oscar?' Saskia looked aghast. I wasn't sure if it was because she thought Harry would lower the tone or whether it was some bizarre taboo in Upper-Class-Land.

Alex looked more shamefaced, which was nearly impossible; his expression almost reached his knees as it was. 'We would have had to put his name down before his first birthday, so I wanted Rosie to see what the place was like.'

'It's very nice,' she put in. 'And Oscar does like Harry.'

'Oscar *knows*?'

'Good God, no. Look Sas.' Alex tilted her chin down so that she looked him in the eye. 'Rosie and I – there never *was* a Rosie and me. We've been trying to deal with the repercussions as best we could without anyone getting hurt. I'm not sorry you found out, but I *am* sorry that you feel so betrayed. I do love you, I always have.' Then, after a pause. 'But maybe counselling might be a good idea?'

Ben, Jason and I repaired to the kitchen to allow the three of them to talk more privately.

'Anyone else think they're protestin' way, *way* too much?' Jason asked succinctly, around a rich tea biscuit.

'Yes, but they're obviously happy to have it over. Maybe they only carried it on for something to do, some kind of physical connection. After all, Saskia hardly looks like she's handing out the cuddles on a nightly basis, and life must be pretty lonely for Rosie sometimes. Maybe they both got caught up in the excitement of being illicit. Alex obviously loves Saskia.' Ben looked at the closed door. 'And she must love him to have done all those shitty things to you. I guess she wanted you both to pack up and leave, so she'd got him to herself again.'

'You look happy, Jason. Family conflict turns you on, does it?' I eyeballed him sternly.

'Nah. But now things are out in the open, it all works for me. Rosie told me, yeah, that she wanted to go public with everything but she couldn't risk Sas taking the work away. So she had to put up and shut up and she wouldn't go to the States with me 'cos it would mean taking Hazzer away from his dad.'

'It still would.'

'Yeah, but now Sas knows, Alex could fly over and visit or be there at the end of the phone. Now, just maybe, she'll start making a new life that isn't full of secret rendyvooz.'

'With you?' Ben looked square at Jason and raised his eyebrows. I gathered that Jason and Rosie had been the subject of some Man-Talk.

'Hope so.' Jason gave a grin. 'I really hope so.'

'Yeah. Secrets are no basis for a relationship.' There was an edge to the way Ben looked at me. 'Let's go home, Jem.'

'Oho, please excuse my presence,' Jason exclaimed. 'You two want to do the nasty thing, you just carry on.'

I was feeling a bit shaken. Saskia's meltdown had reinforced my opinion that love meant you left yourself open. 'Yes. Let's go.'

Ben gave me that look again, joggling the car keys from hand to hand. 'Come on.' He dipped his head to whisper in my ear. 'Let's get away from the high drama.'

Jason winked at me and mouthed 'ice cubes', then helped himself to another biscuit.

# Chapter Twenty-Two

We made love slowly, stretched out on the huge bed in the attic, surrounded by printed sheets of music and lit by a single streetlamp. Ben's room was like him, rumpled and spare, full of half-written tunes and as colour-co-ordinated as a litter of kittens. His skin, barred with light from beyond the blinds, was cool over mine, his eyes were black, then yellow as he moved over me, into the beam and then back into shadow, staring into my face as though he was waiting to see my soul rise.

'Jem,' he was breathing my name. 'Jem. You and me …' I opened my mouth to reply but he pressed his lips to mine to cover the words, and then it was too late to speak. Too late for anything but mounting heat and motion that built until I was catching at his back with my nails and stammering meaningless syllables while he raised himself above me and groaned my name. He held his weight on his arms a moment longer, then let himself slide so that our faces were level once more. 'I've been thinking.'

'Mmmm?' I could hardly bring myself to talk now. It was so easy here to forget the doubts. My arms and legs were heavy and my head was drowsily full of the sense of his closeness. I wanted to lie here and just enjoy the feeling while it lasted. 'What about?'

Ben propped himself up, his face animated. 'How would you feel … I can't believe I'm about to say this … if, maybe, we could, you know …'

'No. No idea, I'm afraid. How many syllables?'

He grinned widely and stroked my shoulder. 'How about if *we* bought a place out at Little Gillmoor?'

'*What?*' Claustrophobia snatched my breath. I sat up sharply, gathering covers to my naked chest.

'Hey, don't panic, Jem. It's okay. Like I said, no pressure. I just thought it might be good, one day, to have somewhere out of town. I'm going to need a studio and you need a proper workshop space, and – you know we're good together. Couldn't you stand more of this?' He waved a long-fingered hand. 'Us. Properly.' Ben sat up beside me.

Blood thundered in my ears as he pressed a kiss to my hot skin, his hair painting a pointillistic design across my collarbone. 'I'm … not sure …'

'I want to be with you, Jem. Committed. No half-assed "seeing each other", but a real couple, living together. Security.' Under the covers musician's fingers stroked my leg, my back.

'I don't know. Ben …'

Another firm kiss covered my mouth. 'Don't say anything yet. Sleep on it.' He was sliding next to me, slipping already into sleep and curling his long legs and strong arms around my body. Pulling me tight against him. 'We'll talk in the morning, babe.'

I lay very still until he fell asleep, carefully judging the moment when his restlessness settled into heavy slumber. My heart was beating so hard that I felt sick and my head buzzed. My mouth tasted like bleach, but I didn't dare move. At last Ben sighed and turned over and I slipped out of the bed. One good thing, I thought, about sleeping with a deaf guy, you didn't have to worry about floorboards creaking and waking him up. I dressed and sidled into the guest room where my rucksack squatted in the middle of the bed, fully packed. Even now with all that had passed between us, I'd kept it zipped and buckled. I'd sneaked clothes from under its flap as though stealing from myself, returning them furtively each night. The simple task of unpacking, of taking up space in the cupboards Ben had cleared for me, had felt fraudulent. Couldn't do it. To empty the bag would be to settle, to admit to feelings that I couldn't understand, let alone come to terms with. And now I knew why I'd never settled – because I never would. It simply hurt too much. I swiped an arm through the strap and hauled it to my shoulders. The weight felt familiar, comforting, with all my belongings hanging down my back. *This* was how it should be. Everything contained, clothes, possessions, books. *Feelings*. All wrapped up and ready to move on.

Down the stairs. I gave the place one last complete glance. Even in my panic I recognised this would probably be the last time I found myself in such luxury and I wanted to remember it. All of it, from our last panting embrace in the untidy bedroom to the exact way the moonlight gleamed on the top of the scrubbed pine table. There was a new picture on the dresser, an old photo, five years old maybe, from the length of Ben's hair and the acute boniness of his hips. It looked as though it had been taken during a live performance of Willow Down; it had that kind of almost-blurredness of people who have hardly stopped moving long enough for the shutter to freeze them. Zafe and Ben stood with their arms locked around each other's shoulders, shirtless and sweaty and wearing two identical expressions of total bliss. Ben was grinning out at the photographer, eyes wide, and Zafe was half-turned towards him, guitar slung over his back, total elation shining from every sweat-soaked pore. Ben must have had this image in his mind every day, locked away in a cupboard to stop it reminding him of everything he'd lost; the band, Zafe, the music. And now he'd taken it out. Somehow he'd found the courage to put the picture where he could see it, where it would remind him of everything that had gone.

Something deep in me broke like a china doll. I'd seen that look on Ben's face. Not just in a photograph but when he'd talked about buying a place in the village, when he'd looked at me and spoken aloud his hopes and dreams. He'd had that same shining look of optimism and anticipation. How could I destroy that? How could I walk away from a man who looked at me like that?

But I had to. Had to go, or risk that terrible pain of loss once more. And I couldn't stand it, not again.

Saskia had showed me what it would be like. You put all your trust in one person, left yourself open to them, and that gave them the power to hurt you. I'd *so nearly* fallen for it, been so close to loving Ben. So close to giving him everything. But doing that only got me hurt. So now – time to go before things got worse.

Ben had been wrong. Running *was* the only answer. Sooner or later everyone went. And what I felt for him – my insides squeezed as the enormity of my feelings made themselves known – it was something I couldn't bear.

I looked at the photo again. Two men having the time of their lives. No inhibitions, no holding back, but throwing everything into their music. No worries about what would happen tomorrow, no foreshadowing of the terrible disease that would strike the heart from the band. Living for the day. For what was now, not what had been or what was to come. Proof that, even while you had the world at your feet, it could be breaking your toes, one at a time without you even knowing.

Life really was shit sometimes.

I swung the rucksack onto my shoulders and tightened the straps. Hefted the weight from side to side, and turned for the door.

There he was in the moonlight in front of me. Completely naked, bleached by the white light except for the dark shining circle of the Celtic mark around his bicep. Softly he trod the floor that separated us. He smelled of sleep, of clean bedsheets and, smokily, of sex.

'So,' he said carefully. 'You lied again, Jem. You said – and I think I quote here – that you'd stop and think before you ran again. Is *this* stopping to think? Or is this a knee-jerk reaction?' He reached out and touched the rucksack.

'I can't stay, Ben,' I whispered. 'I'm too afraid of getting hurt.'

He hardly looked real, his body pale and ghostly in the weird glimmer, hair dark as blood. 'Everyone's afraid of getting hurt, Jem, me included. But sometimes you have to gamble.'

'I've been left alone too many times to want to put myself through it all again, not for anyone. I'm sorry Ben. I have to protect myself.'

'Oh, Jesus.' Ben leaned against the counter. 'I can't

believe I'm having this conversation, naked in the middle of the night. Is this all because you think I'm going to wake up one day and realise you were a big mistake? That I felt *obligated* to you because I told you about the deafness? Jem, my love, you have got some *seriously* warped ideas, haven't you?'

'I only know what I can see. You,' I waved a hand. 'All this. You say that you love me, that you want me. But how long does that last Ben, really? And I've got nothing but myself. You'll always have Willow Down to save you. But there's nothing to save me.'

He moved so quickly I hardly saw him coming, and then he had me by the shoulders. 'But you are saving yourself, don't you see? Do you not see what you've become? Jemima, you ...' He broke off, shaking his head and dropping his hands from me. 'Christ. You really don't. You don't know. Okay. When I first met you, you were someone else, someone defeated. What had happened to you, it had you running scared. And over the time I've known you, look at what you've achieved! Tonight, when you faced down Saskia because you were afraid of what she was doing to Rosie ... Would you have done that before?'

'Ben ...'

'You ran to Glasgow, but you came back. You faced up to what you'd done. You told me, you told Rosie, about your past. You've confronted what you were, and you've become someone stronger as a result. You *don't* have to be with me. You could be anywhere.' His voice dropped. 'But I want you here. And, believe me, Jemima, you aren't the only one who's afraid of being hurt.' A slow hand raised and touched my cheek. 'Please.' His voice was a broken whisper now. 'Please, don't leave me.'

My breathing snagged. Tears began to dribble towards my chin. 'I'm still so *scared*.'

'We all are. We're all scared, Jem. Everyone. But we have to trust someone, sometime. I trusted you when I told you about what had happened to me. In fact, I trusted you from the beginning.'

I did a snorty laugh. 'Yeah, right. You didn't even *notice* me until I asked you to dinner, and scared you half to death!'

'Oh, Jem.' He sounded so regretful now, so sad. 'Hold on, stay there a minute.'

'What? Ben …' But he was gone, vanishing upstairs with a pad of bare feet against the polished wood of the staircase. I wiped my face on my sleeve and managed to smear tears across my cheeks, leaving them sticky and stiff. This had never been so hard.

'Good, you're still here.' Will-o-the-wisp-like he was back, jeans covering his lower half now, and a small bound notebook held out in front of him. 'Here. Read this. It's a diary that Doctor Michaels wanted me to keep. To help me manage my emotions, or something equally farty, but it did help. Look.' He flipped the pages. 'It's all about *you*, Jem. It's what I think, what I feel.' He laid the book down on the pine table and backed off, swinging a leg over a stool in the far corner of the room and tipping it to lean with two legs against the wall. 'Read or not. Your choice. Everything is your choice, Jem. It always has been.'

I riffled the pages. The book was slim and not all

pages were written on. Some contained sketches, little thumbnails of portraits, a guitar, even an unpleasantly lifelike gun. Others were makeshift staves with bars of music scribbled down and much amended. 'So. You can draw, you can write music and lyrics, you can cook … is there anything you can't do, Ben?' I kept my voice steady, despite the continuous motion of the tears down my cheeks.

'Embroidery. Just read it.'

So I read. And gradually the tears stopped and I gave a little laugh. 'You self-centred bastard.'

'Did you just call me a bastard?'

'What do you think?'

'I don't know. It's hard reading your lips in this light.'

I raised my head and moved my mouth exaggeratedly. 'I called you a self-centred bastard, actually.'

'Yeah, that's me. But a self-centred bastard who loves you. Do you see? *Now*, do you see?'

I let the book fall. It landed on the flagstones, splayed open, a loose page protruding to show scratched notes and words. Ben came across the room and picked it up, pulling the page free. 'Here. It's the first song I've written for the new band line-up, still needs a bit of work but …' He held the page out to me. 'Called "You Are All I Have".'

I sniffed. 'Isn't that a Snow Patrol song?'

He ran both hands through his hair. 'Bastards always beat me to it.' Now his eyes were enormous, unblinking.

'Is everything you wrote true?'

'True as I'm here. True as I'm breathing. True as I would personally knock down and kill anyone who tried to hurt you.' A single tear left the corner of his eye and rolled down to his top lip. He ignored it.

'Did you really want to die?'

An embarrassed shrug. 'Sometimes.'

'And you honestly think I have fantastic legs?'

Now he smiled. A slow, deep smile. 'Jemima, you have fantastic *everything*.'

'And you need me?'

'Oh, *so much*.' Now he came close and the moonlight made his tattoo look deep and dark against that white skin. 'Don't do this to me, Jem. Don't do it to *yourself*.' Another step forward and he hooked a finger under the strap of the rucksack, slid the strap down over my shoulder, my elbow. The rucksack tilted under its own weight and fell to the floor.

I looked again at the book in his hand. If what he'd written was the truth then he'd loved me a long time. Loved me even when I ran, even when I treated him so badly that he had no *right* to love me. Needed me, when I was scared to death that it was I who needed him. My heart scudded against the walls of my chest and I put a hand on his tattoo, tracing the lines.

He looked down at my finger dancing along the pattern on his arm. 'Do you love me, Jem?' The strain in his voice told me how scared he was of the answer.

I kept my eyes on those intricate swirls. 'Everyone I've ever loved has died.'

'Not cause and effect. Do you love *me*?'

Now I looked up. Met those grave-deep eyes. Knew. 'Yes,' I said into them. 'Yes.'

'And do you believe me when I tell you that you are a

strong, lovely woman, who can grab life by the bollocks when she chooses, and doesn't need to take shit from anyone?'

'I'm trying to be.'

'Good.' Ben smiled and wiped the last of my tears from under my eye with one finger. 'Then let me be the one that you were running to, all this time. Let this be the end.'

I reached out. Switched on the kitchen light and stood directly underneath, fully illuminated, where he could see my lips move and have no doubt. 'Yes.'

There was a surprising number of ice cubes in Ben's fridge. We used them all.

# About the Author

Jane was born in Devon and now lives in Yorkshire.
She has five children, four cats and two dogs! She works
in a local school and also teaches creative writing. Jane is
a member of the Romantic Novelists' Association and has
a first-class honours degree in creative writing.

Jane writes romantic comedies which are often described
as 'quirky'. She has two previous novels published in
the US: *Reversing Over Liberace* and *Slightly Foxed*.
*Please Don't Stop the Music* will be her first novel
to be published in the UK.

For more information on Jane visit
www.janelovering.co.uk
www.twitter.com/janelovering

# More Choc Lit

Why not try something else from the Choc Lit selection?

**New home, new friends, new love.
Can starting over be that simple?**

Tess Riddell reckons her beloved Freelander is
more reliable than any man – especially her ex-
fiancé, Olly Gray. She's moving on from her old
life and into the perfect cottage in the country.

Miles Rattenbury's passions? Old cars and new women!
Romance? He's into fun rather than commitment.
When Tess crashes the Freelander into his breakdown
truck, they find that they're nearly neighbours – yet
worlds apart. Despite her overprotective parents and a
suddenly attentive Olly, she discovers the joys of village
life and even forms an unlikely friendship with Miles.
Then, just as their relationship develops into something
deeper, an old flame comes looking for him....

Is their love strong enough to overcome the past? Or will
it take more than either of them is prepared to give?

ISBN: 978-1-906931-22-3

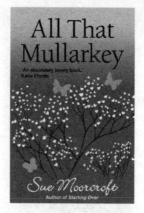

**Revenge and love: it's a thin line …**

The writing's on the wall for Cleo and Gav. The bedroom
wall, to be precise. And it says 'This marriage is over.'

Wounded and furious, Cleo embarks on a night out with the
girls, which turns into a glorious one-night stand with …

Justin, centrefold material and irrepressibly irresponsible.
He loves a little wildness in a woman – and he's in
the right place at the right time to enjoy Cleo's.

But it's Cleo who has to pick up the pieces – of a
marriage based on a lie and the lasting repercussions
of that night. Torn between laid-back Justin and
control freak Gav, she's a free spirit that life is trying
to tie down. But the rewards are worth it!

ISBN: 978-1-906931-24-7

"Refreshing, funny and romantic, it's like a breath of fresh sea air with a cast of terrific characters." KATE HARRISON

Turning the Tide

CHRISTINE STOVELL

**All's fair in love and war?**
**Depends on who's making the rules.**

Harry Watling has spent the past five years keeping her father's boat yard afloat, despite its dying clientele. Now all she wants to do is enjoy the peace and quiet of her sleepy backwater.

So when property developer Matthew Corrigan wants to turn the boat yard into an upmarket housing complex for his exotic new restaurant, it's like declaring war.

And the odds seem to be stacked in Matthew's favour. He's got the colourful locals on board, his hard-to-please girlfriend is warming to the idea and he has the means to force Harry's hand. Meanwhile, Harry has to fight not just his plans but also her feelings for the man himself.

Then a family secret from the past creates heartbreak for Harry, and neither of them is prepared for what happens next …

ISBN: 978-1-906931-25-4

CHRISTINA COURTENAY

Trade Winds

'A lush setting, vivid characters and a wonderful romance make this a delicious treat!'

**Marriage of convenience – or a love for life?**

It's 1732 in Gothenburg, Sweden, and strong-willed Jess van Sandt knows only too well that it's a man's world. She believes she's being swindled out of her inheritance by her stepfather – and she's determined to stop it.

When help appears in the unlikely form of handsome Scotsman Killian Kinross, himself disinherited by his grandfather, Jess finds herself both intrigued and infuriated by him. In an attempt to recover her fortune, she proposes a marriage of convenience. Then Killian is offered the chance of a lifetime with the Swedish East India Company's Expedition and he's determined that nothing will stand in his way, not even his new bride.

He sets sail on a daring voyage to the Far East, believing he's put his feelings and past behind him. But the journey doesn't quite work out as he expects …

ISBN: 978-1-906931-23-0

**A modern retelling of Jane Austen's *Emma*.**

Mark Knightley – handsome, clever, rich – is used to women
falling at his feet. Except Emma Woodhouse, who's like part
of the family – and the furniture. When their relationship
changes dramatically, is it an ending or a new beginning?

Emma's grown into a stunningly attractive young woman,
full of ideas for modernising her family business.
Then Mark gets involved and the sparks begin
to fly. It's just like the old days, except that now
he's seeing her through totally new eyes.

While Mark struggles to keep his feelings in check, Emma
remains immune to the Knightley charm. She's never
forgotten that embarrassing moment when he discovered
her teenage crush on him. He's still pouring scorn on all her
projects, especially her beautifully orchestrated campaign
to find Mr Right for her ditzy PA. And finally, when the
mysterious Flynn Churchill – the man of her dreams –
turns up, how could she have eyes for anyone else?

*The Importance of Being Emma* was shortlisted for the
2009 Melissa Nathan Award for Comedy Romance.

ISBN: 978-1-906931-20-9

**If life is cheap, how much is love worth?**

It's 1914 and young Rose Courtenay has a decision to
make. Please her wealthy parents by marrying the man
of their choice – or play her part in the war effort?

The chance to escape proves irresistible and Rose
becomes a nurse. Working in France, she meets
Lieutenant Alex Denham, a dark figure from her
past. He's the last man in the world she'd get
involved with – especially now he's married.

But in wartime nothing is as it seems. Alex's marriage
is a sham and Rose is the only woman he's ever
wanted. As he recovers from his wounds, he sets
out to win her trust. His gift of a silver locket is
a far cry from the luxuries she's left behind.

What value will she put on his love?

ISBN: 978-1-906931-28-5

**Money, love and family. Which matters most?**

When Diane Jenner's husband is hurt in a helicopter crash, she discovers a secret that changes her life. And it's all about money, the kind of money the Jenners have never had.

James North has money, and he knows it doesn't buy happiness. He's been a rock for his wayward wife and troubled daughter – but that doesn't stop him wanting Diane.

James and Diane have something in common: they always put family first. Which means that what happens in the back of James's Mercedes is a really, really bad idea.

Or is it?

ISBN: 978-1-906931-26-1

March 2011

**Abducted by a warlord in 17th-century Japan
– what happens when fear turns to love?**

England, 1611, and young Hannah Marston envies
her brother's adventurous life. But when she stows
away on a merchant ship, her powers of endurance
are stretched to their limit. Then they reach Japan
and all her suffering seems worthwhile – until
she is abducted by Taro Kumashiro's ninja.

In the far north of the country, warlord Kumashiro is
waiting to see the girl who he has been warned about by a
seer. When at last they meet, it's a clash of cultures and wills,
but they're also fighting an instant attraction to each other.

With her brother desperate to find her and the jealous
Lady Reiko equally desperate to kill her, Hannah faces
the greatest adventure of her life. And Kumashiro
has to choose between love and honour …

ISBN: 978-1-906931-29-2

# Introducing the Choc Lit Club

Join us at the Choc Lit Club where we're
creating a delicious selection of fiction
for today's independent woman.
Where heroes are like chocolate – irresistible!

Join our authors in Author's Corner, read author
interviews and see our featured books.

We'd also love to hear how you enjoyed *Please Don't Stop
the Music*. Just visit www.choc-lit.co.uk and give your
feedback. Describe Ben in terms of chocolate and
you could be our Flavour of the Month Winner!

Follow us at twitter: www.twitter.com/ChocLituk

# *Forthcoming titles*

**April 2011**

*The Untied Kingdom*
Kate Johnson

**1**

*Chain*
ames
rilogy)

**June 2011**

*Love & Freedom*
Sue Moorcroft